FANG

VOLUME 5

Edited by Ashe Valisca

Bad Dog Books

2014

FANG Volume 5
First publication 2014

Edited by Ashe Valisca

Cover by AtomicBoyX
www.furaffinity.net/user/atomicboyx

Published by Bad Dog Books
www.BadDogBooks.com

An imprint of FurPlanet Productions
www.FurPlanet.com
Dallas, TX

TABLE OF CONTENTS

PREFACE

When I was asked if I wanted to work on FANG 5, I was overwhelmed with glee. Little did I know the roller-coaster I was signing up for and how much my life would want to turn everything upside down. Since I have started this project I have moved across the country and bought a house to name a few items. However, that isn't what this note is about. This note is about the collection you're about to read; the collection that I have worked on, forced my husband to work on, and mostly driven Fuzz and Teiran up a wall waiting for me to finish the damn thing.

So what are you about to read? That's what you want to know. Well we, I am including the wonderful cast of authors here, have put together a few different types of stories. We are going to take you from superheroes and secret agents, through slice of life and realism, and then to the extremes of cyberpunk before rounding it out with a romantic tragedy.

With that all said, sit back, relax, and turn the pages because you're in for a treat. Finally for your viewing pleasure, FANG 5: Best Enemies.

Sometimes you have set your differences aside for the greater good. Doesn't mean you still can't have a good time.

WHITE/BLACKMAIL

Whyte Yoté

With no more sound than the breeze of a ghost, Knorr Wheldon stepped out of the hedge through a gap no wider than his trim shoulders and emerged onto a brightly lit sidewalk. Brushing down his fur with his fingers, the border collie adjusted what little clothing he wore and looked across the lightly-trafficked drive.

An imposing wrought-iron gate loomed in the glare from the streetlamps. It towered over fifteen feet high, topped with spikes and bordered on both sides by brambles of barbed wire. In the center of the gate were the letters "SP." Stanley Pedrescu: tiger, kingpin, technological tour de force—and the owner of some very important information Knorr had been charged with retrieving.

The Ministry had provided him an excellent cover and gone to the trouble of arranging an appointment with the tiger this evening. His mission was simple, but without this cover the complex would have been impregnable. Fetching things was what he did best, after all, and the Ministry knew that fact and exploited it for the greater good. He had dedicated a great deal of time as an agent to covert tactical extraction. The Ministry's mission was near and dear to him; the interests of the people was their goal at heart, and it wouldn't be a lie, but it wouldn't be a complete truth either.

Knorr lifted his right ear, tapping the custom-molded receiver/transmitter there to make sure it was secure and hidden. With the physicalities this particular job entailed, a blown cover could stem from as little as an emphatic nod or stray inappropriate whisper. Satisfied with his ear, he did the same to the auxiliary microphone disguised as a filling in his lower back molar. That one was cemented in, and wouldn't move unless yanked or punched. Knorr hoped this evening would result in neither.

A whiff of scent passed by his nose just before he heard a click from behind. A swift kick in the back stopped him before he could shift into a defensive posture.

"Don't you fucking move. Paws up, where I can see 'em. Now." The voice was soft but still gravelly, deliberate and purposeful. A sharp pressure jabbed into his back as the mystery figure slunk up behind him from the shadows. Fingers slithered around the collie's side and gripped his stomach, claws raking down to his skin with calculated precision.

Raising his paws Knorr said, "I don't know who you are friend, but I can assure you I don't know what this is about." He added a little delicacy to his voice, if not a nearly-undetectable lisp. If this guy was one of Pedrescu's goons, he could play off the suspicious behavior as mere curiosity. If this was a random mugging, Knorr carried nothing of value besides the sound equipment in his head.

The paw rubbed over the dog's tight stomach, the fingers snaking between the mesh loops and making for a not-unpleasant sensation. "You know exactly what this is about, *Whelpdon*." The voice had changed, now smoother with just a hint of a familiar accent. By the time the paw slid down and squeezed between his legs—Knorr was more than a little hard—he realized he'd been had. However, when he whipped his leg into a roundhouse kick, the unsurprised hare merely jerked his head and sent him face-first into the ground using his own limb against him. "You should be grateful this is a truce mission, Knorr." The dog opened his eyes to the hare's extended white paw, grabbed it and hoisted himself to his feet, refusing help in dusting off. "If we were in actual combat, I would have snapped your neck by now. Especially since I just held you up with only my finger."

Chuckling despite his runaway heartbeat, the dog replied, "Reilosz, you would sooner come back to the Ministry than kill me."

"You have a point; fortunately for you, we're on the same side." Rei's paw remained on the collie's shoulder, not unpleasant. "This time."

Knorr fiddled with his fur, suddenly missing his markings. Any reason not to make eye contact. "Tonight. Then you can get the hell out of my life again."

"I love you, Knorr." The toothy shit-eating grin showed through the hare's tone. And then Knorr looked up and made the mistake of seeing Rei as he used to be. Damn his turncoat tail.

Running his paws up over his ears, the collie let them flop back down again, wishing they were long enough to cover his eyes. "Fuck you," he muttered, feigning interest in random middle-distance objects.

"You may have to, before we're done with this guy," Reilosz quipped before breaking into a maniacal grin. Then he threw his arms around the dog. "I don't care what you think. It's good to see you." The embrace brought back memories, not all of them bad, and Knorr accepted the hug for what it was. He even reciprocated, as lightly as he dared. When they parted, the hare looked the dog over "What'd they do to you?"

Knorr clicked his tongue, offering an arm. "They made me bleach it."

"All your beautiful merle fur?" Rei ran his fingers lightly along the dog's wrist sparking more memories.

"According to our files, Stanley prefers blondes."

"Well, yes, but …" The hare gave a melodramatic sigh, looking Knorr over with a critical eye. The mesh tank top and leather shorts he wore could have been described as either high fashion or a costume. Rei's clothes weren't much better: a purple vest, tight black leather pants, and wraps to protect his padless feet. The gay-bar border collie and the casino-tramp hare. "I knew I never should have left the Ministry."

Knorr fought to keep a straight face. "You were kicked out for treason."

"Yeah, there's that, too." Rei's trademark insouciance hadn't faded one bit.

"Besides, the mucky-mucks said an all-white border would score points for originality. Did they say the same about you?"

"I've just molted," Rei said, smiling and obviously pleased with himself. "I'm a natural blonde until springtime, remember?"

The dog resisted the urge to make a snarky comment, because somewhere, deep down inside, it was good to see the hare again. Being partners for eight years in the Ministry, three of which they spent as lovers, made some feelings harder to dismiss. The pain of Rei's deception and treason still stung, burning hotter in his company, but still there he was again.

Knorr checked the time. Still early. "Uh, so anything new at the Order?" While "Ministry" stood for the Ministry of the Common Good (McGee internally), the "Order" was merely that—an organization allied against the public interest and focused on its own goals, both politically and financially. Referred to both as a cult and as a movement, the Order existed along the full spectrum of arbitrary and subjective morality. It required of its members loyalty only to itself. Despite Rei's claim that his defection had been an "awakening," he'd turned tail both on his employer—and his relationship. "No, just your average plotting, scheming and general ne'er-do-welling," replied the hare with not a scrap of sarcasm. "Things are going well, in spite of your attempts to spoil the fun."

Knorr's whiskers twitched. "You guys do keep us busy. I suppose I should thank you for keeping me in a job."

"Welcome!" Rei beamed. "I do try my darnedest." While the Order stayed within the law for the vast majority of its operations, it strayed when its goals wandered into the egregious. That was the difference between the two organizations, along with their members: what the Ministry saw as righteousness, the Order saw as haughty weakness.

Turning to look at the gate, Knorr sighed. "I have to say, though, I'm glad we haven't met up since you left. I think that's why the Ministry hasn't sent me on missions where that would be a possibility."

"Why?" the hare prodded, his face suddenly sultry. "They don't want you fucking your adversaries on the job?"

Knorr's ears perked before he knew what he was doing. "No," he said, and it was true. Until just now, he hadn't honestly entertained that idea. "Probably because, if the situation required it, they couldn't count on me being able to kill you."

"Oh." Rei's ears splayed like broken antennae. The mood didn't last long though. "Well, you won't have to kill me tonight. I hope. Nobody would say shit to me about why we're here."

Knorr's jaw dropped. "You weren't briefed?"

"All I know was, my guys and your guys agreed to a truce for as long as it took to get some files out of this Stan guy's house, and it was me and you. And that was from the Order. The Ministry didn't tell me anything because they probably didn't trust me." The hare shrugged. "Don't blame 'em."

"And you like working with people who don't keep you informed?"

"I have a big house and a big car," Rei replied. "It works for me." Suddenly Knorr wasn't quite as sorry things had ended up as they had..

"Right then. We're undercover as... escorts."

"No shit. So, Stan's got an eye for males. That's gotta be worth something by itself."

The border collie rolled his eyes. "What you do with *that* information is none of my business. What matters is that you're able to get inside his safe and grab the drive in there."

"Oh. Oh, hoho! I get it. The Ministry is that desperate? Wait, where's your own safe-cracker?"

Knorr tried to maintain a straight face, keeping his eyes low.

The hare deadpanned. "You couldn't find one as good as me. All that training and all those resources, and the Ministry still couldn't replace me."

"Not with your level of skill—no, but we are still looking."

Rei wiggled the slim radar dishes atop his head. "It's the ears. Did you know that the top safe-crackers are all either lagomorphs, Fennec foxes, or bats? Oh, and that one tawny owl, but he's just creepy."

"My superiors are confident you can do it. My job is to be a distraction while you get the drive."

"That's because I'm the best," said Rei. "What's in it for me? I mean, what's in it for the Order?"

"Diamonds," said the dog. "Stanley doesn't trust banks, so there are some loose diamonds in with the drive. They're blood diamonds, though, so it's on your conscience to use them for personal gain."

"Wouldn't want all that illegal labor to go to waste," said the hare. Knorr found himself wondering how Rei had been accepted by the Ministry at all. It wasn't the first time he'd wondered. "So, how're you going to distract this guy?"

Knorr looked at the hare and his getup. Was Rei really asking that question? "Look what you're wearing."

"Y-you mean we have to sex him up?" Genuine incredulity flashed across Rei's features.

Knorr had rarely seen him like this, even when they were in love. "Didn't you hear the part I said about us being escorts? It's not like sex has ever been difficult for you."

"Are you calling me a slut?"

"If the condom fits…"

Rei stamped a foot. "I don't have to put up with this shit."

"You might want to check your facts on that one," Knorr spat back with a pointed finger. "Talk to my guys first. Then talk to your guys. You're a free agent as of now. If you don't follow through, we turn you in and the Order forgets you ever existed."

Thankfully the hare paused to process before responding. Knorr had been hoping it wouldn't come to having to reveal the until-now joint agreement. The Order may have had the upper hand in Rei's unequaled auditory faculties, but they wouldn't hesitate to sell him out to save their own skins.

"Well…" started the hare, looking around more for words than anything else. "Well, I guess we should get to the sex, shouldn't we?"

"You know, you could always come back." Though that was a slim-to-none chance, on both Rei's part and the Ministry's.

Rei shook his head, smiling sadly. "I like my things too much. We're just a better fit, even if they try to screw me wherever I turn." Knorr didn't believe that for a second, but he said nothing. "When do we go in?"

Knorr checked his wrist again. "Anytime. We're still early in terms of our appointment, but I don't think he'll mind if his playthings arrive slightly ahead of schedule." Without waiting for the hare to assent, the dog grasped Rei's paw and pulled him across the street. Knorr glanced up to see the cameras mounted on the wall followed their movements, and he wondered how long they had been trained on the action near the hedge.

Before the border collie could press the call button on an expensive-looking security pad to the left of the gate, the doors began to swing open.

"Automatic?" Rei asked.

"They're watching us," Knorr replied. "They've been watching us." He felt the hare squeeze his paw as they both noticed a shadow moving against the building's façade.

"How much do we gay it up?" Rei asked from the corner of his mouth.

"Up to you. Just don't overdo it, and if someone asks questions, let me speak. You can be the cute dumb one."

"Just like old times. Except I wasn't the dumb one," said the hare, adopting a more fey posture than Knorr had ever seen.

When the approaching shadow passed under a sconce, a slim polar bear in a tailored black suit emerged. He approached the gate, eyeing the two with more amusement than derision. Whether their perceived sexuality or their purpose wasn't clear, but if the bear was on Pedrescu's payroll he shouldn't care either way.

Knorr leaned one shoulder against the stone wall and crossed his arms. Rei, in character, draped himself limply around the dog's shoulders. His breath smelled of wheatgrass toothpaste. It brought back a rush of more intimate memories.

"Evening," said the polar bear in a voice whose pitch matched his build.

"Hey, sweetie." The border collie kept his tongue just close enough to the back of his teeth to feminize his speech. It seemed to convince the bear, whose muzzle scrunched in a chronic sneer.

"It's a long way to Tipperary." Knorr could hear absolute disgust in the code phrase as the bear spoke, and he reveled in the *Schadenfreude*.

"But a fox in the head is worth two in the mess." The clumsy mismatched innuendos lacked grace, but it was unsuspicious enough to be trustworthy. Rolling his eyes and nodding, the polar bear pressed a button and the gate on that side began to swing back into place. Knorr pulled Rei inside before it had traveled halfway.

"Follow me." The ursine turned on his toes and walked toward the house, not even bothering to look back to make sure the two followed. Security was not up to what the border collie had expected, but what he saw outside was no indication of how the tiger's private documents would be protected. Cameras, maybe, but they wouldn't be on as long as Stanley occupied the room, and especially not with two hustlers keeping him company.

The courtyard behind the gate reeked of modern simplicity: steel, glass and concrete dominated the compound's architecture. Rei held Knorr's paw and allowed himself to be led through a large entryway and into the main foyer. Spartan in decor but very expensive, the living space had an open floor plan that allowed for an uninterrupted view from the front door to the back patio.

"So this is what being an asshole gets you," murmured Rei. If the polar bear had heard, he made no indication of it, mounting the suspended concrete staircase with continued professional disinterest. "I like it." A fresh wave of contempt settled into Knorr's gut, and he jerked his paw away. He felt the hare's eyes but ignored him.

At the top of the stairs, a hallway curved off to the right toward the rear of the house. Rooms branched off to both sides, all closed, but they passed all of these as they approached a pair of ornately-carved doors at the end of the corridor. A bit closer and Knorr realized they were carved from solid jade.

The polar bear pressed a nearly-invisible button. After a few seconds' pause, the doors parted sliding into recesses in the walls. The dull grind of the stone being dragged against the tracks revealing the private rooms behind.

"You may... enter," the bear sneered. Rei gave him a withering look. Just before stepping over the threshold, Knorr thrust his paw against the bear's crotch, meeting the surprised look with daggers. Only a second later, he felt the sheath throb in his grip.

"Yeah, that's what I thought," said Knorr before taking his paw away and slinking into Stanley Pedrescu's bedroom and office. "Sorry, this is a private show."

With that, he turned and walked away, tail high and inviting. He didn't care what kind of reaction he got; if that ursine wanted to keep his job, he would keep quiet.

"Are you through molesting my employees?" boomed a voice from around the corner, presumably the bathroom. The tiger's private chambers spread out, exuding his expensive and refined tastes. To their left sprawled the bed, closet, and lavish side tables while a large writing desk and computer station occupied the opposite side. Directly ahead sat a bar with stools, and at the foot of the bed was a mahogany chest with rampant-tiger hardware. Bingo. If the Ministry's information was accurate, the safe would be behind the leftmost drawer, and after that it was up to Rei and his ears.

"Only the ones who deserve it," Knorr sing-songed.

Rei poked the border collie in the arm. "Where is it?"

"Chest, foot of the bed, left side, combo lock. Should be easy stuff."

"Ah, ah, ah," said the tiger, coming around the corner looking freshened up and recently relieved. "We share our secrets around here."

Stanley Pedrescu cut an intimidating figure in a navy double-breasted suit with a matching vest over a brilliant white shirt. He wore an orange tie that struck a stark contrast with his neck, but complemented the rest of his body. The lines of his suit worked to disguise the slight softness around the tiger's waist.

Hips canted to the side, the border collie threw an arm around

Rei's shoulders. "How's it supposed to be a surprise then, hmm?"

"Look at this guy," the hare said with an appreciative stare. So fake, but to a tiger with an itch to scratch, testosterone would paint a prettier picture. "Rich and handsome."

"Two out of three is good," Knorr said sultrily. "If he's hung as well, it's a perfect score."

Smiling, the tiger crossed the room, his tail curling and uncurling itself as if barely holding back a prey-pounce. "I'm sure you will be quite impressed, and pleased."

Rei intercepted the businessman a few steps from Knorr and made a show of throwing himself at the tiger. "We lucked out. Usually we get the fat ugly rich guys who either can't get it up or get it in." He squeezed the already bulging fly. "Oooh, Mr. Tiger's packin'!"

"Stan's fine, really." Stan was more than fine; he was practically drooling. Knorr moved to the other side and added his paw to the hare's. The hardness within felt average at best. When the dog looked at Rei, the hare rolled up his eyes. "What do I call you fine boys?"

"I'm just a bunny," said Rei. "He's just a puppy. We're used to it, and it's simpler that way."

"Names are so…" Knorr was about to say bourgeois, but even as a joke it might put the tiger off, being a rich bastard and all. "So… personal. I like being a puppy anyway. I wanna be a good boy." Eschewing intelligent speech was starting to hurt his head, which the tiger scritched affectionately. God dammit if that didn't feel good.

Stan said, "You're both being good boys so far. I see the agency went above and beyond to assure I received two towheads."

"I'm a natural blonde," Rei said.

"Five months out of the year," Knorr replied.

"Don't be a bitch just because they had to bleach your splotches out." Even though the hare was playing it up for Stan, the comment stung more than the border collie would have liked it to. His merle coat was a source of pride, and it would take months of brushing and growing before anything resembling his pattern would begin to show again. But the job had to be done, and he was the one to do it.

"No fighting, boys, please," ordered the tiger. "We're all here to have a good time, and you're here to make money while doing it. What could be easier than that?"

Giving us the combination to your safe, Knorr thought. Instead, he said, "I make a better blond anyway," and stuck his tongue out. He got claws on his scruff for his trouble. Rei was subject to the same treatment. Should their cover be exposed, the tiger could easily throw them across the room... or out a window, open or closed.

"Alright, both of you. I think it's time you kissed and made up." Rei's surprised look mirrored the dog's own. Stan let them both go and stepped back, paws on hips. "Go on," he said. "You do this all the time anyway, don't you?"

Knorr fought to remain in character. The pain he'd been trying to hide was now as fresh as it was when Rei had left the Ministry. Trying to tell himself it was just a job would have worked better with any agent besides Rei, but the Ministry didn't care about their past. It cared about the drive, and if getting perilously close to the hare again—even as a ruse—meant a successful mission, then it had to be done. So he stepped up to Rei and embraced him.

The hare had no qualms about pressing his muzzle up against the dog's, or about sliding his tongue halfway to Knorr's throat. Rei's paws found their way around to the back, where they immediately began working the flimsy flap above the border collie's tail. It was maddening to feel the spark of passion after so long, knowing how Rei had betrayed him and the Ministry, but damn if those paws didn't feel good sliding the already-loose shorts off his hips. Knorr heard Stan growl-rumble at his lack of underwear.

Heat crawled its way up and down Knorr's spine, settling below his stomach and filling his sheath. It would have been a convincing show for the tiger, had it been a show at all. Ashamed of his own traitorous heart but dutiful above all else, he allowed his tongue to play around inside Rei's mouth while he undid the hare's pants and shoved them down. Rei pulled them together, and suddenly it was as if they had never broken up at all.

"Oh, that's beautiful," Stan rumbled. "I could sit here and watch you two all night."

Rei pushed away, looking horrified, though it was clear he had enjoyed the kiss just as much as Knorr had. "You can't mean that!" he exclaimed dramatically. "You're paying good money for a couple pieces of tail."

"Very fine pieces of tail," Knorr chimed in. Making out in front of Stan wouldn't get the safe open. "Here we are, half-naked, and you're still all dolled up in that suit. Don't you think he needs to lose the duds so we can get at his cock?"

"Absolutely." Rei doffed his vest and stepped out of his pants, cutting the same athletic figure that had attracted Knorr years before. "And that's what you're gonna get. Naked time." With that, the hare padded over to the tiger and went straight to work on the belt. Stan looked over at Knorr with the grin of a john who thinks he's getting more than he's paid for, and the dog responded by skinning his sheath back over several inches of hardening flesh. He tried to believe it wasn't Rei's round rump that was keeping him hard.

With Stan's help, the tiger became bottomless in a matter of seconds, already erect and dripping. Knorr licked his lips and went to join Rei in removing the jacket, shirt, and tie. His guess about the businessman's body type was spot-on; Stan's belly was there but not substantial enough to encroach upon his sheath. If the tiger were anyone else—other than a rich, cruel, egomaniac—he would have been attractive.

Rei took Stan's cock in his paw and stroked over its length. "Looky here, we got someone wound up pretty tight. Didn't we, Puppy?" He seemed to be enjoying himself a bit too much. Now that they were in the thick of things, Knorr had no way to overtly communicate. Ear signals wouldn't work with his being folded down, and Rei didn't have enough out back for the tail code. Lip reading it was.

The safe! Knorr mouthed.

I know what I'm doing, Rei replied. *Follow my lead.* Fury boiled up from the dog's gut, but practicality trampled it back down. The hare was crucial to the mission, and if he had to take charge to get that safe open then that was how it was going to be. Once they had the files (and Rei the diamonds) it was a matter of wrapping up. But how was the hare going to communicate with the tiger's dick in his muzzle?

Stan grunted, holding onto Rei's shoulder and watching the action unfold between his legs. "Whoof... you boys are talented!" Mixed praise indeed, since Rei's oral action had always left Knorr wanting more. But if it worked, who cared?

Slurping off the tiger's member, Rei said, "You know, Sir, Puppy just loves to kiss. Don't you, Puppy?" The look was pure evil, the wink even more so. Knorr had to work hard to mask his revulsion, both at the idea and at the hare.

"Oh, I just adore it." *You fucking bastard*, he thought in the hare's direction.

Rei swirled a down-facing finger: Turn him around. Yes, it would be an effective method for distracting Stan, but it certainly wasn't the only way. The hare had remembered Knorr's phobia of kissing foreign muzzles and decided to exploit it. The Order had done well in training sadism into Rei, if he'd needed training in the first place. He could have been like this all along, lying during his entire Ministry tenure.

Stan looked nonplussed. "You would do that? No one else has... yet." A measure of small relief, then. Whether or not it was the truth, Knorr could believe it if that made the act easier.

"Isn't that why you're paying us, big guy?" asked the border collie before planting a peck on the tiger's lips. Rei took that as his cue to slide around behind them, as Knorr turned Stan to face the opposite side of the room. But when the tiger's ears pricked backwards, Knorr had no choice but to jump into his arms and distract the rest of him. Stan caught him easily, with a big dumb grin.

"Hey there," Stan said, spreading the dog's cheeks while extending his claws slightly, making Knorr yelp and nip at the tiger's cheek ruffs. Knorr licked a line forward until he could clamp his lips around the black rubbery ones. Stan melted, kneading the canine's rump with vigor.

"You don't... get out much... do you?" Knorr asked between licks, amazed that his gag reflex hadn't decided to kick in like it usually did. That Stan had evidently brushed his teeth just prior to their arrival helped a great deal.

"A man in... my position... can't afford to take chances."

"Our lips are sealed, sir."

"You bet they are." Warm fur enveloped the border collie's length, his body's natural response at least making the ruse bearable. It was nothing he hadn't done before, at least. Thankfully Stan was too involved playing tongue-tag to care about where Rei had gone. From his high vantage point, Knorr watched the hare, with one ear plastered to the safe, listening intently to the tumblers within.

His initial revulsion now past, the dog went along for the ride, making sure to groan and grunt here and there to give the impression his lust was growing.

Stan pulled back with a long, rough-tongued lick to Knorr's snout. "I wanna do so much to you."

Definitely more growl than purr.

"Why don't you show me?" Knorr practically lilted. "Whoa!" And the tiger did, by hoisting the border collie over his shoulder. As they both swung around, Knorr watched Rei go from shocked to suave in a split second, closing the left side of the safe's chest and opening the right just as Stan caught him.

"What are you doing?" asked the tiger. Knorr's brain went into calculation mode: excuses to make, martial-arts attacks to stun him, routes of escape or at least hiding spots within the compound. But Rei looked as cool as ever. In fact, he was smiling.

Twirling a finger around his whiskers, the hare asked coyly, "Where do wealthy men keep their rubbers, huh? I was expecting some jewel-encrusted dish next to the bed."

For a moment the tiger studied Rei with glowing yellow eyes. Then he grinned, beamed, and guffawed, bouncing Knorr like a plush toy on his shoulder. "There's no dish, but they are next to the bed."

"Ah, silly me!" Sitting on the floor, naked and cross-legged, the hare's attempt at looking naïve could fool even the border collie. He was good, but unfortunately he was good at being bad. Then again, "bad" was relative. "You two get on the bed, and I'll handle things down at the end."

"I was hoping you'd want to join us again," said the tiger, flopping onto his back and taking Knorr with him into an instant cowboy position.

Rei sauntered over to the side table and pulled open the top drawer. "Oooh, this looks expensive!" He pulled out a condom and a small green vial. "What kind of lube is this?"

"It's tailored to my body chemistry," Stan said huskily while Knorr busied himself licking each of the tiger's nipples in turn. "It's about two hundred a bottle."

"I sure hope it works better than AstroGlide," said Knorr.

Stan grinned broadly. "Why don't you find out, boy?"

Putting the items on the bed within easy reach, the hare replied, "I told you I'd take care of you. Don't you trust me?" He lowered his ears but couldn't quite pull off the lop rabbit look. Before the tiger could answer, he was behind them and out of sight, back to work. They wouldn't get another chance.

The border collie licked across Stan's teeth, but resisted the tiger's attempt at a second kiss. That was enough of that and besides, he had another task with which Rei had so aptly "saddled" him.

Knorr wasn't a bottom. Even so, he slid down Stan's belly until he felt the barbed tip prodding between his cheeks. Not substantial, but it had been God knew how long since he'd sat on a cock. It didn't feel bad, but it was intimidating.

"Let's get you ready," said the canine, reaching for the vial and the foil packet. The material inside felt like nothing he'd come across, or in, before. "What is this made of?"

"Comes from the same company as my lube. It's actually designed to feel like skin."

"Feels good, but I know it'll feel better once it's inside me." Knorr lolled his tongue to the side, leaning back just enough to see Rei. Still working the combination. Good. He turned back, grabbed the vial and slicked up Stan's shaft with quick rotary strokes, happy to keep the tiger distracted and moaning. The condom rolled on easily, and after slickening that up as well the border collie raised his tail and bore down.

White-hot pain erupted almost immediately, Knorr's whimpered gasp out of his mouth before he could help it.

Stan stopped immediately. "What's the matter?" He started to sit up, but Knorr pushed him back down. His mind spun, but only one thought entered it.

"I'm a virgin." Which was a complete lie. He could just imagine Rei's face; it was a miracle the hare could keep from busting out laughing. "Never had anything up there."

"Your company hired you as a virgin?" the tiger asked, genuinely shocked.

"They said I was gonna lose it anyway, so why not?" Knorr shrugged. The lust in Stan's eyes burned brighter. He almost looked like he was contemplating backing away.

"How old are you?"

"Nineteen." Another complete lie. Rei probably had his paw over his mouth as hard as he could clamp it.

"I'll be gentle."

"Thank you," Knorr said truthfully. He reached behind and placed the tiger's tip back under his tail and pushed. The pain returned, but when Stan saw the struggle he began to stroke the dog's sides, easing him down as he soothed. It would have been romantic, save for the espionage. After the tapered head and the barbs, which stimulated rather than scratched, the rest was only a matter of girth.

"You weren't kidding." Stan hunched up to meet Knorr's hips. This time the pain was a memory, supplanted by a pleasant fullness he hadn't felt in too long. He didn't know how much he'd missed it. The last time he'd been fucked was... well... it had been Rei, actually.

"Can't really lie with a hole that tight," Knorr lied.

"Beautiful. Rock those hips, if you wouldn't mind." Not that Knorr would mind too much, as long as it kept the tiger distracted. He situated his body across Stan's waist and began to ride. Not too long after, he did start to enjoy the pleasure he was giving both of them. But every time he wanted to close his eyes and just feel, he had to remind himself his job was as a decoy, not as a boy-toy. It was, however, turning out to be one of his most fun missions to date.

Knorr had just begun to stroke himself when he felt the tiger jerk and cry out. "What, did I hurt something?" the dog feigned concern.

"Oh, no, quite the opposite," said Stan. "Your bunny friend has his finger somewhere very sensitive."

Knorr twisted around and smiled. There was Rei with his thumb rubbing over the tiger's hole and making him squirm. On the floor in front of the chest were a small jump drive and a pile of diamonds, glittering against the carpet. With his free paw, the hare shut the safe and pulled the door closed before making a throat-slash signal: We're done here. He stood, maintaining his thumb massage.

"I thought you would like that," said Rei to Stan without actually being in the tiger's line of sight. "You think you would like that replaced by something more substantial?"

"Oh, shit! Nobody's done that before! I've... always wanted, but... oh fuck me, I want it!"

"I didn't see any other condoms, though, Sir. But, to tell the truth, I don't mind if you don't." The hare winked at Knorr, pointed to the member still thrusting into him, and thumbed over his shoulder. This kind of communication had become second nature toward the end of their relationship, but the border collie had in no way forgotten its subtleties.

"Oh, fuck..." moaned Stan.

"In fact," said Knorr, "I... I think I'm thinking the same way." In a deft series of movements, the dog rose off the tiger, peeled the condom off, gave it to Rei and settled back onto the newly-bare flesh. "If it's gonna be my first, I'd prefer you make a proper dog of me."

"Oh, fuck!" It had worked perfectly. Stan was now busy enjoying unimpeded sensation while he worked to hump into Knorr, while Rei busied himself with emptying the safe.. Upon reflection, however much reflection one could do while riding a tiger, Rei'd been smart to shy away from giving up his tail for that very reason. He'd likely store the booty in the rubber and stick it where the sun didn't shine.

Whatever plan the hare had in mind, he didn't have to worry about making noise. Knorr couldn't have watched Rei if he'd wanted to, occupied as he was trying to keep from falling off the bouncing, thrusting tiger. Without the condom in the way, those barbs were doing a number on his prostate, along with the stimulation from Stan's white—and soon to be sticky—belly fur. The tiger strained while holding Knorr's thighs down, obviously given over to pleasure and not caring a whit about anything else.

Straddled as he was, Knorr sensed something had changed behind him when Stan stiffened. No warmth splattered deep up inside him, so when he looked back he saw Rei lubing himself with runoff from their coupling. Then—rather roughly, thought Knorr—he slid into the tiger, his flexible body wedged between Stan's legs and the bed

Stan roared. He roared but he never moved away. A big man like him could take Rei's relatively slender member, especially as worked up as he was. The hare merely stood still and let the tiger do the work for all three of them, his hips twitching between the two males. When Knorr sent a bemused glance toward the hare, Rei merely shrugged and mouthed, Let him do it, I guess. So they did.

The rest was a matter of watching a grown man work out his rent-boy fantasies in a heated fashion that completely belied his professional status. Seeing the wealthy techno-giant writhe about underneath him gave Knorr the sweet satisfaction of knowing Stan's empire would likely come crashing down in the coming weeks. Once news of his overseas dealings, labor violations and insider trading came to light, Stanley Pedrescu would cease to be relevant in the world of business. One small victory.

Smiling a devious smile, Knorr bent over to lick at the tiger's heaving chest. "Breed me good and hard. I wanna feel it splash." Stan snarled and picked up the pace, the border collie finally finding the wherewithal to clench on his upthrusts, until he finally dug his claws in and held them both still. And Knorr did, in fact, feel it splashing inside him. He missed that, too.

Rei wasn't too far behind. The dog and tiger held each other while the hare took over and sped up to his usual breakneck pace, Stan whispering, "I can't believe how good this feels," into Knorr's flopped-over ear. Then Rei grunted and pounded through his usual power-climax. Shortly thereafter, the tiger's afterglow began to wear off.

Clearing his throat, Stan said, "Well... that was fun. That was very fun."

"You're not gonna finish the poor worked-up puppy?" asked Rei, stroking the base of Stan's cock as it softened and slid slowly from Knorr's backside. As soon as it left, the hare shoved something much smaller in to replace it. It wasn't a finger. Knorr clenched to hold it in, but after what he'd just done, it would be a task to keep it that way. He faked a disappointed face to mask anything revealing.

"It's okay," Knorr said. "Mr. Stan is the client, and he makes the decisions." Before the tiger could even think about reciprocation the border collie dismounted and padded toward his clothes. Rei made a show of approaching the side of the bed, and went as far as smooching the big cat.

"Didja have fun, at least? Learned a few new things about

yourself?"

"I did," replied Stan, though he didn't look as if he liked everything he'd done. As near as Knorr could tell, he might even be regretting it. He wondered if that was something that happened every time he bedded a male. Either way it wasn't his problem. His and Rei's work was done.

All three dressed quietly, awkward not only because the tiger was definitely down from his oxytocin high but also because Knorr wanted to make sure he and Rei got off-property before anyone was the wiser regarding the safe. But once they were dressed, Stan did them a huge favor by walking them all the way to the front door. Even if Stan went directly to the safe, Knorr and Rei would be long gone.

"Thanks for the fun," the hare said when the tiger opened the door.

Stan cleared his throat again. He wouldn't even look at them now. "Welcome."

Knorr took a chance. "Can we look forward to a repeat performance sometime in the future?"

"I ... don't really do those." The tiger's face told a different story.

"I suppose I can understand. Any specific reason?"

"You have a safe trip back to, uh, work."

Knorr nodded, looked at Rei and led the way. "Let's go, Bunny." The gate was even open, anticipating their departure. Once outside they made a beeline for the hedge. Once clear of the hedge, they ran until they couldn't breathe. Knorr kept pace with the hare's longer strides and springier steps.

"You're still pretty fast," Rei panted. "I thought you'd gone soft."

"Nope. The Ministry's agent regimen keeps us all in shape." Knorr caught his breath for a few more seconds. "I don't suppose I need to confirm what you stuck in my ass."

"Your precious little jump drive, what do you think?"

"You put a delicate electronic device in my cum-filled tailhole."

Rei palmed his face. "No! You idiot, why do you think I needed that rubber?"

"Oh," Knorr said, running his fingers through damp head fur. "What did you use for the diamonds?"

The hare shrugged. Grinned. Made a vague drinking gesture.

"You just... swallowed them."

"They come out eventually," said Rei. "My superiors're just gonna have to wait a couple days to get 'em all. There's probably a couple mil in my gut about now."

"You're crazy. You'll be lucky if you don't bleed to death."

"We do what we do to get ahead."

"Like I said, crazy."

"We both got what we wanted. You should be happy. And you should be thanking me, Knorr Wheldon. I was your golden boy. Plus, it's not every day you get to have a threesome with your ex and a rich tiger." Rei paused, looking the border collie over. "You never did get off, did you?"

Knorr replied, "I didn't think it prudent to deal with that right then."

"Want to deal with it now?" Instead of waiting for an answer, the hare cupped Knorr's sac and rubbed. His erection returned within seconds. Traitor.

He could have said no, flat out. What came out of his muzzle was, "Don't you have a car to catch?"

"They're waiting for me to show up at an address near here. You?"

"They'll track my position when I call them, and drive to me."

Rei grinned and went to his knees before the dog. Two seconds later Knorr was naked again from the waist down. "Sounds like we're both still off the grid. I don't think anyone will ask questions," the hare murmured, sliding the bleach-white sheath beyond Knorr's knot and closing his lips around his shaft.

The darkness and trees and cool, humid night all disappeared. Knorr was back in the downtown apartment they had shared not as long ago as he'd thought. They were fresh off a dangerous mission, taking out the sexual thrill of escaping death on one another. And he was just as powerless to stop it as he'd always been.

And as Rei held his balls with his soft padless fingers, Knorr gave himself up to that fantasy, as impractical as it seemed. Those days were gone and he could never get them back. The hare had changed too much to take back what he'd done. But for those moments, there in that place, he allowed himself to feel again. He clung to it when he felt his climax rise and then spill out of him, confirmed in Rei's hums of appreciation.

When the hare came to his feet, he was licking his lips. "You haven't changed. At least in flavor," he said. Knorr considered asking the question he'd been thinking about since he'd mentioned it before they went into the house, but Rei beat him to it. "You know, you could always join us."

"I could never." It was so easy to say it, too. It proved his conviction to the Ministry over all. But was that really a good thing?

Smiling sadly, the hare said, "I would've been surprised if you'd said anything else. You're good people, Knorr. I wouldn't want you to change for me." He stroked along the border collie's cheek, his nightshine darting this way and that within his eyes.

"Same here. Though sometimes I wish you would." This time Knorr did the holding, with both paws. A part of him felt like crying. Over the old Rei, maybe. Not anymore.

"You know it's too late for that. Hey, maybe I'll do something really bad and you'll have to come get me. Then we can have this little *jeu de pions* again. Pointless, but fun." Rei kissed Knorr lightly, the ghost of his body heat lingering on the dog's lips. "I still love you, you know."

"Yeah. Me too." But he said it to the back of Rei's head because the hare was already trotting away through the trees, back to the Order. He doubted he'd never see him again. That was the way those things worked. Knorr tapped the tiny transmitter in his tooth. Ten seconds or so later, he heard three beeps in his ear. The Ministry had heard him and were on their way. His only hope was that his knot would deflate before the car swung by to collect him.

Every hero has a weakness; sometimes it is his villain.

Super Complications

Ianus J. Wolf

People of all species and sizes fled and cowered in fear as the robust bank doors exploded inward. That was good. The bull loved it when he made an entrance that caused even the bravest souls to seek shelter. The servos whirred as he pushed his massive armored frame through the front entrance. He hadn't made any effort to muffle them because he knew the sound amplified the intimidating presence of his mechanized suit. The helmet's glowing red eyes scanned the crowd, the sensors taking in everything. He imagined what he must look like to them as the smoke and dust settled to reveal his featureless visage and the shining silver against the matte black of the power armor covering his hulking, muscled frame.

"Yes! Tremble citizens!" he shouted through the speaker in his suit. "For the mighty Taurus Maximus has returned!"

It was gratifying to see the looks of fear etched onto every single face in the lobby. Even the armed guards knew they were outmatched by the bovine terror armored from his hooves to the tips of his horns. He watched as the Doberman, panther, and komodo security guards all simply crouched and cowered behind the most solid looking structure with their paws and claws clearly visible. He probably wouldn't have to fire a single weapon to complete this job. That was good too; he didn't want to be here long. A bank robbery felt so … pedestrian at this point, but his latest upgrades after this jailbreak hadn't come cheap. He slammed a gauntlet against the closest wall to amplify the imposing terror. Hearing the marble crack, he smirked behind his faceless mask in satisfaction.

"Do not interfere, citizens! My business is not with you. I shall merely make my withdrawal and take my leave!"

Seeing the crowd was properly convinced to keep still and silent, Taurus stomped towards the back of the building. He tore open one of the gates leading behind the tellers' counter as if it were paper and checked on the clerks behind their station. They all trembled as he came close, but his sensors informed him that the silent alarm remained inactive.

The bull diverted power in his suit to increase his strength even further and gripped the wheel of the vault door. This would take a bit more effort than his entrance and the gate, and he could feel the wheel bending even as he pulled at the rest of the door. Soon enough, the suit wrenched the vault open, revealing the stacks of cash and neatly locked safety deposit boxes. Only the green interested him, and he grabbed a nearby treasury sack and began to fill it with all the banded stacks within reach, knowing he could carry a great deal and jet away before the police arrived. Not that they were a threat at all, but it was an inconvenience he didn't need.

Taurus barely heard the rustling behind him before, with a metallic clang, something slammed into his back. Nothing should have been able to force him off balance with the new modification, but somehow that attack had hit at just the right point of leverage to make him jolt forward. Despite the bulk, the suit could move and turn quickly, and Taurus shifted about just in time to see a familiar mustelid frame flying at him with a weighted boot forward that hit him in the chest. He staggered a bit more as the hooded, caped marten flipped back off of him and landed out of arm's reach.

"Mystic," the bull muttered as he began to rebalance power in his suit for strength and reflexes. "I should have known I'd have to deal with your meddling!"

The pine marten spread his arms in a casual gesture, a smirk showing just under the mask that hid the top of his face. The dark blue cape fluttered behind him as the hood cast deep shadows on his brown fur. The rest of his body was shrouded in tough black leather that moved fluidly with his sinewy form. "What can I say? I had you pegged the second you broke out of Harper. No one escapes justice for long."

With a flick of his wrists, flashes flew from Mystic's gloves as tiny smoke bombs filled the air, blanketing both of them in a thick cloud. Taurus only chortled under his helmet as he steadied himself and prepared to knock the little marten into next week. His new sensors could cut through the smoke that his nemesis used; he had a clear view of the hero taking one of his many fighting stances. It would be quite a prize to jet out of here with both the cash and The Mystic in his clutches.

The bull thrust forward with a mighty blow aimed squarely at the mustelid's chest. He could tell he had surprised Mystic, but it was not enough to land the hit as the lithe frame twisted quickly out of the way and back towards the teller windows, crouching and ready for the next attack.

"Those tricks will not work on me any more, Mystic. I've learned since our last encounter. And you have escaped my wrath for far too long!"

As Taurus strutted forward out of the short hallway, he saw the marten looking at him, concentrating and focused directly on the armored bull. This would be good. He took another step and Mystic dove to the right to come around, leaping for Taurus's helmet. Without a second thought, the bovine shot an arm out and caught Mystic out of the air, holding him up by the throat. It felt wonderful to have the struggling mustelid in his iron grip, knowing he would attempt this trick. He took a step forward and brought Mystic's face up to the red eyes of his helmet.

"This new armor has dampeners to block your little telepathic illusions." He gave a light squeeze around the marten's neck. "My sensors will see every move you make."

Without waiting for the move or gadget Mystic undoubtedly had up his sleeve, Taurus hurled him as hard as he could through the open gate and towards the unyielding marble of the bank's wall. A good hit would take down even his well-toned body and then the bull would have him. But already the marten's quick thinking had saved him as he twisted and turned his body to roll along the wall and come to a stop on the floor outside of the gate. Taurus could see that the hero was not completely unscathed from the wince of pain as he righted himself; however, he'd personally witnessed Mystic come back from worse.

As the marten backed into the lobby to gain some open ground, Taurus stomped through the gate and turned to find there were no hostages. Of course The Mystic had helped them leave undetected while Taurus was busy with the vault. He must have shooed the tellers out just before getting the bull's attention. Taurus turned to see his opponent. Mystic had fully regained his balance and was watching him from the other side of one of the podiums used for customers to fill out forms.

Mystic smirked. "You know you won't win this, Maximus. Why not just come quietly? Your cell is just the way you left it, nice and cozy."

"You forget one thing, little hero. With these dampeners, you cannot tell my next move either. You must simply face me as any mere mortal; you cannot stand against my superior strength and intellect!"

Before he had even finished speaking, Taurus shot the high-tensile cables from underneath his wrists, sweeping them at

Mystic in order to wrap up the marten. Capture would be easy when the mustelid didn't see it coming until it was too late. In the split second before the cables would reach him, Mystic let out a soft squeak as he leaped straight up into the air. Taurus snorted in frustration as the cables swept by each other just below the marten's boots. Just a hair's difference and his whips would have at least wrapped around Mystic's legs. He had to remember not to underestimate the mustelid's strength and agility.

As he reached the height of his leap, the marten's paws whipped from beneath his billowing cape and two shining objects blurred through the air. Mystic's glaves neatly sliced through the cables that should have been nigh unbreakable just in front of the bull's gauntlets, making the metal whips fall useless to the floor. Bellowing in frustration, Taurus flipped his right arm up and aimed the mounted stun ray where Mystic was falling. With the suit aiding the bull's aim, even the marten could not twist his body fast enough, and the blast sent him sailing through the air across the large lobby.

It was already clear that the hit had knocked the wind out of the mustelid and done some damage through the leather armor as Taurus watched Mystic slump to the ground and wheeze. A sense of triumph surged in his breast as he stalked around the tables and podiums towards the hooded figure, hearing a little cough as he struggled to rise. The bull's tail struggled to swish where it was pinned by his armor, and he fought to keep the rest of himself under control. Seeing the hero prone before him like this, knowing that he'd have him in his grasp shortly … it all sent a thrill through Taurus's entire body.

Looming over Mystic, he leaned his featureless silver mask down to the marten, speaking low in a way only his nemesis would hear, "And now, little hero, I'm taking you back to my base for—"

The bull's words were cut off in a bellow as a sudden flash of light burst before his face. With a little warning he could have altered his sensors by a stray thought to block out the blast, but caught unaware, Taurus took the full force. Blinded by the stars exploding in his vision, he could hear the marten rising, still coughing slightly.

"Just needed a moment to adjust my goggles, Maximus. I'd hate to take a light burst to the face, you know?"

The armored bull staggered back, flailing his arms in front of him in wide arcs. He tried to concentrate on his other sensors, to engage his personal radar, but every time he almost had the neural input right, another afterburn would flash in his eyes. Mystic could move as silently as he needed when he chose, a fact Taurus knew too well, and soon he felt the weight of the hero on his back just before his head was forced to turn to the left.

"Sometimes you just have to take the bull by the horns," Mystic's voice said with a clear smirk in his tone.

Taurus groaned as he knew the forced turn would move his helmet enough to expose a gap in the armored suit. "Oh, Mystic, even for us, that one is ..."

He couldn't help but trail off as he felt the sting of one of the hero's knock-out darts at the back of his neck. Unable to even let out a last bellow of frustration, Taurus Maximus was unconscious before he clattered to the ground, defeated.

***

When the bull began to come to again, the first sensation he noticed was being in motion. Lying on his side, he slowly pushed up from the black unconsciousness and realized he was out of his armor and clad only in the boxer-briefs and undershirt he wore under his powersuit. Even out of the armor, he cut a tall, impressive frame; thickly muscled under his russet fur with almost perfect definition. Of course it did him little good now, with his wrists cuffed behind his back while he rested in the back seat of Mystic's custom SUV. One thing he had to give the hero, those darts didn't give the woozy, hung-over feeling of some of the other incapacitations he'd dealt with. Just a refreshed sensation, almost like a good nap. He grunted a little bit and tried to stretch, only to remember that the bench seat afforded little room.

"How do you feel, Hank?" came the voice from the driver's seat. A small light switched on over the back seat, allowing the bovine to see. Mystic's car had no outside windows; the hero navigated by some kind of mental power related to his telepathy.

The bull sighed. He hated losing like this, but there was no sense getting bitchy about it now. "Not so bad, I guess. Where's my armor?"

"It's secured in the back. Those telescoping plates over your horns were kind of a pain to get off. I figure after we're done this time, I'll take a look at your newest toys. That was a close one."

"It was, wasn't it?" Hank couldn't help but smile as he fidgeted to relieve some of the pressure on his shoulder. "A split second's difference and I'd have had you in those cables."

"I noticed. And that laser did sting quite a bit, I'll admit."

"Well it's supposed to. Thought I had you again, once it hit." Taking a deep breath, the bull tried to relax, already feeling a quiver of anticipation. "So you've caught me. I take it next stop is the police station?"

Mystic just chuckled. "C'mon, I think you know me better than that by now, Hank. Not going to waste an opportunity like this. Would you?"

Despite himself, Hank could feel his groin twitching and swelling just a bit. "You know I wouldn't. I was hoping to be taking you and the cash back to the lair at this point."

The bull felt the car slowing and coming to a stop as the marten said, "I'm sure you were. But it looks like this time, I have the upper paw."

As the front door opened and Mystic stepped out, Hank leaned his head back a moment and tried to gain control. He was already getting half hard, and he didn't want to give the hero complete satisfaction. Didn't want it to be so readily apparent just how much he was actually looking forward to the next few hours.

When the back door opened, the bull expected to be pulled out and on his feet in Mystic's hideaway. Instead, the marten was suddenly on top of him, pouncing into the car and pressing his thin muzzle to Hank's broader snout. As the lips met his and Mystic's tongue slipped into his mouth, the bull broke down and returned the deep, passionate kiss. His groin responded, member swelling and stiffening as the marten's paw reached down and rubbed it through the elastic fabric. Kissing up at the hero, Hank no longer cared about appearances or self-control. There was only that lithe body pressing to his, and how much he wished he could wrap his arms around the little marten as they kissed.

Mystic's hood remained up as he broke the kiss and nuzzled down the bull's body in the back seat of the car. Hank just snorted and sighed as a paw ran delicately down his side and the marten rubbed against him, the other paw continuing to massage his thick package through his underwear. The bull bellowed loudly as the paw deftly slipped into the flap of his boxer-briefs and fished out his turgid cock, urging it stand fully at attention. He felt Mystic's tongue washing up the underside to the sensitive head and looked down to see his thick meat disappearing underneath the dark hood.

Wet slurping and moaning filled the air as Hank felt the hero sucking and pawing at his member, making the bovine bite his lip as his hips pushed up towards the enthusiastic muzzle. His horns scraped the car door as his head moved back and forth in the intense pleasure as Mystic hungrily devoured his member, the bull panting and trying to keep control. It had been long enough in prison this time, and the hero knew all the places to lick and tease along his shaft to take him to the edge of pure pleasure.

Just as he thought he might pass beyond his threshold, the soft muzzle slipped off his slick member, and The Mystic slipped off of him and back out of the car.

"Mmm," the marten moaned, and Hank thought he saw the pink tongue sliding across his muzzle, "It's been a long time, and I just had to have a taste."

Groaning as he came back slowly from the edge, the bull panted and looked at Mystic. "God, you are such a fucking tease. Help me out of here."

The marten crossed his arms, his eyes still covered by the hood. "Say 'please,' villain."

Rolling his eyes, Hank felt his member twitch as he looked at the hero's frame, noticing the smirk on his muzzle. "Would you get me out of your car … please?"

Mystic leaned forward and gripped the bovine's thighs, letting his fingers work over the muscles there before pulling them down and out of the SUV. As Hank tried to get his legs under him, the marten's paws slipped up to his rump, groping and squeezing the sensitive cheeks, making the bovine squirm as he finally stood up. Standing in front of the car, his hands behind his back and his malehood hanging out of his shorts was humiliating. Even worse was how aroused Hank felt, standing there at Mystic's mercy.

Before he knew what to do, the hero had him pressed against the car and was kneeling down again, licking at his exposed member. The bovine let out a lowing whimper as the soft, wet strokes began to pull him closer to the edge again. His body was trying to slump down against the car as his knees weakened, with no way to grab for purchase.

Then as he once again thought he couldn't hold out, the muzzle retreated and a paw on his chest helped him slide back up and regain his footing. Hank panted and tried to shake out the head rush from the intense sensations.

"Oh, not yet, Hank," Mystic said as his paw slowly stroked the broad chest, "Just tastes too good to leave it alone."

"Man … and people say *I'm* evil."

Mystic simply chuckled and hooked two fingers into the waistband of the bull's shorts. "C'mon, stud. Let's get you back to my bed."

Grunting as he was led through the hideaway, Hank followed dutifully around the computers and trophy cases. He tugged at his wrists, still secured behind his back. "At least take these off. I want to hold you. I promise I won't try anything."

"Sorry, Hank, I can't trust you that much." Mystic looked back and grinned under his hood. "Besides, I kind of like it this way."

"Well if it's going to be that way; before I forget … *GADZOOKS!*"

Mystic turned, his ears swiveling as a series of popping and sizzling sounds erupted from the back of his vehicle. Tipping his head back with a sigh, he asked, "What was that?"

"Just the sound of most of my equipment becoming useless to you. Can't have you knowing all my secrets." Hank grinned at the marten. "You may have some clean-up to do in there."

"Of course, should have seen that coming. And seriously, 'gadzooks'?"

"Well no chance I'm going to say that in a fight, am I?"

Mystic just shook his head and began leading the bull back into the hideaway again. "I swear, next time you're getting a ball gag."

The thought sent a little shiver up Hank's spine. *I really shouldn't like that idea so much.* "Next time, you'll be waking up in one of my cells, lubed up and ready for my amusement."

"Heh. Promises, promises."

Walking dutifully behind his captor, Hank came to the door that he knew all too well. The pine marten tapped in a code on a keypad next to the thick steel plate, and it opened into an opulent master bedroom with a four-post king-sized bed as its center-piece. The entrance to the room always closed to reveal a bookcase that seamlessly fit into the wall, as if no doorway was present. The same soft carpet met his hooves as before and he looked around at the antique furnishings, trying to determine if anything new had arrived since last time. He was almost positive that this was a bedroom in the home of Mystic's secret identity, but there was no way to be sure. Still, the cost of the furnishings and of the hero's equipment, he had to be a major player in the city. How many fab-ulously rich pine martens could there be in the area? Then again, Hank could never be sure how much of this was illusion to throw him off the scent.

As he mused over all this, Mystic turned and pushed him back against the bookcase, almost climbing his body to kiss him as the big bushy tail thrashed behind the marten. The bull leaned his head in and closed his eyes as their lips met, working his muzzle against the hero's. More than anything, he wanted the cuffs off, not to try anything against the marten, but just to hold and ca-ress the smaller male's body. He wanted to feel his fingers running through that fur and stroking that tail as their tongues wrestled against each other, to hold the marten like a lover. Hank could accept defeat more than he could accept not being able touch and grope the body pressed against his.

Mystic broke the kiss, that damned hood still obscuring his eyes as he pulled a small blade from his utility belt. Working with all the dexterity he did in the field, he quickly cut the straps of Hank's undershirt with a smile. The hero slipped steadily back down his body, taking the cloth with him. As his feet were on the ground again, the marten leaned forward and let his tongue tease Hank's now exposed nipples, the bull gasping as the soft, wet strokes ran over the erect nubs. His member strained at the stimulation, throbbing as Mystic gripped the band of his shorts and began pulling both undershirt and underwear down around his legs. The bull felt a paw gently manipulating his shaft to work the boxer-briefs around it before everything slid easily down to his ankles, leaving him naked.

One hoof at a time, he stepped out of the pile of cloth as Mystic already knelt down to nuzzle at his shaft once again. The bull's horns disturbed several books as his head turned against the shelves, his hips desperately trying to push forward. Moaning loudly, the marten opened his muzzle wide and engulfed the bull's thick shaft almost down to the root. Hank could feel the sensitive head pushing into the hero's throat as he looked down to see his meat disappearing into Mystic's mouth. Pressure was building as the tongue lapped along his shaft and he felt delicate fingers rubbing and rolling his heavy balls. His hands struggled by nature against the cuffs while the bull tried to hold back from the edge.

Soon he realized that this time, Mystic had no intention of letting him come back down or hold his load any longer. The mustelid sucked and slurped hungrily, moaning and humming around Hank's cock with every relentless caress his mouth could produce. Unable to hold back, the bull let the pleasure crash over him, feeling his climax come in heavy spurts as a bellow echoed around the room. All the while, the marten swallowed and lapped as if trying to get every last possible drop out him, extending his pleasure through several more waves.

As the orgasm reached its end, Hank felt the muzzle slowly slip off of his shaft, gently sucking all the way. He looked down to see the marten's tongue licking the short muzzle completely clean. Before the bovine could catch his breath, Mystic was up on his feet and craning his head up while pulling Hank's down for another kiss. He could taste the remnants of his seed on the hero's breath as he leaned readily into their muzzles' embrace, sighing as his softening erection twitched just a bit at the touch of the marten's lips.

When the kiss broke again, Mystic was smiling. "Mmm, I've been waiting for that since you broke out," the marten said as he began to strip his way out of the one-piece suit he wore. Hank could see the bulge straining at the skintight leather over Mystic's groin, and as the pine marten pulled the suit off, his glistening erection stood free.

Leaving his hood and cape on, Mystic pulled the rest of the suit off and tossed it aside. For his species, he was quite well endowed, making up any lack of thickness with extra length, and Hank quivered a little as he got a good look at the mustelid's naked, sinewy frame. With a beckoning gesture, Mystic turned to the bed and Hank stepped away from the wall.

"You know you can take the hood off. It's not like you'll let me remember your face anyway," Hank said as he moved to the foot of the bed where the marten was leading him.

"Oh, I think I'll leave it on this time. For my own amusement."

As the hero sat on the bed, his erection jutting up from his hips, Hank wondered for a moment if that was the real reason. Had something in the fight taken its toll on the marten? Did he not have the concentration for his mental powers? Or it could really just be the way the marten wanted to play the game this time. In any case, he couldn't wonder for too long with that body in front of him just waiting for attention.

Rubbing up against the seated mustelid, Hank leaned down for another short kiss and felt Mystic's paw caressing his cheek as their muzzles entwined. Carefully he slipped down to his knees in front of the marten, almost an expert at this point in keeping his balance with cuffs on. He leaned forward and lapped his broad tongue over the long cock in front of him, just licking and savoring the scent and flavor of the marten's musk as he heard light chittering of pleasure from above. Paws stroked his head and cheek as he let himself enjoy licking along the smooth shaft, his eyes drifting shut for a moment.

For several moments, he lost himself in the taste of marten musk, the feel of the shaft against his soft tongue, and the little moans Mystic made. Hank leaned slowly forward and wrapped his thick lips around the slick meat, delighting in the little squeak of pleasure he heard. The marten's cock stiffened further and throbbed in his lips as he slowly sucked and licked, wondering if he'd get to bring him off completely this way. The bull could already feel another little twitch at his own groin as he sucked a little harder and felt the musk intensify. Precum dribbled onto his tongue and he greedily lapped it down, swallowing around the malehood in his lips. A tug on his horns pulled the bull gently away from the hard member and made him look up. He could see the smile on Mystic's muzzle as a paw stroked his head.

"God that's good. But you know what I really want." The mustelid slid to the side and stood up, leaving Hank on his knees at the foot of the bed. "Get yourself up on to the bed, villain. You must be punished for your crimes."

A little low escaped Hank then, a mix of desire and shame as Mystic walked away to one of the nightstands. Knowing exactly what the marten expected, he leaned against the foot of the bed and worked with his hooves to push himself up until he was leaning over the edge and ready. His arms instinctively struggled against the bonds of the cuffs, muscles straining just a little as he found them holding fast. He was getting hard again when he heard Mystic slip up behind him, the bull whimpering slightly as a paw ran over his perfectly sculpted rump.

"Seeing you like this, part of me just wants to get right to it," Mystic said as he groped Hank's buttocks, "but I think you need a little discipline first, after what you pulled."

The paw moved to lift up Hank's tail. A shudder ran through the bull's body and he braced himself just as the leather paddle swung through the air to hit his right cheek with a loud smack. The intense sting still made him jump against the bed, even being ready for it. Feeling utterly powerless in the hero's clutches, his fresh erection throbbed as another quick crack landed on the same section of his rump.

"Now you aren't going to go shooting me again, are you?"

Another swat landed, this time on the bull's left cheek as he panted. "No …"

"That's a good bull."

Hank couldn't help but grin. "No … promises," he finished between breaths.

He was rewarded with a quick, hard swat across his cheeks, feeling the burn as the sting faded. The bovine's entire body quivered as a few more hard smacks landed on each side. Moaning, he pushed his hips against the bed, trying to rub his arousal against the soft comforter as each smack made it jump.

"Some people just never learn," Mystic said through his own panting breath. The smell of their arousal was thick on the air and as his rump felt the low burn from the swats, Hank could tell what was coming next.

As if on cue, he felt the marten's paw spreading cold lube between his cheeks and pushing a digit forward towards his tight hole. The bull pushed back as he felt the finger slide in and begin to slick up his insides, moaning as it opened him for the first time in a long time. He winced and sighed as another thin finger joined the first and spread the lube within, eager for something more as the discomfort from being spread faded, for that special warmth that only one thing could provide.

The paw moved and soon the marten was gripping both cheeks and spreading them with his fingers. The little claws dug in where the hardest smacks of the paddle had taken place, but the burning tingle there soon took a sideline to the feel of the marten's tapered cock tip pressing in against the bull's pucker. Hank groaned and lowed, his head thrashing about as Mystic pushed into him. The marten buried the length of his shaft quickly, making Hank cry out as it warmed him from the inside and made its first contact with all the right places within him.

Arousal already dribbling against the comforter under him, the bull let out panting gasps as Mystic began a steady thrusting in and out of him, the length of the thin shaft probing deep inside. He bit his lip as he spread so easily and perfectly for the marten, feeling the thrusts push deeper and press the marten's tip against his most pleasurable point. Hank's fingers clenched at his back, the bull wishing he had something to grip as Mystic rode into him, chittering and rumbling in pleasure the whole time. This was where the hero truly claimed his victory for the day, his real triumph as the bull squirmed and bucked under him, being used for the mustelid's pleasure. And even at this ultimate defeat, Hank could feel his own bliss rising at the full feeling inside.

With each bump against his deepest insides, the bovine could feel arousal growing. His member grinding against the bed as Mystic sped his rhythm, the marten grunting and panting along with his other vocalizations now, Hank knew that a climax was not far off. The tingle inside spread through his balls and up his shaft, and even before the hero was finished, the bull felt the wonderful eruption between the bed and the muscles of his belly. He bellowed as the throbbing spurts of his orgasm took hold, still feeling Mystic behind him pushing furiously in and out, the smaller marten working himself almost to a frenzy as he used

Hank's ass.

Moments after his own climax had faded to leave the bull panting and writhing against the bed, he felt the marten suddenly stop deep inside him and the pulsing against his stretched ring. Heat filled his insides, making Hank groan low in his dizzy afterglow, enhancing the wonderful feeling as Mystic shot his load deep within the bovine, the hero grunting and chattering with each throb that delivered another shot of warmth.

Both of them trying to catch their breath now, Hank was grateful for the bed's support, feeling himself almost ready to slide off the end while Mystic leaned against him. When it was clear that he was entirely spent this time, the marten slowly slipped himself out of the bull. Hank whined just a little as he felt that moment of emptiness, just as the marten stumbled to help him slip up onto the bed the rest of the way. When Hank was on the mattress completely, the caped, hooded form walked slowly around the bed, his bushy tail gently swaying, his glistening erection steadily going down.

"I have missed that. That was nice," Mystic muttered in a dozy voice. "You relax there a little bit. I'm gonna go get cleaned up."

Without much other option, Hank just settled in as best he could. He lay on his side on the bed, his head propped up by pillows as he tried to avoid his horns scraping anything. Even with the discomfort of his hands still trapped behind his back, the bull began to doze on the soft mattress. He wasn't sure how long Mystic was gone, but Hank was reawakened by the feel of the marten climbing onto the bed with him and brushing a paw across his cheek.

"Hey there," the hero said softly.

The hood was finally off, but it didn't matter. To Hank's perception, the face that looked into his was as generically handsome as possible, a result of Mystic's mental abilities. But the loving smile there seemed genuine enough as the naked marten rubbed gently against him, so he leaned a little and kissed the muzzle.

"Hi, you." Sighing, Hank looked into the eyes he could see, wondering what those eyes actually looked like. "Really just want to hold you now."

The hero exhaled and seemed to grapple with it for a moment. "And I'd like nothing better than to feel those arms around me. But I know how strong you are and what you're capable of." Mystic's arm reached out to stroke along Hank's side. "I've got to be responsible and not take the risk."

It was always like this. Even as Mystic pressed up against him on the bed, their bodies and sheaths gently touching, the bull could feel that distance between them. He wanted to lighten the mood.

"Of course, last time, I had you trapped in my last lair, remember?"

Mystic chuckled just a little. "How could I forget? You managed to knock me out and cart me off to that warehouse you'd kitted up. Two weeks I was hostage there, and I don't think I've ever been that sore."

"Hey, I thought I took good care of you at least. Just made sure you couldn't concentrate enough to get away."

"I meant my ass, after I actually did get away."

Hank laughed and they kissed, a long gentle press before they looked at each other again. The bull grinned, "It was nice having you all to myself like that. Amused me that while the rest of the Protectors were out scouring for you, you weren't really complaining too much. Gotta say, maybe the best two weeks of my life."

"Yeah, until I finally escaped," the marten said, rubbing Hank's neck.

"Right. You left me fucking a pillow, thinking it was you and made sure I didn't remember your face." The bull mocked an angry look but an amused smirk. "Bastard. By the time it wore off and I was cleaned up and trying to get away, you had the cops and half the Protectors there."

"You should have monitored the equipment and the drugs you had me on a little more carefully, made sure they were getting into my system. But I'll tell you a little secret."

"Oh? What's that?" Hank asked.

The marten leaned his face in close. One of his claws traced the bull's muscles gently while his bushy tail thumped on the bed. "I actually had the drug cuff beat after the first week. I was just having too much fun in there. Something about getting fucked every night made it hard to leave"

Hank shook his head and laughed as the marten wrapped his arms around the bull and pulled himself closer. He pressed his body forward, his arms straining again against the cuffs. They nuzzled for a moment before Mystic looked at him.

"It could be easier, you know. You and I, we could make a pretty unstoppable team."

Hank rumbled a little. He'd heard this one too many times before. "What? You're finally ready to come down off that pedestal?"

"Don't be like that. Really, what do you get out of all the intimidation, the pointless displays of power, out of trying to rob banks? A cell that you go back to every time. We get these few moments when one of us catches the other. You're having to set up your lab again over and over, always rebuilding. That genius of yours could be put to better use."

"Yeah, right." Hank snorted. "I could be at the beck and call of every weak, idiotic sap that can't be bothered to defend themselves or think their way out of a paper bag. No thanks."

"It doesn't have to be like that. I'm not saying join the Protectors with me, or anything like that. Just … knock off the criminal activity. Do a couple rescues, make a show of turning over a new leaf. Then I imagine I could make some things happen, get you on parole. Be easier to have more nights like this, that's for sure."

"Until everyone starts expecting it. How many times do you have to drop everything to help some moron that likely got himself into his own mess?"

The marten rolled his eyes. "Look, we were lucky with our gifts. That kind of luck carries a certain responsibility."

"Oh don't give me that," Hank snorted. "What I do isn't about luck. It's work, study, and figuring things out. Exercising my body and mind, anyone can do it, but they choose not to. It's what makes them weak and what makes me sick to death of sharing space with them. Not like I'm going to go on a massacre, I just want to be able to set up someplace better."

"But your brain power is a gift. A lot of people just didn't get the raw intelligence you have," Mystic stroked the side of the bull's head. "But that's beside the point. This isn't just about getting more time or not wanting to have to take you in every time. After the last few times we've done … whatever this is, I'm starting to worry about you."

Hank leaned his head back, "What, you think I'm going to go nuts and start killing people?"

"It's not that, though some of the injuries you've caused do get me worried. It's more …" The pine marten took a breath. "I'm afraid that if I miss getting to you sometime, it'll be someone like Commando that might try to maim you or even kill you. I don't like to think about that."

"You think I haven't worried about you? Like if you decide you have to be the hero with some psycho like Lord Shadow, you might not catch a death-blade or whatever insanity he's using that week?"

Mystic looked down, "I … honestly wasn't sure it meant the same thing for you."

"It's started to," the bull admitted. "I've caught the TV sometimes when you've been out on a big mission. I haven't thought about it too much, maybe because I don't like to. But every time there's this pain in my chest and I wonder if I'll suddenly hear that you're down. And I have to be honest, that scares me."

With a sigh, the marten looked up and grabbed Hank's head. As their muzzles met again, the kiss was deep, passionate. Their tongues wrestled and they moaned together, and despite the gravity of their conversation, Hank's groin twitched as his arousal grew. Some part of him began to want what Mystic was offering. A chance for them to be together. As the kiss broke, the marten pressed again.

"Look … now that we both know—well—that there's something more to this, do one thing for me. Think about it, would you? Because the idea of having you any night like this, being able to truly trust you …" Mystic ran a paw over Hank's cheek. "It would mean a lot to me."

The bull felt his heart flutter a little bit, despite trying to ignore it. "Okay, being with you whenever we like would be nice for me too. I'll consider things, but no promises."

"I can hope. So now, as a little show of faith, I'm going to take a risk here."

The pine marten slipped off the bed, his tail brushing Hank's chest as he did so. He reached into the nightstand and pulled out one of the drawers, coming back to the bed with a small key. He reached around the bovine's body and Hank heard one click, then another as his wrists were freed and the cuffs were tossed off the bed.

As soon as his arms could move again, Hank reached for the marten and rolled onto his back, sweeping the mustelid into a tight embrace on top of him. As he pressed Mystic close against his muscled frame, Hank saw the bushy tail swaying and heard a little churring sound of pleasure escaping the hero to match his own deep moan. Mystic nuzzled his chest and gripped his sides while the bull stroked his soft fur with one hand. He sighed happily as their sheaths rubbed softly against each other, feeling his twitch and swell as he pulled the mustelid up for another deep kiss.

While he suckled at Mystic's tongue, the mustelid's nimble hips ground against him, both of them growing to the moment as they rubbed against each other. A paw left Hank's side to rummage in the closest nightstand, the marten clearly not willing to stop the dance of their muzzles and tongues while he searched. Finally Mystic arched his back and pulled himself up, looking down at Hank with the bottle of lube from earlier in his smaller paw.

"There's something else I've been missing since those two weeks," Mystic said with a lascivious grin.

Chuckling, Hank smiled back and moved his hands to the marten's hips as Mystic helped to slip himself up against the bull's body. The marten flipped open the bottle and squeezed a bit of the lube onto his fingers, then reached back to spread it under his tail as the bushy limb lifted and swayed. As he did, Hank reached a hand around his rump and let one of his thick fingers help with pushing the material up into the marten's elastic hole. Mystic was already moaning as the digit pushed slowly into him, moving his paw to get some more lube while he looked down into Hank's eyes.

Any thoughts of taking the opportunity to try to escape or gain some advantage over the hero had fled from the bull's mind. Earlier maybe he could have attempted something, but not now, not after what he and the marten had shared with each other. That sort of betrayal would go against all rules of even their little back-and-forth game. And as he felt that paw slowly stroking lube onto his thick, erect cock, all Hank wanted was a little more time with his companion, this one extra act of passion as he looked up at that wonderful chestnut body.

Fingers running through the soft fur, the bull gripped the marten's hips and began to slowly slide and position him, meeting no resistance as the marten lifted himself up over the erect bovine shaft. Mystic panted in passion as Hank's hands guided him and he lowered himself slowly against the waiting head. At the moment the cockhead began to push up into the tight hole, the marten's eyes closed, the hero gasping passionately as Hank felt the ring stretch slowly around his member. The tight, hot grip made the bull grunt and snort as his hips pushed up and his hands continued to guide the mustelid frame around his erection. Vision blurring, he quickened the pace, impaling the hero on his shaft and hearing a high pitched squeal of pleasure from Mystic.

"Oh God, yes!" the hero called out as he was settled with the bull's cock deep inside.

Hank could feel every little ripple around his malehood, the grip of the marten's slickened walls around his shaft, barely able to grunt out between breaths. "I've missed this too."

Thrusting his hips upward, Hank gained a tight grip on the marten and let out a feral grunt. He began to work the smaller male up and down, using him in that rough way he knew Mystic loved while the mustelid bounced his hips in time with each push and pull. A chorus of chittering and exclamations escaped the marten between his panting breaths as he rode the bull, his inner channel squeezing Hank's cock in the smooth heat and milking the bull as their scents mingled once more in the bedroom.

That joined scent meant more to Hank than almost anything, bringing him back to every time they had been together, even as his balls began to try and draw up for another climax. He willed himself to hold back from the quickening pace of the marten moving along his entire length, burying it in himself only to slip back up and plunge back down again, crying out with every movement. He wanted this moment with Mystic to last just a little longer, just a moment more of the two of them being nothing more than friends on a bed enjoying each other's bodies. But soon the heat and pressure all along his length was more than he could withstand and his fingers moved from the smooth hips of the marten to the bed sheets as the most powerful orgasm of the night began.

The bull's eyes shut tight and his fists gripped great handfuls of the sheets as he shot up into the marten, bellowing with every throb and spurt as the bliss washed through his entire body. He was dimly aware of the marten crying out above him and the feeling halfway into his climax of warm, sticky fluid splattering across his chest from Mystic's own orgasm. That moment, the feel of their bodies against each other and the smell of their arousal and their seed all mixing in the air at once, was overwhelming for Hank. His mind was gone for several moments in the afterglow, visiting all the other times he'd had the marten or the marten had had him, every tawdry dalliance in every hidden lair, back alley, or this very room. And in the moments as he softened and Mystic slipped slowly off of him to lay close on top of him and his arms wrapped around the smaller male, the bull couldn't stop himself.

"I love you."

"Love you too."

Hank's eyes shot open to look at the marten, seeing the hero's eyes wide and staring back into his. The bull was locked up, no clue what to do next as the awkward moment simply stretched between them. Try to take it back? Dive into another conversation and see where it led? He was completely at a loss.

As Hank's mouth opened to try and find something resembling the right words, Mystic's paw darted to the lamp on the bedside table. In one more quick movement, the bull felt another sting at his neck as the marten trembled on top of him.

Well ... that's one solution, he thought as he drifted back down into unconsciousness.

***

Reclining on the bunk in his cell, Hank sketched on the pad of paper in his hands. The next suit needed a few new features, especially something to deal with the gaps created in the armor if anything got twisted. Working out the facts and figures and diagramming wasn't the same as being able to experiment in one of his labs, but it was at least a way to get a start for the time that he was stuck in Harper.

Thankfully the understanding he had allowed him to work in peace. Because he didn't have a habit of going on killing rampages like some other folks he'd run across, he wasn't stuck in a hyper-max facility or an asylum. And the few gangs or hard cases in Harper had learned during his first stay that it was wise to just leave Taurus Maximus alone and give him no cause to notice them. Even outside of the suit he was an imposing figure, and he always found a way to get his armor or other toys back. So he was content to work on plans for modifications to his equipment, and as long as they didn't resemble actual escape plans, the guards couldn't really hassle him for exercising his mind.

He needed to keep his mind busy now more than ever. Hank hadn't seen or heard anything from Mystic since that evening, but the whole conversation had been circling in his head since he woke up to be booked back into the prison. He'd thought about the idea of going straight for the marten. It was attractive at times, just letting everything go and being with the male he ... whatever they were to each other. If the hideaway and bedroom were any indication, they wouldn't want for resources. Then he thought about someone else being able to pull his strings, about having to just blend in with society. Plus most people wouldn't simply let him forget the past. It just wouldn't work and he couldn't change that much even if he wanted to.

Exhaling as he finished a round of theoretical diagrams for some lightweight adaptive under armor in the suit, Hank tapped his pencil against his snout. He'd always gone for external adaptations and didn't like the idea of surgery, but he couldn't deny that turning a few designs into implants would be useful. The psychic dampeners, for one, would make sure that Mystic or any other mentalist could never use their tricks on him. A lock-pick of some kind in a sheath in his wrist wouldn't be a bad idea either. If he really wanted to win the next round, it might be time to bite that bullet and allow for those couple little things. Taurus didn't have to go nuts with it like some of the cybernetic monstrosities he'd seen, just a few little extras that could never be taken from him.

Flipping a page, he began to work out what would be necessary to make the dampeners smaller and the points on the skull where they'd have to fit for maximum effect. He'd also need to make sure there were no damaging effects on the brain, but the external models had shown no issues in the couple years of experiments before finally applying them.

As he sketched on the pad, his mind started to drift again to his feelings about the hero. Did he really love him, or had that just been the moment? Mystic had said it back too, but that could have been just a reflex. Their secret flings and trysts after almost every battle were one thing, but actual serious feelings complicated everything. And he thought and worried about Mystic more than he'd even admitted during that night. The reality was that he was keeping his ear open all the time for news of the hero and hoping that he'd be safe. Before, he'd chalked it up to the idea of a final victory; having Mystic firmly in his possession before anyone else could get to him, with no chance to play his mental games. After that night, the thought of seeing his face and remembering it as he held him and kissed him brought on a whole different feeling.

He had a special high-tech collar waiting for the marten that was originally going to be used to keep him like some kind of trophy or pet, maybe even to be loaned out to friends on occasion as proof of his triumph. But now Hank only wanted to use it to keep him safe and figure out just what they were to each other. No more worrying about his little marten going up against the wrong villain or ruining the bull's own plans. No one else would have a chance to know Mystic's identity; that would be for Hank and Hank alone. They could be together, simply on Taurus Maximus's terms. And at night when no one was watching, behind secure doors, he might even have Mystic tie him up ... with a few precautions of course.

Hank lost focus as his hand drifted down to the growing bulge at his groin. He sighed as he momentarily became lost in the fantasy of the marten being pressed to him whenever and for as long as they liked, never having to worry about when they had to go back to their rivalry. But he couldn't stay there, couldn't let his mind wander like that right now. It simply wasn't time for that kind of activity, and it did no good sitting in a cell to go back and forth on questions he couldn't answer yet. He needed to just focus on finishing the designs.

Shaking his head and coming back to the cold, uncomplicated science, Taurus let the wondering and fantasies about Mystic fade away. He had to be ready for the next breakout, for the next act to bring his pine marten out into the open, and for their next battle.

Next time, lover, things will be different ...

Spy games and love games sometimes mesh all too well.

DUPLICITY

Sorin

Lucan dropped into a three-point crouch, the 9mm like an extension of his hand. The lithe panther sprinted down the hall, stopping at the corner with precise movements born from natural agility and intense training. Coming around the corner, his suppressed weapon popped twice, and he was past the pair of security guards before their bodies hit the ground. Pressing himself up against the wall by the door, he placed a small box on the panel that protected the door's security lock. A second later a low buzz and a clicking pop sounded, and the door opened with the faint smell of burnt wiring. Plucking the box from the wall, Lucan tucked it back into his pocket as he pushed open the door and slipped inside.

His eyes adjusted quickly to the dim light as he crept across the floor towards the computer terminal. Finding a USB port, he connected the small flash drive and watched the dark screen light up, small command windows flashing in and out of existence as the instruction device began its work.

"Intruder alert. Intrusion in Data Storage Detected." The calm tone of the alarm system filled the room from recessed speakers in the ceiling and walls. Lucan snapped up the flash drive, preparing his escape. He cursed softly, hoping that the program had finished and captured the needed data. Alarms blared through the speakers, dismissing the surreal calm voice noting his intrusion. Movement broke the thin line of light under the door, and without a thought Lucan pressed himself up against the wall to the right of the door. The door slid open, and Lucan caught the barrel of the rifle before his active mind recognized it. With a sharp tug, the guard stumbled into the room and would have fallen if the panther's shoulder hadn't been there at throat level to catch him. A crunch and a gurgle were the last sounds the guard made as he tumbled to the ground.

He fired the guard's weapon into the pair standing just behind their fallen comrade. Lucan stepped over the pair, dropping the rifle to the ground and drawing his pistol in one smooth motion. The sound of boots behind him and a shout indicated how close his pursuers were. He ducked around another corner as a burst of automatic fire ripped into the wall where his head had been only a second ago. Sprinting, head down, he heard the sound of feet rounding the corner.

With only a moment's hesitation, he threw himself into a roll as another burst of fire zipped past him so close he could hear the snap of the bullets. Senses honed to a sharpness reserved for field agents of F.L.A.G. he fired a shot behind him, the bullet taking the lead guard between the eyes, whipping the running male's head back, and making him crumple, tripping his two companions as they ran behind him. The hall continued to the left and right, and he could see guards running towards him from both directions, cutting off his escape.

Even later, after the commotion died down, he couldn't think what brought him to do it. With a casual cockiness, the panther snapped off a casual two finger salute to the lead, hard-faced wolf guard, and leaped through the fortieth-story window behind him out into the night air. Wind whistled past him, faster and faster, the lights of the cars rushing up to meet him. The snap of the parachute deploying jerked his mind and his body back into reality.

***

"Lucan, I don't know how you did it." The young terrier looked up in a mix of awe and disbelief as he typed quickly. "You even managed to get the data."

Lucan grinned down at the kid, basking a little in the praise. He would never admit it, but he loved this almost as much as the thrill of the work. "So it's all there, Lee?" He asked the dog, leaning on the wall next to the tech's work area.

The desk in front of the young dog was covered with computers, and while it looked cluttered Lucan knew it was organized to the terrier's own needs. Lee was the best tech in the business despite—or because of—his checkered youth. He had been recruited right out of high school by F.L.A.G, after he had bypassed some of the organization's encryption at age sixteen, as part of a smoke-screened contest to find young talent. Despite his age he had settled in nicely though and become an indispensable part of the team.

Lee nodded eagerly "Account records, Information stockpiles, even phone numbers of Margrin's mistresses." The dog giggled in that teenage way that spoke to hormones at war and smiled up at Lucan then back to his screen. "Hold on a second …" he typed in a few more commands and frowned.

"What is it, Lee?" asked Lucan, leaning over Lee's shoulder to look at the dog's screen.

"A hidden file." He opened the document and frowned. "Just an address alone in a file, and it's here in town. It's not listed under any of his accounts, almost seems like an afterthought." Lucan picked up a notepad from the desk next to the computer and wrote the address down, pulling off the paper and returning the notepad.

"I suppose I should check it out then," said the panther, idly slipping the paper into his pocket and patting the dog lightly on the shoulder. "Let me know if you get anything more ok?" He grinned at Lee, who had already turned back to his screen, lost in the flicker of the monitor.

***

The address was an apartment building, four stories, and looked to contain eight expensive lofts. Not surprising with the upscale neighborhood. Seated at a small sidewalk café the panther sipped overpriced, subpar coffee and casually watched the building. It seemed normal enough. No security beyond a doorman and some cameras. He noted plenty of comings and goings into and out of the building.

Taking a final sip of his coffee, he stood, dropped some money on the table, and made his way over towards the building. He made a show of strolling along the street, stopping to look into a few of the kitschy little shop windows until he reached the fence that marked the apartment's property line. Pausing and kneeling to tie his shoe, he casually slipped a small camera into the foliage of the decorative plants on the corner of the property so that the little spy eye watched the building. Standing after finishing with his shoe, he walked over to his car and took a roundabout route back towards F.L.A.G.

***

"See, Lucan, it's this fox; it has to be." Lee held his finger over one of the keys on his computer. On the screen, frozen, was a frame of the footage from the camera. "The address said 4B. According to the building blueprints that's the top floor, corner room there to the left of the main door." The terrier hit a key, and the video began to play again. "See, he comes in, and five minutes later the lights come on in 4B" he typed a command and the video jumped ahead. "Next night, fox comes home, lights come on four minutes later" Lee looked over at Lucan, a wide grin on his face.

"So what else do you have for me Lee?" the panther asked, looking down at the fox on the screen.

"I ran him through Facial Recognition, CIA, Interpol; no one had anything on him. Then I ran him through local city police records." The dog was grinning more, tail going a mile a minute. Lucan knew he loved this kind of stuff, the suspenseful reveal, like in the mystery movies. Pressing a key his screen popped up a file "Our fox, a one Tylor Marks, appears to have a criminal record for prostitution." The dog smiled proudly, leaning back in his chair and crossing his arms over his chest.

Lucan chuckled. "Good work, Lee. I suppose it's time to pay Mr. Marks a little visit."

***

Mr. Marks wasn't especially quiet coming up the stairs. The fox had his paws full. Backlit from the hallway lights, he clutched a bag from a high-priced clothing boutique in his teeth, a set of keys in one hand, and a cup of coffee in the other. Lucan watched the lithe vulpine bump the door closed with a shapely rump and drop the keys into a basket that hung by the door. He fished a stack of mail out of his shopping bag. Setting down his coffee, he started going through it, tossing the envelopes into a trash can by the door one by one.

The fox was definitely a looker, lean with soft russet fur, immaculately cared for. He was dressed pretty plainly, but in clothing that spoke volumes about how the fox had paid a lot of money to look like he hadn't spent a lot of money on his clothes. The clothing clung to his body though, leaving very little to the imagination.

"You've been a very bad boy Mr. Marks." Lucan's voice was soft, yet he couldn't hide a slight smile as the fox jumped at the sound and spun to face him. Lucan had to give the vulpine credit; he had no idea where the male had kept the can of mace he now held. Not that it mattered, since he was too far away to use it. He watched the fox peer into the darkness over by the couch where the panther sat. *Pretty green eyes*, he thought to himself before reaching over to switch on the light.

The fox looked at him steadily, mouth shut, though he thought he detected a bit of nervousness in the vulpine face. "What are you doing in here?" Marks finally asked, tail flicking behind him, catching the light from the recessed lamp above him.

"I want to talk to you about a man named Margrin." He watched the fox's face as his expression shifted from fear to confusion to downright dumbfounded.

"Why would you break into my house to talk to me about Mari?" He asked curiously.

"Because … your 'Mari' has done some bad things, Mr. Marks," he purred, watching the fox for any duplicity. The vulpine just seemed so startled about the topic and the intruder, it was hard to think it was anything but the truth.

"Mari is a sweetie; I can't imagine his being on the bad side of anyone," the fox admitted after a moment. "Look, I'm going to get some water, you going to freak out if I move or some stupid thing like that?" he asked. Lucan shook his head, watching the fox with a slightly bemused expression on his muzzle. To his credit, Mr. Marks hesitated for only a moment before lowering the mace and heading for the kitchenette.

Marks came out of the kitchen carrying a glass of water and sat down across from Lucan. "You seem pretty calm for having a stranger in the house," commented Lucan dryly, to which the fox only shrugged.

"Comes with what I do, which I'm sure your aware of, since you seem to know almost all the other stuff that I don't normally share … including where I live." The fox looked at Lucan with a slight sigh then settled back. "So what do you want to know about Mari?" He took a sip of water, looking at Lucan over the rim of the glass.

"How do you know him?" He asked after a moment watching the fox for subtle hints of body language and movement.

"The same way I know a lot of guys, discreetly." He added after a moment. "I'm pretty sure Mari is married, at least I've seen the mark of a ring on his finger." Marks set his glass down on the table and leaned forward towards Lucan as he spoke. The fox reached out lightly grabbing the panther's ring finger giving it a little wiggle to emphasize what he meant. It was then that the panther's nose first caught a tingle of the fox's scent.

Lucan pulled back slightly from the paw's touch. "And I'm sure you're very good at what you do, Mr. Marks." He cursed himself inwardly for the stammer, trying to concentrate on the fox's face. "I mean how did you meet him?"

Marks smiled "Call me Ty, please, much less of a mouthful than 'Mr. Marks.'" Lucan couldn't help noticing the flick the fox's eyes downward as he spoke. "And I met him in Cabo San Lucas when I was on vacation."

Sex had never been much on the forefront of his thinking. Ever since the army, the academy, and his work, it just never came up. There was something about the fox's scent though. His voice was thrilling, unusual, and enticing. His ears perked listening to the melodic roll of the fox's words, his tone.

"Had you been to Cabo before?" he asked, almost yanking his eyes away from the fox's face, his delicate muzzle, the lovely graceful line of his jaw … With a soft curse he realized he hadn't even heard Ty's answer. The fox's scent was in his nose, like a drug, a delicious intoxicant that reminded him, all at once what he had been missing with his years of abstinence and dedication.

Ty leaned forward to pick up his water, and before he even realized it had happened he had dragged the fox onto the couch with him, muzzle pressed to his in an eager kiss, tongues brushing each other. Lucan vaguely remembered a soft tug on the fox's paw pulling him from his chair and into the panther's lap, but not what had inspired him to make such a bold move. His mind, hazy with lust, was glad the fox hadn't resisted the urging.

His other hand slipped around the fox's lower back pulling him closer as muzzles and tongues danced languidly, breathing hot, heavy pants. Lucan felt the fox's fingers trailing along his chest, over his shirt, and up under the cloth, running through the short silken fur of his abdomen. It felt exquisite, his skin tingling under the touch.

Fingers worked at the buttons of his shirt, pushing the article open and running through the fur of his bare chest. His own paws, far from still, slid down the fox's hips, caressing softly and cupping his rump in a delicate gesture belying the strength in the panther's fingers.

Lucan was a bit surprised when the fox pulled away and slipped out of his lap. He looked up at the sly, excited expression on the fox's muzzle as Ty slipped his shirt off, taking a bit of time while the panther watched. As the light silk fluttered to the ground Ty reached out, gently drawing on Lucan's hand, pulling the panther to his feet, and sliding his shirt off one shoulder with his free hand. Lucan leaned down to pluck another kiss from the fox's muzzle but was thwarted when the vulpine coyly turned his muzzle away and drew him towards the stairs.

Navigating the stairs took more time than usual. Half way along Lucan pinned the fox with a thump against the wall stealing his kiss and getting a caress along his arousal as it strained against his slacks. The initial touch on his erection, even through his pants, was so intense he almost snarled. Both panted softly as they reached the top of the stairs and began to shed clothing like the casualties of a war along the carpet leading to the bed.

Lucan's pants were the first to go. He was surprised to find himself cognizant of the need to catch his gun before it fell with its holster attached to the waistband. He was careful to leave the weapon discreetly bundled with the pants to avoid giving its presence away. His shirt joined Ty's pants on the floor, his phone kicked some place under the bed. He couldn't bring himself to care about anything more than the soft, skilled hand gently teasing his cock, the smell of the aroused vulpine in his nose and the blood rushing in his ears.

Pushing the fox languidly down onto the bed, he fell on him like a drowning man would reach for a rope. Muzzles met again, hot and furious, Lucan's fingers closing around the fox's excited length. He smiled slightly despite himself at the eager gasp from Ty. Insistent paws pushed him onto his back, and he rolled looking over at Ty. The vulpine eagerly moved, trailing his muzzle along the line of the panther's hip, and licking languidly along the underside of his erection.

A growl escaped Lucan's muzzle despite himself, claws digging into the bed as his arousal was treated to a most exquisite bath. The fox's tongue seemed to be everywhere, at once caressing and soothing, burning, tingling, and tantalizing. The suddenness and intensity of his orgasm shocked him. His hips arched, and he let out a surprised, almost barking growl as he throbbed, spatters of his seed streaking across his tummy and Ty's muzzle while the fox sought to catch the warm pulses.

A shudder ran through the panther's body, an almost pained groan escaping his muzzle as he relaxed slowly from the intensity.

Ty lifted his muzzle, licking a few of the stray spatters from his lips and grinned

"You did need that, didn't you?" he murmured, trailing a finger through one of the slippery trails on the panther's belly. After the intensity, Lucan found he was blushing only slightly at the eager, quick release more like a teenager than a disciplined male.

"Seems so …" he purred, drawing the fox up against him and spooning against the vulpine back. Reaching down he began to tease the aroused fox and was surprised to find he was as hard as when they started. Ty's scent was still enticing, clinging to the fox's throat, so he pressed his nose into the thicker ruff of fur gently prodding at the slender rump with his already eager arousal. Ty was breathing quickly, soft little breathes as Lucan's paw trailed along his member. His hand fell to Ty's hip stroking the luscious curves of the vulpine rump and thigh. Lucan arched his hips forward, feeling the heat on the tip of his arousal, then tightness wrap around the slick head. He felt Ty stiffen, a sharp gasp hardly registering it on more than a primal level as he pushed himself into Ty's heat pulling back on his hips.

Coherency left, reduced to memories of snarling eager thrusts, yelps, and cries of pleasure and pain from the fox. The throbbing surge of pleasure, primal and deep with need and a bit of desperation, claimed him. He remembered the heavy, musky smell of the fox's release across the sheets. The shimmering glow as they both basked in post release almost brought him back to his senses.

***

Lucan woke to the sharp light of dawn in his eyes. He was in a bed—that much he knew—and the scent of sex still lingered in the room. His eyes slid over to the fox, asleep under a light sheet next to him, the fabric rising and falling gently with Ty's breathing. Lying back with a smile, the panther closed his eyes reveling in the warm, pleasurable flashes of memory that darted through his head.

A paw came to rest on his chest. "How about breakfast?" Asked the familiar, warm voice of his lover. "You can use the shower while I cook." Ty slipped out of bed and padded across the room, taking his time, letting Lucan's eyes linger on him.

Smiling, the panther picked up his cell from the bedside table and flipped it open to check his messages. One from Lee, from the previous evening saying he had found out more information and would talk to Lucan when he got back. He sighed, knowing he should check in, but seeing that the message wasn't urgent he got up and made his way into the bathroom for the proffered shower.

Breakfast was delicious, coffee much better than the café from the other day, and the fruit was fresh. His phone rang, and glancing down to see Lee's number, Lucan glanced over at the fox who was sipping coffee with a dainty motion born of natural grace. He excused himself and made his way out onto the patio to take the call.

"Lucan, where have you been? I have been trying to call you all night, and the director has been looking for you." The dog's voice was terse, annoyed at something outside the scope of the call.

"Calm down Lee, I was out … handling a bit of intelligence gathering and had my phone off. Why does the director want to see me?" he asked, scowling at the phone despite himself. He heard the patio door slide open behind him and felt the soft caress of arms draping around his waist.

"He says someone pulled strings, Senator Avrium ordered a halt to the Margrin investigation, some sort of pressure from high up."

Senator Avrium maintained oversight of F.L.A.G. and a few other black book projects and was one of the only government officials even aware of the group's existence. Lucan looked back over at Ty, smiling a little and mouthing the word "business" to which the fox nodded resting his head against the panther's back. "The director says you're supposed to return for reassignment, other cases have piled up while we have been focused on Margrin."

"Right, so I'll be into the office in about an hour, hummm?" he purred, casually smiling down at Ty, who returned the look.

"Is someone there with you, Lucan? Where are …" The panther hung up the phone mid-sentence and turned in the fox's arms, looking down at him.

"Something has come up at the office; I don't think I'll be able to stay for breakfast," he murmured as paws warmly rubbed the small of his back. "Can I see you again?" He asked, surprised at himself even as the words left his muzzle.

"I'd like that," the fox replied softly, accompanied by a tender kiss. The kiss broke, leaving a hungry look in Ty's eyes "Are you sure you have to leave this minute?" he asked, his voice slipping into a sultry purr that made Lucan's knees weak.

"I think I can spare a little while …" the panther murmured quietly.

***

"Director, you're making a big mistake."

The mid-fifties husky hardly looked up at the panther. "Mistake or no, Senator Avrium is in charge of our budget, one of the few people we are actually accountable to, so when he says 'stop', we stop." Lucan could feel the frustration in the director's voice, the annoyance at having his orders questioned.

"It doesn't make any sense, Director; we get close, start to gather real information on Margrin, and suddenly we're told to cease and desist. It's politics, or it's money, or both, but you can't tell me you're not even a little suspicious." Lucan leaned forward slightly as he spoke, noting the twitch in the Director's ear that told him he had made a point, even if the husky would never admit it.

"Fine!" growled the dog. "I'll have Lee keep up the data probe on the accounts we found, the senator will never know, since it's not budgetary. But if he doesn't find anything else, I expect you to drop the issue. And no more field activities related to Margrin until I say so, understood?"

Lucan nodded and stood slowly. "Understood completely, Director."

"And take some time off fieldwork; you're getting agitated about nothing, it's a bad sign." With a wave he excused Lucan, and returned to his paperwork.

***

"Lucan, are you seeing someone?" The dog's voice squeaked, like it always did when he was nervous about a question he was asking. The panther looked up from his desk, a bit surprised to see Lee out of his computer room. He pushed a folder to the side closing it and smirked.

"Why would you think that, Lee?" A bemused expression crossed his muzzle as he watched the little dog fidget.

"You're never around anymore; you used to be here late all the time. I haven't seen you working later than five for the last two weeks." Lucan leveled his gaze more on the dog as he started to fidget more.

"The chief told me to take some more time after the Margrin case, so I am." He held the dog in his gaze a moment longer. The buzz of Lucan's phone on his desk broke the silence and Lee slunk off back to his computer room. Waiting until the pup was out of earshot he flipped open the phone "Hiya fox." He grinned, imagining the fox's surprised look on the other end.

"How did you know it was me? The number's blocked," came the slightly surprised vulpine voice from the ear piece. Lucan glanced at the Caller ID, showing the fox's unlisted number, one of the many perks of his job.

"Lucky guess." He commented, a grin in his voice. "So are we still on for tonight?" His tone was upbeat, though he kept his voice low.

"Of course we are. Will the office let you out on time? I'm cooking tonight." Lucan felt his tail twitching slightly and a larger smile spreading over his muzzle.

"Yup, I'll be there at five." They exchanged a few more pleasantries before Lucan hung up the phone. His ears twitched at a soft pop in the receiver just before the connection ended and was out of his seat and into the tech room like a streak.

"Lee, what the fuck! Do you know what the director would do if he knew you were listening in on my calls!" He pushed the door closed before his voice could carry.

The little dog almost fell out of his seat in a scramble to put it between him and the angry panther. "I didn't mean anything by it, Lucan! Honest, I was just curious, and you've been blocking me all week!" He whimpered as the panther stood glaring at him darkly from the door way.

Lucan sighed, leaning back against the door. "Your smarts are going to get you into trouble someday, Lee, if you don't watch it." He felt the anger draining out of himself, leaving behind a soft burn of annoyance. "You can't tell anyone, okay? You know field agents are discouraged from having significant outside ties, especially with persons of interest to the agency." He glanced back at the door and growled softly "Keep this secret for me, and I'll owe you, okay?"

Lee peeked out from behind his chair and nodded. "Yeah, okay,

Lucan, I won't tell; I promise." He rose up a little more when he was sure that the panther wasn't going to come after him. "So who is it?" he asked, and Lucan felt a flood of relief run through him that the dog's cell sniffer hadn't retrieved Ty's ID.

"No one you know, Lee."

***

He was barely inside the door before Ty was in his arms, muzzles locked in a deep kiss, tongues pressing eagerly against each other. To anyone watching from outside, the embrace would have seemed almost violent in its eagerness. They melted onto the couch in a soft, intimate, snarling dance filled with gasps and yips of pleasure, the call of primal, lustful hunger.

Later they lay quietly in each other's arms, basking in the glow of satiated urgency. "Dinner is probably cold," came the quiet amused vulpine whisper in his ear, and Lucan chuckled softly.

"I wasn't in any great hurry … to eat," he said, giving the lithe vulpine form in his arms a soft hug. They lingered together in the soft warmth of each other's embrace. Finally Ty slipped out of Lucan's embrace and licked his nose.

"I'm going to get a glass of wine." He grinned to the panther that looked at him with languid, half-lidded eyes. "Would you like some?"

Lucan nodded, watching the pretty red tail wag as it made its way into the kitchen.

"I am going to get in the shower actually, kitty, will you wait for me?" The fox's sultry voice drifted in from the kitchenette. A moment later he heard the sound of the water running.

Lucan's phone buzzed in his pants by the door. With a languid purr and stretch the panther made his way over fishing, his phone out of a pocket.

"Hello?"

A soft crackle greeted him like a phone left off the hook in a mostly quiet room. He was about to hang up and try calling Lee back when a soft sob broke through the connection.

"L-Lucan … th-they're all dead … and … and I think they're going to find me …" Lee's voice was a scratchy, terrified whisper. The connection cut, leaving Lucan staring at the phone for a long moment.

He stared at the phone, his hand pulling on his pants automatically. A moment later his mind caught up and ground into action. He was out the door with a purpose, hardly registering the surprised shout from Ty as the fox came into the living room with two glasses of wine. Down the stairs and into his car he flowed and hit the street at reckless speed.

Driving up onto the curb in front of the secret underground back entrance to the F.L.A.G. compound, he slipped from the car leaving the keys in the ignition. Darting into the run-down travel office that served as a front for the secure entrance, Lucan made his way through the room, hardly taking in the stunned faces of the office workers.

None of them knew of the entrance, Lucan was sure. Meant only for emergencies, he doubted that the door had ever been used in the time they had worked there. He passed into the back room and closed the door locking it. Pushing open the secret panel, he typed in his personal access code and waited impatiently. The machine scanned his thumb before the wall opened with a soft click, and he pushed it further into the dark tunnel beyond.

***

F.L.A.G. was in shambles as Lucan peered out of the tunnel that ended in a utility closet behind the cubicles in the middle of the office. Most of the lights were out, some flickering faintly, a few sparking, and he could see a body near the elevator. From here it looked like Lisa, the agency's receptionist, slumped against the wall.

Shifting his grip on his pistol, the panther slipped out of the utility closet on silent feet, moving through the ghost-lit room. A slight crunch of footsteps around the corner perked his ears and alerted him to movement on the other side of the wall. A quick glance showed the outline of a figure in tactical gear checking a pair of cubicles. In a smooth motion, Lucan slid around the corner, his gun hand coming up in the same breath. The figure turned slightly, surprise on his face. The panther pulled the trigger.

Click.

It was the loudest sound he had ever heard, or so it seemed. The gun was empty. A split second passed between the pair, and as the gunman brought his submachine gun up Lucan threw the gun in desperation. The pistol hit the jackal between the eyes, causing him to stagger, his gun going off kilter as it spat fire in a series of soft suppressed pops. Darting forward without thinking, Lucan felt the sting of a bullet grazing his cheek as he grabbed the male's wrist and pulled him into an elbow slam.

The panther grimly registered the dull pop as the Jackals neck broke against his elbow, and he caught the submachine gun from the suddenly slack fingers before it hit the ground. Guiding the body to the floor quietly, he checked the clip and pulled a second one from his dead foe's belt, slipping it into his pocket. The computer room was at the end of the hall and through the lunch room. Lee would be there if he was still alive.

Voices in the lunch room tipped him off to the presence of more intruders. Silent, terse talking reached his ears, and he paused for just a moment to listen.

"He said there would be twenty three, and that the panther

would be taken care of. Find the fucking little mutt; he's the only one not accounted for." It was spoken in a soft growl. *Probably a wolf*, thought Lucan as he stepped around the corner into the lunch room. His gun spoke back, almost as quiet, but the male it was speaking to got the message. The bullets caught the otter in the neck, just below the ear, and he went down without a sound. Two of the other men in the room spun, trying to see where the attack was coming from, their eyes falling on Lucan as the panther emptied the last of the clip into them leaving their broken bodies draped and moaning softly on the cafeteria table behind them. He dropped behind the cover of the table, starting to reload the weapon on instinct.

"It's the fucking panther! He's not supposed to be here; kill him!" It was the wolf again, his surprised shout cut off by the snapping impact of weapon fire hitting the table where he had taken refuge. Lucan rolled slightly to his right, glancing along the table.

"Three, and the wolf," he murmured to himself before rolling out from behind the table in a crouch. His gun popped, met by a surprised yelp and a crash. He didn't wait for a response before rolling behind the cover of the lunch counter as bullets smacked into its metal surface. Picking up a discarded apple from the floor, he pressed back up against the corner of the counter.

He waited for a brief lull in the barrage of weapons fire, before leaning out, throwing the apple at the pair of intruders to the right. Both reacted as they were trained, ducking to the left in case the apple was a weapon. The real weapon in his hand made short work of the cougar as he turned back, realizing a second too late that the apple wasn't the attack. Lucan was moving again before the body hit the ground. He pulled the trigger as the other intruder spun and caught the male in the torso, finishing his spin and depositing him in a crash among some of the fallen chairs.

Lucan turned and found himself face to face with the barrel of a suppressed submachine gun. The wolf on the other end displayed his teeth in a predatory grin that left no doubt he was enjoying this. He squeezed the trigger, and nothing happened. The look of surprise on the wolf's face would have been comical in another situation.

"Same thing happened to me today," purred Lucan in a deadly soft monotone, and before it even registered on the wolf, the panther pulled the trigger. This time his gun fired.

***

Lucan stood over the raccoon still slumped against the table where he had fallen at the beginning of the fire fight. Blood pulsed through his fingers, and he looked up at Lucan, his eyes wide with pain.

"Tell me who sent you. How did you find this place?" His voice held no rancor, business, it was all business. Always would be now, he knew that.

"M-Margrin sent us … traced a call back here …" The male—not much more than a kid, probably enlistment age—stammered, terrified. Lucan almost felt sorry for him, still at that age where he thought he was invincible, until now.

"How did Margrin get a number to trace? Ours are all secure." He asked, knowing from experience that the boy was beyond caring about what he was saying.

"From your phone …" groaned the raccoon as he slumped lower, a little sob escaping his muzzle. Lucan left him on the floor of the cafeteria. He had all the information he needed.

His training was all that kept him moving. Every door he opened, every corner he rounded had the potential to reveal one more dead face, a co-worker, friends he recognized despite the violence done to them. The raccoon and his friends had been thorough ... so thorough.

***

Lucan pulled up in front of the condo. The neighborhood was so quiet, so normal in that sleepy way of neighborhoods unused to violence and crime. Lee was alive; it was something. The panther had found the young dog huddled under a desk, almost petrified with fear. It had taken a few moments to coax him to crawl out from where he had almost wedged himself and get him out of the building. The dog was in a safe house across town, the FBI had been called as protocol demanded, and Lucan was sitting, looking up at Ty's condo.

His feet carried him out of the car and up the front stairs. The panther brushed past the door man, the no-nonsense lion looking about to stop him until he saw the look in the panther's eyes and the blood that had matted his neck fur where the near miss had cut open his cheek.

Lucan took the stairs two at a time. He wasn't expecting to find Ty still there; he knew it was a long shot, but he also knew he couldn't leave it. He went through the door with a solid kick that smashed out the lock, stepping into the living room.

What surprised him first was the strong scent of incense hiding the fox's musk. What surprised him more was that there, on the couch was Ty. In the fox's hand was a slim, lethal-looking pistol. For a long moment, the pair looked at each other, weapons leveled, the callous pieces of metal aching to kill.

"You set me up, Ty." The fox nodded slightly, eyes fixed on the panther. "Why?" The question surprised even him, he had never cared before.

"Because Margrin paid me, Lucan, and because it's what I do."

The fox's voice was the same, teasing, seductive, but the edge was hard now, stinging. "Sex was a nice bonus to be sure, but in the end, it was all business."

"You got Lee's number from my phone, and the encryption code from the firmware, traced his call back to the agency. You found the data probe was still running and sent men to kill everyone." The panther had worked it all out on the drive. "And somehow you beefed up your pheromones to drive me nuts, draw me in, so you could get them."

Ty nodded. "A little chemical treatment some of Margrin's people cooked up; very useful in my business."

He glared at the fox. "Margrin is a terrorist and a killer. How can you work for him, Ty?" The sudden need to understand, something the panther had never felt before in all his time at war, in killing and hunting people like Margrin. Now as he faced down Ty he needed to know.

There was no denial when Ty spoke. "It's really simple, Lucan. I love him." The vulpine lowered his gun, and Lucan suddenly caught a flicker of movement, a sorry half smile on the fox's face. Something hard hit him on the back of the head.

***

Lucan was surprised to wake up. Evening light burned in through the windows aggravating the headache. Looking up with a soft groan, the panther confirmed his suspicions; the apartment was empty. He was slumped over the couch where he had obviously been dragged and left. He staggered to the bathroom splashing a bit of water onto his face to calm the throbbing in his head.

The soap tray was filled with bullets, the rounds that had been in his gun when he had arrived the night before. The bullets that had almost gotten him killed at F.L.A.G. and under the soap bowl was a folded note.

"Lucan, I hope you appreciate the gift I have given you in letting you wake up." The panther scowled at the note almost imagining he could hear the fox's voice as he read. "I suppose we can chalk your life up as one more. I doubt you will ever understand what would drive a person to work for a man like Margrin." Lucan closed his muzzle his ears twitching slightly. "We're fated to meet again, and there is little chance, I think, that both of us will walk from that meeting alive."

***

Ty dropped his bag by the door with a tired sigh. It had been a long trip, throwing the feds off his trail had sent him half way around the world. Margrin had been right about the hit on F.L.A.G. but the feds were crippled now. They would chase their shadows and get nowhere. Now that F.L.A.G. was out of the picture, it would take years to recover the intel on Margrin's organization, years his lover could capitalize on. His phone rang, and he slipped it out of his pocket glancing at the number. It was Margrin, and that brought a smile to his face.

"Hello my sweet, no need to call, I just got ho—" A soft recognizable voice purred in his ear, cutting him off in mid-sentence.

"I do understand, Ty. Love can drive us to do inconceivable things." The fox opened his mouth for the first time at a loss for words. "But we do what we must. Margrin's dead, Ty. I'm coming to see you next."

The line went dead and the fox dropped his hand, the phone falling from his fingers.

.

When in doubt all problems can be solved with coffee.

False Impressions

Roland Jovaik

Winter winds sent a chill down Kevin's spine as he sat under his favorite tree outside his dorm. It had been stripped of all its leaves in preparation for the season's first snowfall. The seasons had fallen behind and, given that the wolf's winter coat was late coming in, he was grateful for it.

He dipped his muzzle into the rose that had been left mysteriously on his dorm room desk and took a deep breath. Its fragrance was still strong and fresh leaving a lingering tingle in his nose. He wondered who could've left it in his dorm. He lived alone and no one else had a key—not even his boyfriend, Jordan.

Kevin fiddled with the silver ring that rested on his left hand as petals slowly fell from the rose, blown away in the biting winter winds. He watched the petals drift along each snow bank until they flitted out of sight, leaving behind the delicate inner petals. When the wind picked up it quickly got to be too cold out for the wolf's late winter coat and he was forced inside.

The bustle of activity and studying students was a pleasant contrast to the silent winter vista outside. Steam rose from Kevin's mochaccino, enriched with an extra shot of espresso, as he took his usual table in the campus coffee shop, Weasel Shotz. He pressed his paws into the side of his cup for warmth before taking his first sip. The taste, along with an exorbitant amount of sugar and too much espresso, was like winter.

This was how he wanted to remember his college years. He idly spun his ring around his middle finger; relaxing after a long, hard semester, enjoying overpriced, decadently titled, lattes.

The wolf had almost convinced himself to crack open one of his biology textbooks when he was interrupted, a familiar face taking the seat across from him with a smug grin on his muzzle. Kevin smiled, dropping the book back into his bag. He definitely wasn't getting any studying done now. "Hey babe," he said, leaning back in his chair, taking another sip of his latte.

"Hey yourself lover boy." The rabbit's devious grin was obvious, and in the time they had known each other that grin had become a crystal clear signal.

"I'm not getting any studying done now, am I?" Kevin's grin mirrored Jordon's, his tail thumping against his chair.

Jordan looked at his non-existent watch and rolled his eyes before giving the lupine his signature *fuck me* look. "The odds don't look good, Sweetheart."

Kevin barely had time to collect his bag when Jordan grabbed him by the collar of his jacket and dragged him to the nearest bathroom. Kevin resisted, but only a little as he swatted at the rabbit in a fit of giggles, trying to maintain at least a little dignity in public.

As luck would have it, the first bathroom they visited was empty. Their giggles echoed against the tile, the room quickly filling with deep panting and lusty moans. They slipped into the handicap stall. Kevin's pants were down around his ankles before he could fumble the latch closed on the stall door.

Kevin leaned back against the wall as Jordan went to work, his short muzzle working wonders on the canine's swollen shaft. Jordan's white cotton-ball tail wiggled back and forth as he wrapped his lips eagerly around the wolf's thick cock. The sexual chemistry between them had been good since day one.

The wolf had to pull the rabbit's head back before he blew his load right in that pretty white muzzle. Jordan really was too good at his blowjobs. It made it hard to save himself for the real fun.

Jordan licked his lips with a grin. He stood, letting his pants fall to the floor before pressing himself up against the wall, his powder puff tail twitching back and forth. Kevin didn't need any more of an invitation than that.

The scent of arousal filled the bathroom stall as Kevin positioned himself behind the rabbit, placing a paw on either side of that pert rump, spreading them as he pressed the tip of his throbbing cock against the rabbit's flexing pucker.

Jordan scratched his dull claws against the bathroom wall with a gasp, pressing into Kevin's throbbing maleness. Kevin had to hold back from thrusting into the rabbit right away, even though his cock ached for the tight warmth of his boyfriend.

He rubbed the leaking tip of his shaft just beneath the rabbit's tail. Jordan squeaked and whined, his tail twitching uncontrollably as Kevin teased the needy lapine.

"C'mon baby, don't tease me," he whimpered. "You don't want us to get caught, do you?"

Kevin relented, positioning himself before he plunged his maleness deep under the bunny's stubby tail, eliciting a deep moan from the lapine.

The wolf started out slow, but quickly gained speed. Grunting echoed throughout the room. Kevin had to keep from biting his lip too hard as the rabbit pushed his tight ass against the wolf's impressive girth. The tight passage squeezed and massaged the wolf's cock as they fucked, pushing him closer and closer to the edge. Kevin wished the rabbit wasn't so good at working him up. They had barely begun and he was so close to blowing his load already.

The rabbit's squeaks and moans weren't helping. With each bump and grind, Jordan's moans got louder and louder as Kevin's knot stretched the rabbit's hole to its limits.

Kevin tried not to tie, but Jason was persistent. The rabbit pushed back, pressing the wolf's thick knot deeper under his tail.

"No, no, oooh," Kevin tried to pull back, but Jordan insisted, pushing until Jacob's knot popped inside. The wolf gasped and grabbed feebly at his boyfriend's fuzzy hips and jerked forward, spilling his seed into the bunny's bowels. Strangled moans echoed against the bathroom tile and died down as Kevin managed to restrain himself.

Jordan showed off his sticky paw with a grin. Kevin rubbed his claws through Jordan's fur and along his back with a giggle and a sigh. "What do I do with you, Bun? We're gonna be stuck like this for a little while, you know."

"I do," he replied with a chuckle. "I like how it feels when we tie like this."

Kevin said nothing in response and enjoyed the silence between them, running an aimless paw up the curves of the bunny's backside.

The bathroom door creaked open and the two of them froze, still pressed up against the wall. Hollow footsteps walked into the stall beside them. Kevin focused on staying absolutely still, keeping his paws planted firmly on the rabbit's hips.

Jordan, on the other hand, wiggled back and forth. Kevin jerked and stifled a moan. That was enough to catch the attention of the visitor next door.

"Aw gross, dude. Save that for your dorm room."

The footsteps hurried out of the bathroom with the door slamming shut behind them, followed by silence. Kevin gave the bunny's ass a smack that made him jump and giggle.

"I don't see why that was necessary." Kevin grunted, pulling back with a small gasp as his knot slid free, letting a small amount of cum dribble down the rabbit's thigh. He stuffed his package back in his pants and zipped up.

"It got him to leave, didn't it?"

Kevin grinned before stepping out of the stall while Jordan pulled his pants up. He hobbled over to the counter and ran the tap before pulling some Old Musk out of his bag, applying it thoroughly. "I'm not going to be able to walk straight for the next half hour with this boner in my pants, you know that?"

Jordan laughed without a hint of remorse and walked up to the sink, grabbing the masker to apply it under his tail. "Maybe it wouldn't be such an issue if you weren't so hot. Otherwise I wouldn't have sex with you at all and you wouldn't have to worry about random bathroom stiffies."

"Flatterer." Kevin splashed water against his muzzle and twisted the taps off, drying himself off with a hand cloth from his bag before pushing the bathroom door open.

Jordan soon followed, giving the wolf a slap on the ass before taking his place beside him. "You always carry around cosmetics in your bag?"

Kevin looked to the side and smirked. "I have to be ready for you, don't I?"

"Touché," said the rabbit as he skipped down the halls.

Kevin glanced back at the cafe where his mocha sat, neglected and cold. Seeing the latte reminded him why he'd gone to the coffee shop in the first place.

He leaned down to kiss his rabbit on the cheek and gave a small wag of his tail. "Hey, I need to get up to the dorms and study. If I don't, this last final is going to kick my ass."

The rabbit leaned back and stared at the wolf's backside with a keen interest. "I can think of so many better things to do than kick it."

Kevin laughed and ruffled the rabbit between the ears before patting his bag. "Cute, Bun. I'll catch up with you later."

Kevin caught a glimpse of the rabbit pouting as he headed for his dorm. As great as Jordan was, he thought, the need for sex was overwhelming at times.

Keys jangled as Kevin turned the knob to his dorm. He was ready to get some quality studying time in. The wolf paused when he noticed a bouqet of flowers sitting in the middle of his bed. He brought the flowers to his nose, only managing a quick sniff before a card fell from between the flowers. The floral scents lingered as he read the card.

I hope you like variety. I thought these tulips and chrysanthemums might brighten your day.

The card was unsigned. Kevin flipped it over, but there was nothing on the back either. They were beautiful and their smells livened up the small area nicely.

A sweet gesture, but it baffled Kevin as to how someone had gotten into his dorm to leave flowers. He shot off a quick text to Jordan. *Did you send flowers?*

His phone buzzed before he had the chance to put it back in his pocket. *no, y?*

No reason, he texted back before throwing the phone in his pocket. His phone buzzed again.

has sum1 been sending u flowers?

Kevin looked back at the unsigned card and tossed it onto his desk. *No, don't worry about it.*

Kevin sat back at his desk and cracked open his first text book before glancing at the bouquet. He sighed and let the aroma tickle his nose as he immersed himself in the fascinating world of biology.

***

"Who sent you flowers?" Jordan leaned over his coffee cup, his floppy ears almost dipping into his brew. This question came just after yet another ten minute quickie in the bathroom next to the campus cafe. It was starting to become a regular rendezvous for them.

Kevin lapped at his latte before setting it down. "I don't know. The card wasn't signed, but it's the second time this week."

"So you've got a secret admirer. That's kind of creepy. I mean, we're in college after all and that's like, grade-school stuff. In addition to being a stalker, he finds ways to get into your apartment when you're not around? Super creepy. Like, three times the creepage." He held three of his fingers up then picked up his coffee and took a long, thoughtful sip.

"I don't know." Kevin picked up his cup, keeping his elbows on the table. "I think it's just a little romantic. Kind of like back in high school, y'know?"

Kevin felt Jordan's paw on his. The rabbit looked very concerned. "It's suspicious, Sweetie. We're not teenagers anymore. That kind of behaviour isn't normal. The next time you see flowers, I want you to report it to campus security, okay?"

Kevin set his coffee down and squeezed the rabbit's paw. He still thought the flowers were a little sweet, but he wanted to respect his boyfriend's wishes, and he was glad to see Jordan so concerned for his well-being. "Alright, I'll tell someone the next time it happens. But," he trailed off, giving him time to take another sip of his coffee.

"But what?"

"Would you send me flowers?" He finished after taking a gulp of his coffee.

"What?"

"Would you buy me flowers?" Kevin repeated.

Jordan looked a little bewildered at the question. "Do you want me to buy you flowers?"

"That's not the point," Kevin said, leaning back in his chair. "Regardless of whether or not I wanted flowers, would you surprise me with flowers?"

"Does it count if I did something wrong?"

"Maybe, have you done anything wrong?"

Jordan tugged his ear, rolling it between his fingers as he looked off to the side. "No, not that I can recall."

Kevin unfolded his hands. "In the event that you were completely unprovoked and the thought just happened to cross your mind, would you buy me a bouquet of flowers?"

"Yeah, I mean, if you wanted me to."

Kevin only smiled and ended the conversation with another slurp of his coffee before they ran off to the washroom for round two.

***

No more flowers arrived the following week. The awkwardly cute display must have grown tiresome for his secret admirer and things were set to go back to normal.

With no more distractions around, Kevin was determined to have a quiet hour alone to study. He had retreated to another corner of the cafe away from his usual spot. Meeting up with Jordan so frequently had been extremely detrimental to his study time. He knew Jordan wouldn't understand his need for a little peace and quiet, so he resorted to hiding away. His grades couldn't afford to suffer, not if he wanted those scholarships he'd worked so hard for.

Kevin had only just found the dog-eared page in his book, a result of his last failed study session, when he was interrupted yet again. A meager coyote, holding a copy of the same book Kevin was currently trying to read, stood in front of the table with his head lowered and his ears flattened.

Awkward silence filled the space between them until Kevin decided he'd given the coyote ample time to try and explain himself. "Can I help you?"

"Oh, I'm sorry," he stammered, clutching his textbook tightly to his chest. "I'm—we're in the same class, you see. I wanted to ask if you could help me study. I'm not doing too well and, well, you're smart and have good grades, and—"

Kevin silenced the coyote with a paw. He watched the coyote stand stalk still, quaking with nervousness. He forced his muzzle into a smile and gestured to the free seat beside him. The coyote nodded and stumbled into the chair, nearly tipping coffee all over his notebooks.

Though the coyote was unmistakably awkward, there was a natural cuteness about him, Kevin thought. For being so shy, he was awfully adorable. From his puppy-dog eyes to his eager tail after he sat down. Kevin was about to go back to his textbook when the coyote spoke up again.

"Thank you," he whispered with his head reclined into his chest. "I'm not too good at introducing myself. I'm Ray." He extended a paw.

Kevin reached out and shook his paw, wondering how he had gone so long without noticing someone so awkwardly adorable. Easy to miss in a big class, he figured.

"No problem," Kevin finally answered back. "I'm just trying to catch up on some of the more advanced stuff myself. If you have any questions just let me know." Kevin picked up his coffee cup for another sip, disappointed to find that it was empty. He shook the cup with a sigh and set it back down.

"I can get you another one." Ray jumped from his chair. Kevin could barely stop him fast enough.

"No, you don't have to worry about that, I have enough—"

The coyote actually shushed him, leaving Kevin to stare with his mouth open. Based on first impressions, Kevin hadn't thought Ray had the capacity to be so assertive.

"I've got it," he said, fishing around for pocket change. "You're nice enough to help me study. It's the least I can do."

Before Kevin could protest again Ray had vanished. He was already at the counter, ordering another drink for the wolf without even asking what he had wanted. Kevin smiled at the coyote's enthusiasm and dipped his nose back into his textbook. He knew he would regret the extra caffeine so close to crash-time, but it would just be this one time.

Ray returned to the table soon after. Both drinks were marked with the same abbreviations. Kevin flicked his ears back a little bit, abashed that he had neglected to mention his finicky taste for coffee. Though the smell of whatever was in those coffee cups was captivating.

He felt bad for saying anything, especially when he struggled to remember the coyote's name. "Thanks, uh, Ray, but I really only drink one thing here." He pointed at his empty cup that was marked with his usual regular.

Ray's ears pointed down a little bit as the coyote bit his lip. "I don't know how to say this without sounding creepy, but, um, I know."

Kevin was about to tell the coyote to pound sand, but Ray interrupted him. "I'm not stalking you," he blurted. "It's just that, well, I come here lots too. I see you around. You're always sitting in the same spot."

Ray's ears perked up again and he handed the drink over anyway. "You'll like this one, promise."

Kevin eyed it and took a tentative sip. He smacked his lips, letting the taste linger before making his final decision. It was sweet, but not overpowering. The espresso was notably present, unlike in most other drinks. It really was quite good, a lot like a Rolo.

With a nod, Kevin took another sip. "You're right, this is good. Thank you."

They concluded the rest of the evening with a relatively quiet study session. Ray would break the silence once in a while to point at something in a textbook and ask Kevin what it meant, and he was more than happy to educate the eager coyote.

It was midnight before the shop kicked them out. Kevin felt his brain might explode from the wealth of information he'd ingested. He imagined Ray felt the same. Both of them were content with parting ways after agreeing to meet up later for another study session.

Kevin quickly found himself enjoying his quiet breaks in the evening. Between his daily activities and his frequent impromptu romps with Jordan, he was beginning to find balance. He and Ray had been meeting up almost every day since their first study session to read and quiz each other. Each study session ended with the coyote having a better grasp on the subject material.

***

A month passed since Ray and Kevin had begun their study sessions. Kevin's finals were long over and he still hadn't said anything about his secret study sessions to Jordan. He wanted to, but telling the rabbit where he'd been going every evening would mean the end of his study sessions, destined to be replaced with the rabbit's sex games.

With Christmas coming up fast, Kevin and Ray had agreed to keep each other company over the winter holidays. Neither of them could afford to travel home and Jordan was off to the Bahamas with his family.

After another successful study session, Ray accompanied Kevin back to his dorm. As they walked the empty hallways, Kevin spotted Jordan peering from around a corner. Kevin raised his arm and waved, calling down the hall. "Hey Babe!"

Jordan stepped out from behind the corner, taking one glance at Ray before turning his attention to Kevin. As Kevin walked to approach Jordan, Ray gave a tap on his shoulder and pointed back down the hallway. "Hey, my dorm's this way. I'll see you later."

Kevin looked back as Ray power-walked down the hall. "Uh, okay. Good study session. I'll see you around later."

Ray waved in acknowledgement and turned the corner without hesitation, leaving Kevin and Jordan to themselves.

Jordan gripped Kevin's sleeve and dragged him down the hall towards Kevin's room. He lowered his voice to a whisper and leaned in. "You haven't been hanging around with that weirdo, have you?"

Kevin cocked his head to one side with his ears canted. Sure, Ray was a little more than eccentric at times, but he had proven to be a genuinely nice guy and was quite intelligent when he put his mind to something. "Yeah, turns out we've been in the same class since last semester. He asked for some help studying about a month ago and we just sort of made a regular thing out of it."

"A month and you haven't told me!" Jordan exploded. "Don't I have a right as your boyfriend to know who you're hanging out with?"

"Whoa, chill out Jordan." Kevin put his hands up, going the passive route to keep Jordan from making a scene. "I didn't think it was that big of a deal. Everyone's going home for the holidays and it would be nice to have someone to hang around with while you were gone."

"You were planning on spending weeks alone with another guy and you think it's no big deal?" Jordan was shouting now, the rabbit's hands balled into fists.

"Jordan, calm down." Kevin looked to the people that had quickly taken notice of the domestic dispute. "It's not like I'm fucking him behind your back. Would you prefer that I lock myself in my room until you get back?"

Jordan sighed and rubbed at his temples, obviously resisting the urge to yell at him more. "Look, I don't mind if you hang out with other guys, just not *that* guy." Jordan paused and sighed. "We have a … history."

That piqued Kevin's interest. He slipped his paws around the rabbit's waist and drew him closer. "What kind of history?"

Jordan shifted, looking off to the side instead of directly at Kevin. "I've known that guy since grade school and we just never really got along. We got into some fights. Mostly just stupid playground shit. I found out he was taking courses here and I tried to make amends, but," Jordan tried to hide a tear as it slid down his cheek. "I guess some people just can't let the past go."

Kevin was flabbergasted. Ray had seemed so sweet, but it was Jordan's word against his. With a strong hug Kevin nuzzled one of the rabbit's floppy ears. "I'm sorry Bun. I wouldn't have even considered spending time with him if I'd known he had hurt you like that."

There was a sniffle from the bunny before he pushed back and wiped a tear from his cheek. "It's okay, you didn't know."

The two of them locked muzzles in the hallway, cradling each other before finding a private place nearby to make up.

***

Ray stopped keeping in contact since the incident in the dorms. Kevin supposed that seeing him with Jordan was enough to scare the coyote off. Winter break was upon them as Kevin leaned in to give Jordan one last kiss before the rabbit left for his month-long vacation.

Kevin watched the bus disappear into the distance with his jacket wrapped around his chest. His winter coat had finally grown in, and he did his best to hide it. Jordan said he liked the extra fluff, but in Kevin's eyes it just made him look like a big Pomeranian.

The school was eerily quiet now. The few that stayed behind were littered about the study halls and the Weasel Shotz café, which remained open over the holidays, with limited hours and even more limited staff.

Kevin spent most of his time in his dorm with little more than his textbooks to keep him company. He wanted to give Jordan a call, but the rabbit had requested not to be disturbed, citing family time and long-awaited time away with old friends.

Because of cell reception issues, Kevin had been given an alternate number to call, with specific times in which he was allowed to call it. It made enough sense, he supposed. It was just lonely knowing he didn't have Jordan to lean on, and there was no one on campus that he knew well enough to hang out with.

As much as Kevin tried to occupy himself in his small dorm room, the solitude was getting to him. He packed his textbooks and set out to wander over to the cafe while it was still open, in the hopes that the ambient nature would calm his nerves a bit. Thankfully no one had taken his favorite table yet, and he was sure to save it before going to order his drink.

Kevin stood in line behind two others. When it came to his turn, he ordered his new favorite, a Café Rolo with extra espresso. He handed over his remaining pocket change when a soft voice spoke from behind him.

"Kevin?"

"Oh," Kevin turned with flattened ears, and his tail tucking between his legs. "Hi Ray." They stood together in awkward silence, neither of them sure of what to say to each other. Kevin grabbed his drink as it was called, gripping the cup with both paws to his chest as he looked off to the side. "I'm not supposed to talk to you."

"Oh, I should've guessed." The coyote's voice was meek, like he knew this would happen.

Kevin made eye contact with the coyote. He wanted to walk away, to forget that he'd ever met Ray, but he couldn't bring himself to do it. Ray deserved a chance to explain himself. "What happened between you guys?"

The flattening of Ray's ears and his creased muzzle at least confirmed there was bad blood between them. Ray said nothing at first. His ear flicked when his drink was called out from the other end of the counter, but he made no effort to reach for it. "Jordan and I go back. Like, way back. We used to date."

Kevin was hardly surprised to hear that. Even though Jordan had been cryptic about his relationship with Ray; Kevin was already aware of Jordan's track record, which had only left him with one conclusion.

"It didn't end well."

"I could've guessed," Kevin dryly stated.

"I broke it off with him," he continued. "It just wasn't working out, y'know? All he wanted was sex and I just wasn't in to doing it all the time. I mean, the sex was great; really, really great, but there's so much more to life than just sex."

Kevin thought back to the last four months with Jordan, and just how many times they'd eloped in public to screw off in some distant corner. "Yeah."

"He didn't like that much, as I'm sure you know. I think he was so used to being the heartbreaker." He finally reached for his coffee, sniffing at the steam before taking his first sip. "He's made it his life's ambition to date every guy I've had a crush on since. He won't let it go, not even now."

They retreated from the counter back to Kevin's usual table, before the study sessions. It was surreal to witness his two worlds mingle together. He'd first met Jordan at the very same table they were sitting at now. To see someone new in the spot that was typically reserved for Jordan was just odd, to say the least.

Kevin sipped from his mug, considering Ray's version of the story. He tapped the mug with a finger, keeping his eyes on the coffee cup in front of him. "So what is he doing that tells you he hasn't let go of the past yet?"

Ray was silent, taking several sips of his coffee before breathing a gentle sigh. He opened and closed his muzzle several times before the words escaped his lips, barely louder than a whisper. "Did you like your flowers?"

That was when the last cog clicked. It all made sense, now. The flowers and the anonymous letters were all just Ray working up the courage to talk to him in person. But if his story were true, then that would mean …

"What are you insinuating about my relationship, Ray? Are you saying I'm just another one of Jordan's boy-toys?"

Ray didn't say anything as he looked down at his cup.

Kevin sighed as he stood up from the table. "I had hoped you were better than that, Ray. Making up a story like that is just as insulting to me as it is to Jordan. He was right about you. You're just trying to sabotage our relationship because of some petty squabble you guys had when you were kids.

"Don't bother getting up." He stormed past Ray, nearly knocking him over. Ray splayed his ears flat against his head with a quiver in his lips. "I don't want you coming near me or Jordan. I've had enough of your games. Stay away from me."

The coyote sniffled once into his cup as Kevin stormed out of the café. Serves him right, he thought. Kevin wanted to call Jordan more than ever now. The bunny would understand if he called just this one time, considering the circumstances.

He got back to the dorm room and dialed the number scribbled next to his desk. The phone rang once, twice, three times. On the fourth ring someone finally picked up, but it wasn't Jordan.

"Hello?" The voice on the other end was gruff and deep.

"Hi," Kevin coughed, a nervous lump slowly growing in his throat. "This is Kevin, may I speak to Jordan?"

There was the scratching the other line, followed by the muffled sound of shouting. "Sweetie, do you know anyone named Jordan?"

The call was followed by a frantic "oh shit!" as the phone tumbled and clanged over the speaker. Jordan was on the other line in an instant. "Hi Kevin, I wasn't expecting you to call so early."

Kevin's heart sank further into the pit of his stomach as his mind raced, connecting the dots. "I had to call. I ran into Ray and, well, we talked for a bit and—I needed to hear your voice."

"That's great, Kev, but—" The call was interrupted by a fit of giggles and little snippets of conversation, the only audible string of words being "I'll get to you in a minute" before Jordan was back on the line. "Look, you shouldn't listen to what he says."

The lack of affection in Jordan's voice was painfully obvious, giving Kevin even less reason to discount what Ray had said. It was all becoming far too clear now. "Tell me you love me."

"What? Kev, now's really not the time—"

"Tell me," he growled, "that I'm not another one of your boy-toys." The wolf was fuming now. He had half a mind to catch the next flight to go and beat the snot out of whomever Jordan was sleeping with.

The line was silent as Kevin waited for an answer, tail lashing and ears burning. He sighed. "Look, we can talk about this later."

"No, we can't."

"Kevin, it's not what you think!"

"Goodbye, Jordan." He mashed the send button and threw the

phone onto his desk, letting it topple onto the floor. He ran his fingers through his hair before falling over onto his bed, burying his muzzle into his pillow as he wept.

***

Kevin received several calls that night which he refused to answer. When he woke, there were five missed calls on his phone. Four had been from Jordan over the span of an hour, and one was from Ray.

His finger hovered over Ray's number. The wolf wasn't sure that he wanted to talk to anyone right now, but he knew the coyote would understand what he was going through more than anyone.

Ring, ring.

"Hello?"

"Hey," Kevin coughed, his voice hoarse from crying. It hurt to talk. "Can we meet for coffee?"

Kevin's dorm was easily closer to their meeting spot, but somehow the coyote had beaten him there. He was sitting at their usual study table where two coffees sat untouched, their steam rising into the air.

Ray forced a smile onto his worried face and pushed the sweetened latte in Kevin's direction. Kevin tried to keep it together, but the moment he curled his tail to sit down it all broke lose.

He'd done everything wrong. He'd been a bad friend for not believing in Ray when it mattered and an even worse friend for the things he'd said. He'd been a bad lover for not being able to satisfy Jordan's active sex drive, and the fact that Ray was still being so nice after what he'd done to him was proof that Ray was the kind of friend that Kevin didn't deserve.

Kevin felt Ray's paw on his shoulder, and he clutched his coffee when he pushed it to the edge of the table, into his paws. Kevin took sips between sniffles and grasped the cup, thumbing around the edge while letting the warmth seep into his paw pads.

The two of them sat in the empty café in silence, Kevin sitting with his nose in his coffee while Ray watched patiently.

Kevin struggled to speak, unable to break eye contact with his coffee cup. His words were weak and hard to hear, even to himself. "I'm sorry."

Ray's false smile faded. "For what?"

"For being me. For the things I said to you." He hid his muzzle with another sip from his cup. "You were right. If I had been smarter, I would have been able see that."

Ray touched a finger under Kevin's chin and brought his nose up out of the steaming beverage. "You're plenty smart. You couldn't have known. Jordan's good at manipulating people. He's had a lot of practice. You weren't wrong here, I hope you know that."

"It sure feels like I am," he sulked.

"Well you're not." Ray lowered his hand and touched it to the wolf's paw, squeezing a little.

Kevin watched the coyote for a few moments. He was a much different person from the first day he'd met him. It was hard to believe the shy and timid coyote that approached him was sitting in front of him with his shoulders broad and his opinions firm. He supposed Ray didn't have much to lose by expressing his feelings anymore.

Kevin scraped his claw along the porcelain cup, thinking about what Ray had said earlier. "So you've been interested this entire time."

Ray nodded.

"Since when?"

It took some time for Ray to answer as he drummed on his cup, chewing the bottom of his lip before answering. "Chem 119, start of last semester. At first I just thought you were cute, but it didn't take long to see you were smart and charismatic to boot. I always sat in the back where you wouldn't notice me because I always thought you were way out of my league.

"Halfway through the course I tried approaching you, but I chickened out at the last moment. I didn't know at the time, but Jordan caught wind of my crush towards you and went after you like a shark smelling blood. He laid it on thick with you and, well, I never stood a chance.

"He's been stealing all of my crushes since high school. Not much I can do about it. He's charming and handsome and I'm, well, me." He gestured to himself and shrugged. "I never thought I stood a chance with you then and, to be honest, I still don't feel I stand a chance with you now."

Kevin felt terrible for passing judgment on the coyote. He was easily the sweetest of any person he had ever met. He sipped from his cup of good will and let the warmth fill him as he reflected on the last several months. He recalled the coyote being in more than a few of his classes, resigned to the furthest corner. He even caught him looking a couple times, trying to pretend he'd been buried in his notes the whole time whenever Kevin's head turned.

With a sigh Kevin looked back to Ray, who looked to be deep in thought. Kevin set his coffee down with a low "thunk" that snapped the yote from his trance, his full attention on Kevin now.

"Ray, I've been unfair to you let me make it up to you. That is, if you'll let me, but I want to know something first."

Ray nodded silently, taking another sip from his coffee.

"Why did you start sending flowers only after Jordan and I had already been dating for so long?"

Ray wiped a bit of whipped cream from his snout and set his drink down. "When you two started dating I just accepted that he had won. There was no way I could challenge him. Each bathroom tryst, each hallway quickie between you two only discouraged me more."

Kevin's ears flattened in embarrassment at the mention of their casual encounters. At the very least he had thought they were being discreet, but if Ray had noticed, odds are others had, too.

"I saw Jordan doing the things he'd been doing for years. I got tired of watching him build people up and then tear them down only out of spite for me; so I bribed maintenance to sneak flowers into your dorm because I was too scared to do it myself."

Kevin tipped his coffee up to his muzzle, getting a mouthful of syrup that had settled to the bottom of the cup. He set the cup aside on another table and folded his hands in his lap. "I have to say, I still think he won but," he looked up, folding his ears back apologetically. "Thank you for trying."

They sat in silence until the awkwardness of the situation got to be a little too much for Kevin. He cleared his throat and looked at the time on his phone. "Look, I really should get back to studying."

Ray's ears flattened. "Oh, okay."

"All of my books are in my dorm," he continued. "I won't be able to talk much but," he paused, rubbing his fingers along his coffee cup nervously. "I'd appreciate the company."

The thumping of Ray's tail against the back of his chair said more than his words ever could.

Upstairs, the two of them sat in silence with their noses buried in their textbooks. They took small breaks in between that allowed them to stretch and to watch a few short videos together.

Kevin felt the brush of Ray's hand more than a few times over the course of the night. Each touch sending tingles up his arm, and each time he had to resist the urge to wag his tail or grab his hand in response.

After hours of countless studying, Kevin's mind was numb; the wolf hardly felt like thinking about anything, let alone Jordan.

Ray had started to nod off on his corner of the mattress as well.

Bed was beginning to sound like a better idea by the second.

"Well," Ray yawned and stretched. "It's late. I should head back to my dorm." Ray sat up and started shoving books into his bag.

"Wait."

Ray stopped in the midst of fitting one last book into his over-stuffed backpack, looking over to Kevin. "What's wrong?"

"I, well, I don't really want to ... I was wondering—"

Ray's smile only grew as the wolf stuttered. He put his bag down and sat back onto the bed. "Did you want me to stay?"

Kevin nodded.

Ray reached out to squeeze Kevin's paw, sending chills up the wolf's spine. "Alright then."

***

The next few days did not come easy for the wolf. He still blamed himself for what happened. Ray's selfless charity only made Kevin feel guilty, turning him into a rollercoaster of emotions.

Christmas day rolled around and Kevin had completely for-gotten all about the occasion. He awoke next to the sound of his phone rattling off the desk. He had to wiggle out of Ray's arms that were wrapped firmly around his torso.

He almost fell out of bed trying to reach for the phone, check-ing the time and caller ID before he picked up: 11:06AM. "Hey Mom, Merry Christmas."

Ray stirred, lazily wrapping back around Kevin, eavesdropping on the conversation.

"No, no, you didn't wake me. I just haven't had my morning coffee yet, that's all."

Kevin stifled a giggle and a girlish shriek as Ray tickled at his sides. "What? No, I, er, have a girl over." He paused and reached over to ruffle the hair between Ray's ears. "Yes mom, I wore a condom. No, I'm not seeing anyone else."

Ray looked like he was about to get ready for a second round of tickles. "Thanks for calling, Mom. Merry Christmas, say hi to Dad for me. Tell him to eat extra for me, not that he needs any encouragement."

Kevin was only just able to end the call before his phone went flying as Ray attacked with a barrage of tickles.

"No, no, stop!" He squealed and fell off the bed in a fit of laughter, his tail thumping against the side of the bed.

Ray looked down at him from over the side and grinned with his head in his paws. "What are you doing down there, mister?"

"You would know," Kevin barked with a laugh. "Wanna grab breakfast?"

Ray's ears shot up and his tail thrashed in the air. "Yeah, I'll meet you there. I have to grab something first."

Kevin had time to order and grab their usual table by the time Ray got back from his dorm. His hands were strategically hidden behind his back. Each time Kevin tried to twist and turn his head to see what Ray was hiding, the coyote countered with a series of impressive maneuvers to keep his surprise hidden.

Ray made it all the way to their table before revealing a beautiful bouquet of neatly arranged red and white roses. Taped to the bouquet was a card with "Merry Christmas" on the side.

Kevin's heart melted when the coyote handed him the flowers. As he smelled each individual flower, Ray produced a small jeweler's box. It opened to reveal a thin silver chain, looping through a snowflake pendant.

Kevin sat speechless as Ray latched the pendant around his neck, giving him a quick peck on the cheek as he stood up straight. "Merry Christmas."

Kevin stood up, knocking his chair back with a clatter as he pressed his lips against Ray's warm lips. They locked lips for only a few moments before they parted, Kevin's tail wagging like a fan behind him.

Ray looked absolutely flushed, his ears flicking back and forth from heated embarrassment. He licked his lips with a smile and sat down, taking Kevin's paws in his own. "Since neither of us really have any family around here, I thought it might be appropriate to celebrate Christmas together."

Kevin was overwhelmed by the incredibly sweet gesture. He felt guilty for not getting the coyote anything for Christmas, especially after receiving such a thoughtful present. "I'm sorry," he stated meekly, "I didn't get you anything in return."

Ray smiled and took one of Kevin's hands with both paws, as though he had expected the wolf's response. "I don't need any gifts, Kevin. I just need to know if you'll be mine this Christmas."

"Oh Ray," Kevin squeezed the coyote's paws and let a tear fall from his cheek. "If you'll still have a foolish wolf like me."

Ray leaned across the table to kiss Kevin on the cheek. "Of course I would."

***

Back at Ray's dorm, the coyote had setup a small Christmas tree laced with tinsel, next to a set of red and white candles that lined the desk and led up to a small TV that sat in the corner.

Ray turned to Kevin, obviously embarrassed by the sparsely decorated dorm. "It's not much, but," he trailed off, his ears pointing out to the side.

"It's lovely." Kevin stepped into the room and gave Ray a peck on the cheek, sitting down and patting a spot on the bed beside him.

The rest of the night was spent sipping peppermint tea and

cuddling up close on Ray's bed while watching Christmas specials until the two of them were too tired to keep their eyes open, and they passed out in each other's arms.

***

When it came time to go back to school, Kevin had forgotten all about the situation with Jordan. At least until Jordan came storming through the doors as Kevin and Ray were passing through with their arms locked together.

Jordan's brow furrowed as he looked to Ray and then to the silver chain around Kevin's neck. Ray hid behind Kevin and the wolf stood with his chest out, knowing Jordan would have no problems starting a scene.

"So after all I told you about him, you still choose to hang with this little faggot. And now you're holding hands! I suppose you two are dating now?" Jordan's hands were balled into angry, shaking fists.

"Nice of you to notice, not that my personal business is any matter of yours now," Kevin glared, reaching around to embrace Ray.

"Who says so?" Jordan stepped forward, pressing noses with the wolf.

"I say so." Kevin took a step forward as well, bumping his chest up against the smaller rabbit. "I thought that was quite clear from our last phone call."

"I told you," Jordan retorted while trying to stand up on his toes to meet eye to eye with the wolf, "that isn't what it sounded like."

Kevin barked with laughter loud enough that more heads turned. "I'd love to hear what excuse you can come up with for staying at another guy's place, one who calls you 'Sweetie' and likes to tease you while you're on the telephone. Admit it Jordan, you've been cheating on me."

"Only because I was so upset that you were hanging out with that, that thing!" He pointed right at Ray, his hand shaking.

Kevin stepped in front of the rabbit's accusing finger and shoved his paw away. "*I* didn't cheat on you with him, and I stopped seeing him when you asked me. I thought you were okay with that, but I guess not. Our relationship was over the second you betrayed my trust."

Jordan lurched forward and clutched onto Kevin's arm, turning on the waterworks as he sobbed violently. "Don't leave me, Jordan! I love you! That's what you wanted me to say, right?"

Kevin pushed the rabbit and stepped back, putting an arm around Ray. "I don't believe you and even if you were telling the truth, it's too late."

The waterworks stopped and Jordan glared at Ray. He lunged forward and ripped the silver chain from Kevin's neck, discarding it to the floor. "You bitch!"

Kevin was too flabbergasted to react. Out of the corner of his eye he saw a brown blur and then Jordan sliding across the floor. The hallway filled with the cheers of people standing by as the rabbit struggled to get to his feet.

"I've had it with you, Jordan. You can't let go of a grudge you had in grade school. Stay out of my life and stay away from Kevin. You've hurt him enough!"

"You tell 'im, girl!" A flamboyantly-dressed buck that Kevin identified as the president of the LBGT social club on campus called out from the crowd.

Jordan growled and turned away, throwing the door open with a bang as he stormed outside.

The halls were silent. There were hushed murmurs until the gravity of the situation had lifted and people gradually milled back into the crowd, leaving Kevin and Ray in anonymity.

Ray rubbed his knuckles with a whine. "Sorry I hit him so hard. I couldn't stand to see him treat you like that anymore."

"It's okay. I would have punched him too." The silver glint of the snowflake pendant drew Kevin's attention to the floor, where it had been tossed in the skirmish. He picked it up, examining the broken links with dismay.

Ray put his paws over the broken chain and bumped noses with the wolf. "We'll get it fixed. The point is that we're okay now, and maybe we can stop worrying about what that hare-brained antagonist has to say about our relationship."

Kevin looked at the pendant before slipping into his pocket. He touched his fingers to a ring that Jordan had given him on their first date. He had continued to wear it, just in case it really had been one big misunderstanding. It was bittersweet knowing that this was how everything was supposed to end, but when he looked into Ray's eyes, he knew this was what he wanted. With a twist, the ring slid off of his finger. He set it down on a nearby counter.

Ray laced his hand in with Kevin's and squeezed. "Café Rolo?"

"You read my mind."

"Leave it" is the hardest command to teach.

OLD DOGS NEW TRICKS

NightEyes DaySpring

The glow from the computer monitor gave the tips of Sebastian's fur highlights, accenting his broad canid muzzle. It was already dark outside, but he liked to leave the lights off when he was working late. It made it easier to admire the view of the city below in the large window behind his desk. Tonight though, Sebastian was fully focused on work as he fired off another email to one of his direct reports. If they thought the fact the akita was taking tomorrow off meant they got a free day before a three day weekend, they were going to be sorely disappointed.

Chuckling, he leaned back and considered if he needed to give them any additional instructions for tomorrow. The deadline for the Patterson contract was looming, but no one was going to be paying much attention to it until next week. He'd already typed in specific guidance for what he was looking for in the proposal, but was that going to be enough?

His musings on additional instructions for his staff were interrupted by the ringing of his cell phone. Sebastian glanced at it and gave off a low growl of annoyance as he checked the id. A picture of Joshua had popped up on the phone. The red fox was smiling up at him from the screen. Sebastian hit the answer button as he put the phone up to his ear.

"Hello Joshua." He mumbled into the phone.

"Sebastian," said the fox on the other end of the line, pausing. "You're still at work?"

Sebastian scowled straining to keep his voice neutral. "Why do you think that?"

The fox chuckled. "You think after all these years I don't know the voice you use when I've interrupted your concentration?"

"It never seems to stop you from talking."

There was a slight pause at the other end of the line. Sebastian was pretty sure Joshua was shaking his head in annoyance. Over the years, he'd mastered pushing his ex's buttons.

"Remarks like that Sebastian are exactly why we broke up." Joshua's retort was the type of comment Sebastian expected from the fox. "I was calling to see if you've got time for an early lunch tomorrow. I know you'll be taking off early to head up country sometime in the afternoon."

Sebastian sighed, Sam, their mutual friend, had obviously been talking too much. "I'm actually leaving in the morning. What about Tuesday, after I get back? I have some things to take care of up at the house when I get there."

"And what types of things would those be?" asked Joshua in his *tell me what I already know* voice.

"I see Sam has been gossiping. Is this call 'cause you're jealous I'm dating someone new, and you're looking to rattle my cage?"

Joshua laughed. "Always assuming I still want you Sebastian. It's touching, but I gave that up years ago. No, this call is the, *'I'd like to knock some sense in your head before you go scare the poor boy away'* call."

"I think I still remember how to date; thank you though."

"Very well, lunch on Tuesday?"

"So now it's a post weekend debriefing?" Sebastian asked.

"Whatever you want to talk about; my prodding to get you to open up only works if you're willing to talk."

Sebastian chuckled; Joshua did know him better than anyone. It was a shame things had never worked right. "Tuesday then, 11:30 at PJs."

"Excellent, I'll see you then," said Joshua. With that, he was gone. The line went dead, and Sebastian pulled the phone away from his ear. He turned in the chair to look out at the city. The fox was definitely digging for dirt. With barely a conscious flick of the finger, he hit speed dial on his phone and called Hector. Automatically, he reached up to loosen his tie; there was something about talking to the coyote that just made him hot under the collar. The phone only rang twice before Hector picked up.

"Hey baby," said the coyote in a smooth rural drawl.

Sebastian smiled, the expression carrying into his voice. "Hey handsome. Did you get tomorrow off from work?"

"Ya thought I wasn't going to be able to sweet talk my way out of work for ya?" Hector's voice was thick and rich and washed over Sebastian, making the tips of his fur tingle.

"Not really. You can be very persuasive."

"I got t' take Mama to her doctor's appointment at 1, and then I'm free for the night. What'cha got planned for us this weekend?"

"I was thinking of playing it by ear. Just spend some quality time together up at the house," said Sebastian slyly.

Hector giggled. "Ooh, I don't know. You're kinda a big boy down there; little old me can only take so much."

Sebastian shifted his weight in the chair. The coyote knew how to press his buttons, and he was already getting hard. "Well, you didn't complain last time I was up country. I'll pick you up at 2:30?"

"Sounds good," said the coyote. "I'll be waiting on ya. You have a good night now."

"Thanks, same to you," said Sebastian as he hung up. He put down the phone and smiled to himself. One of the many things he loved about Hector was the hot rush he felt whenever they spoke. Talking to the coyote always put him in a good mood. He looked back at the computer screen and frowned looking at his email client. Perhaps he was being a little too harsh on his staff. His fingers clicked on the keyboard sending his staff a follow-up email letting them leave the office early for the weekend; the Patterson contract could wait until Tuesday.

***

The drive up to the high country took about three and a half hours. The road started out flat, but when he left the interstate, the roads became windy as they climbed up through the hills. Sebastian took the turns a little fast, feeling the smooth glide of his car around the curves. He loved cruising the mountain roads with the windows down, the breeze ruffling his fur. His sleek black luxury sedan might seem out of place in the high country with its pickup trucks and jeeps, but he didn't care. Spring had finally come to the Birch River Valley, and the cool mountain air refreshed him after a night of fitful sleep.

The road up from the main valley road to the house crossed through cool pine woods, and Sebastian savored the scent as he pulled into his driveway. He arrived shortly before 11:30; the housekeeper had already come and opened it up for him, leaving him with little to do before he picked up Hector. The house was built with heavy timbers, and one wall was covered with glass. Situated up on the rim of the valley, the mountains rose in front of the house, and behind the earth dropped away to nothing. He walked up to the glass wall, and stepped out onto the deck outside. He looked out over the valley spread before him, the town below was nestled among the trees, and he could almost make out where Hector lived.

It was funny. Since he'd bought the house up in the mountains, he spent less time at work looking out over the city. Sitting out on the deck gazing out over the valley had become so much more fascinating than gazing out over the city. Sebastian pulled himself away from the picturesque view and checked his watch. With so much time before he had to get Hector, he didn't know what to do with himself. He considered fixing himself a drink, but there would be plenty of time for drinks later.

He eventually settled on the couch, with his laptop and checked his work email; however, there was nothing important enough there to keep him occupied. Later, after he fixed himself lunch, Sebastian settled to idly reading the news while his thoughts drifted to the coyote. The akita unbuttoned the top button of his shirt as he sprawled over the couch. He had to restrain himself from reaching down into his pants and relieving himself too early.

***

As he turned down the dirt road Hector lived off of, Sebastian mused how odd a couple they were. Hector was a poor gas station clerk that had never gone to college. He was an advertising executive at a major firm still climbing the corporate ladder; even his clothes reflected his position with the button-up collared shirt he was wearing.

As he pulled in front of the trailer the coyote shared with his parents, he was forced to smile. There, waiting by the mailbox was Hector; his tail wagging. He had a small duffel bag tucked under one arm, and a warm smile painted across his face. Sebastian rolled down the window.

"I see you're dressing sexy for me" said Sebastian.

The coyote had gone all out. He wore tight fitting designer jeans and a fishnet shirt on top that left nothing to the imagination.

"Maybe," Hector drawled as he got in the car tossing his duffel bag into the back seat. "Don't you like it when I do?" He wagged his tail in a slow deliberate fashion.

Sebastian's expression shifted to a toothy smile. "I love it."

Hector slid a paw across Sebastian's lap making him jump. "I see," he murmured as he brushed his paw over the akita's crotch. "My, ya get all excited when ya see me."

Sebastian grunted and spread his legs a little. "Well, you know how to get me going."

"Well now, I can't be doing that while you're driving the car," he said withdrawing his paw. "I gotcha a present, but we'll look at it back at the house."

"A present?" said Sebastian as he turned the car around. "You didn't have to get me anything."

The coyote only nodded, and Sebastian started the car back towards the house. He wanted to ask Hector what it was but knew the coyote wouldn't elaborate. Instead, the akita put the windows all the way down, letting the cool breeze wash over their fur. Sebastian turned up the music, while Hector settled back into the leather seat and closed his eyes enjoying the ride. There was something serene about the way he was relaxed, his body caressing the leather of the seat, that made Sebastian want to watch him. He had to pull his eyes away from the coyote and concentrate on the road. There would be time soon enough for admiring the coyote's body.

Sebastian whipped the car around the corners of the road, climbing up the slope of the mountain, but slowed down as he approached the house and pulled the car up in front with a soft stop. Rolling up the windows, he turned to grin at Hector, who still had his eyes closed.

"I've missed you." he said and leaned over for a kiss. "Three weeks feels like a long time."

Hector opened his eyes and returned the kiss. "Well, come on up more often. I'll be here for ya."

Sebastian leaned over the center console more to nuzzle the coyote and kiss him again.

"Ya reckon we should go inside first?" asked the coyote breaking off the kiss and trying not to giggle.

Sebastian blushed. When he was with the coyote, he felt so free; he was liable to forget they were making out in the driveway of his summerhouse. He got out of the car and Hector followed him into the house. Once the door was closed, he turned towards the coyote, who proceeded to immediately shove his paws down Sebastian's pants.

Sebastian wanted to say something but Hector smirked and leaned in to lick his muzzle.

"I could feel the heat radiating off ya body in the car as you were driving." He drawled as he wrapped a paw around Sebastian's throbbing member. "You feel like it's been ages since someone has taken care of ya."

Sebastian panted. "Well it has been three weeks."

"Mmhmm. And who's fault is that?" said Hector as he dropped to his knees and started to undo Sebastian's pants.

Sebastian just smirked and put his hands behind his head. "I was busy with work."

The coyote snorted. Before he even had pulled down Sebastian's pants, the akita was already fully hard; his cock having slipped out of its sheath. Hector leaned forward, and with his tongue, licked all the way up from the base to the tip of the akita's cock. Sebastian shivered at the sensation and threw his head back and moaned loudly when the coyote next engulfed his cock.

Hector wagged his tail and proceeded to slowly start drawing up the length of the shaft. Sebastian growled a little as he caressed the side of the coyote's face. The coyote knew exactly what he wanted, but he was going to prolong this.

The coyote sucked on the tip of Sebastian's cock for a few seconds before he again went down on it and slowly worked his way back up the shaft.

"You tease," panted Sebastian.

Hector just looked up at him with the tip of Sebastian's cock in his muzzle, tail wagging slowly. As he slowly worked his way down the shaft and back up in a long slow motion, the akita growled and stepped back, freeing himself from Hector's muzzle.

"Where ya going with my toy now big boy?" asked Hector disappointed, looking up at the akita.

"Nowhere," smirked Sebastian. "I've got another itch I need to scratch."

Hector laughed. "Ya aren't gonna last if we do."

Sebastian shrugged as he walked over to one of the end tables in his living room and pulled out a small bottle of lube stashed in the drawer there. "We'll just have to see," he said coyly.

Hector walked up behind him and wrapped his arms around the dog, pressing his hard erection up against Sebastian's rear. "Y'all trying to take advantage of little old me?"

Sebastian closed his eyes feeling the warmth of Hector's body wrapped around him. "You're complaining?" he said as he turned around when Hector loosened his grip on him.

The coyote opened up his mouth and curled his tongue, licking his fangs. Silently he undid his pants and let them, and his boxers, drop to the floor leaving his fishnet shirt tightly against his torso.

Hector pulled away, flicking his tail back and forth excitedly, and walked over to the couch and stretched himself out on it with his rump held up, the leather creaking softly in protest. Sebastian followed the coyote and settled behind him and poured lube onto his paw. He quickly slicked up his hard shaft and then poured more lube onto his fingers. He spread it onto the coyote slowly, slipping a finger into his warm insides.

Hector gasped softly and pushed himself back, and Sebastian pulled back to slip two more fingers in. When Hector didn't say anything and pushed back more, he pulled out satisfied the coyote was ready. He then lined himself up and pushed himself forward. Sebastian wanted to slam himself into the coyote, but he knew that would hurt Hector. Instead, fighting back the urge to hilt, he slowly slipped himself in. The coyote shivered and arched his back a little as he was entered by the akita. The fur on his back stood up, pressing through the mesh of the shirt, and Sebastian ran his paws over the coyote's back feeling the rising tension in him. They both needed this, and Sebastian could feel the heat radiating off Hector.

Once he'd got himself hilted into Hector, Sebastian pulled back and pushed himself back into the coyote faster. Hector had been right; he wasn't going to last long. Sebastian moaned loudly and repeated the thrust trying to start a rhythm. Hector met him by pushing back.

He wrapped a hand on Hector's cock and started working it in time, but he couldn't keep up with his own rhythm. He wanted the coyote and it was hard to do anything but take him. After a few clumsy, fumbling thrusts, Hector pushed his hand away; Sebastian just put both paws back on Hector's hips, gripping the coyote tightly.

The akita let his tongue hang out as he panted, his thrusts growing in urgency. It was hot and quick, but over much faster than Sebastian would have liked. With a guttural sound, he leaned over Hector, pushing the coyote into the couch, and emptied himself deep inside his lover. Hector just panted, moaning loudly, as he emptied himself onto the couch underneath them.

Sebastian waited a few moments before gently pulling out. The first time he had sex with Hector when he hadn't seen him for a while was usually urgent like this. They would make more passionate love later, after each had gotten the initial heady rush of excitement out of their system. Now spent, Sebastian flopped backwards on the couch.

"I told ya, ya weren't gonna last," laughed Hector as he rolled off the couch and sat on the floor. "Sorry about the mess though."

"That happens when you're around."

Hector smiled. "Here let me get you something," he said springing up from the floor.

Sebastian looked up tiredly as Hector jumped up and went to his duffel bag he had dropped by the door. After such an intense romp, Sebastian just wanted to rest. He didn't know where Hector had gotten the energy from. The coyote returned quickly and handed a small wrapped package to the akita.

"Thanks," said Sebastian as he took the present into his hands and started to unwrap it carefully. He frowned softly once he'd gotten the paper off the gift. "A fishnet shirt? I don't understand."

Hector chuckled. "I figured since ya love looking at me in mine so much, you could return the favor. Put it on, and let me see how ya look in it."

Sebastian looked at Hector slightly alarmed. "I can't wear this."

"Why not?" asked Hector, "You allergic to nylon?"

"I just don't have anything that this goes with. It's not me."

"Who said you had to wear anything else with it?" smirked the coyote. "But, I did think of that. I gotcha a nice black nylon bikini brief to match it," he said handing Sebastian another wrapped package. "I would a gotcha a thong, but I figured you'd want something a little more comfortable."

"Hector, you don't understand. I can't wear this. It's just not who I am. It's trashy, and I'm anything but trashy."

The moment he said it, he knew he'd stepped on a land mine. Hector's ears dropped and he looked hurt.

"You think I'm trashy?" he asked. "You think the fact I haven't been to college or that you have two houses makes ya better than me?"

"Hector it's not like that..." Sebastian started but the coyote cut him off.

"You picked me up at that bar. You're the one who started calling me 'cause y'all alone in that big city. I put on the fishnet shirt for you 'cause it excites you, and I love how it make me feel. But at the end of the day, all you can do is say I'm trashy for knowing and admitting who I am and what I like."

"No Hector. I just have certain standards in how I have to present myself for work. I can't make mistakes, it could cost me my job."

"Really?" said Hector rolling his eyes. "Maybe you need to stop pretending that money elevates you above the rest of us, especially when you long to escape from the burdens your life imposes on you... That's your mistake."

Sebastian growled low; he hadn't meant to cause this, but he wasn't going to let anyone talk to him like this. "Or maybe my mistake is that I brought you home that day."

Hector flattened his ears and closed his eyes for a second before he opened them and gave Sebastian an icy look.

"Then let me fix that for ya," said the coyote staring coldly at Sebastian. He started to put the rest of his clothes back on.

"Hector what are you doing?' asked Sebastian.

"Leaving," he said as he buttoned up his pants.

"So that's it then? You're just going to walk out on me 'cause I won't wear a damn shirt? Do you realize how immature that is?"

Hector looked at Sebastian and snorted in disgust. He quietly strode over to where his bag was on the floor by the door and picked it up. Hector then turned and without even acknowledging the dog, let himself out of the house, closing the door behind him. He didn't slam the door, but let it close gently until the soft click of the lock signaled the door had shut.

***

"I screwed it all up Joshua," Sebastian sobbed into the phone. "We got into a small argument, I said some really stupid things, and he stormed out of the house on me."

Joshua sighed exasperated. The akita imagined the fox was probably unconsciously ringing his tail in his paws. Joshua did that a lot when they'd dated all those years ago whenever he was frustrated with Sebastian.

"Knowing you, I'm not surprised." Joshua said softly. "What exactly caused the fight?"

Sebastian gulped. "He got me a fishnet shirt and black underwear to match it."

"Really?" laughed the fox. "That wasn't your style even when you were young. But, you're telling me that caused the entire blow up?"

"I accidently called him trashy when I said I didn't want to wear it," Sebastian confessed into the phone.

There was a pause on the other end of the line. Joshua's eventual response was unexpected, to say the least, "Nice Sebastian. Even for you, that's shows a major loss of tact."

"I didn't mean to start a fight," mumbled Sebastian.

"Well you didn't mean to, but you did. You should have just put them on and sported the look for him."

"What do you mean 'sport the look'? It's not me; I can't wear stuff like that," the akita protested. Maybe calling Joshua wasn't the best idea, but he didn't know who to turn to.

"For an akita approaching forty, you're in good shape. Nobody asked you to take pictures of you wearing it and put them online.

Plus, if it makes him happy, why not? Sam tells me this guy loves wearing fishnets, so what exactly are you worried about?"

"He's young. I'm an established professional. I just don't go around looking like that. Even in private, it feels weird."

"Then stop picking up guys in rural gay bars that are so much younger than you!" Joshua grumbled into the phone. "You like them in their cute club outfits, but you always treat them like they're beneath you."

"That's not true! I love Hector. Yes, I love his body; but he's also gentle and loving. He's," and Sebastian faltered. "He reminds me of you a lot when we were much younger."

Joshua's response was guarded. "Well, telling me how much you love him isn't going to fix anything. You need to tell him that."

***

He tried to call Hector, but he wasn't picking up his phone. After pacing around the house fanatically, Sebastian decided to see if he could catch Hector walking back into town. He ran out of the house, to the car and cranked it up. Kicking up gravel, he pulled out of the driveway onto the road and headed down the mountain, back towards town. Hector couldn't have gotten that far yet, and sure enough, a mile down the road, Sebastian went around a turn and saw the coyote trudging down the side of the road.

He slowed down to pass the coyote and then pulled off to the side.

"Hector," he called jumping out of the car. Hector stopped walking. The akita ran up the hill toward the coyote.

"Hector, I'm sorry. I didn't mean to upset you."

The coyote growled. "You said how you really feel about me."

"I'm sorry, I didn't mean it like that."

The coyote simply walked past Sebastian and didn't say anything.

"Hector?" whimpered Sebastian.

The coyote kept walking.

"Hector!"

He turned as he reached the back of the car.

"I know what ya thinking. If you make nice to me, I'll forget and it will be okay. Well, I am not some trashy trick ya just get to use when ya want, and discard when you don't want me."

Sebastian sighed. "I don't think you're trashy. I just had better opportunities in life growing up than you did."

"Fuck off Sebastian." growled the coyote as he shot Sebastian the bird and turned away.

"Hector, I'm sorry. Please don't do this," said Sebastian trudging downhill after him.

The coyote waved him off. "I'm no charity case. If you can't think of me as an equal, you don't deserve to have me."

The akita chased after him and grabbed his left arm. Hector turned around sharply.

"Don't touch me!" he yelled at Sebastian and pulled his arm away from him. "I don't need your pity for being born poor."

Sebastian let go of the coyote and he started downhill again. The dog watched as Hector walked down the road. His eyes followed the shape of the retreating coyote, and after he'd disappeared around a bend in the road, Sebastian stared blankly at where he'd disappeared from sight hoping Hector would come back. After a few minutes, he got back in the car and turned it around and headed back up to the empty house.

***

It had been a long day at work, and Sebastian had stayed late.

The Patterson contract was proving to be more troublesome than he had thought it would be, but his heart really wasn't in his work right now. Coming home to an empty apartment only reminded him how alone he felt. The upscale studio wasn't huge, but it was open and that's something that he and Joshua had liked about it when they'd bought the place together. Joshua had wanted to sell it when they'd broken up, but Sebastian had the money in order to buy the fox out.

He'd considered upgrading over the years, as he'd moved up at work, but Sebastian had decided that getting a vacation house was more his speed. He'd come to realize he appreciated having something small and cozy when he came home after working long hours. After work and working out, he rarely had energy left to do anything else. The furniture was much fancier now than it had been when he and Joshua had moved in almost fifteen years ago, but the spirit of the place hadn't changed. It just felt emptier now; emptier than it had in a long time.

The ice in his glass was starting to melt, watering down the whiskey he had poured for himself. The desire to drink really wasn't in him; he had poured it out of habit more than anything else. Actually, the desire to do anything was something Sebastian had been having trouble finding this past month. His staff had sensed his weakness, and while they were respectful, he knew he wasn't riding them hard enough on the Patterson contract. He was going soft and in a business like his, that often led to swift unemployment.

Sebastian picked up the glass and sniffed at the contents, swirling the liquid, idly listening to the ice clink. After he and Joshua had broken up, it had been easy to find other men to bring back to the studio. Finding someone to date—that had been hard. He'd sworn off picking up men a few years back, and it was with Hector that he'd finally reentered the fray. He'd been delighted when it had turned into something more. Now, he was back being single.

The ringing of his cell phone broke Sebastian out of his contemplation. He put his drink back down on the coffee table and glanced at the phone lying face down next to the glass. He really didn't want to talk to anyone: he just wanted to be left alone. Reluctantly he picked it up, and without looking at the caller id he answered it, hoping it wasn't work.

"Hello?"

"Hey," drawled a familiar voice.

"Hector!" yelped Sebastian. "Why—why are you calling me now? It's been over a month."

"I've been thinking, an' it's taken me a while to cool down and be willing to talk to ya again. I kept glancing up the mountain towards your house whenever I went into town at night. The next time you came back to town, I was going to go up there and give ya a piece of my mind. I realized after the lights hadn't been on for a month, you were probably serious with that last message you left me where you said goodbye. The more I looked up at that empty house on the hillside, the more I missed ya."

"I haven't had the time really to head out that way, and I just haven't had the desire to make the time either. Work has been busy."

"I figured ya were probably tied down. That's why I called."

"I'm sorry Hector; I didn't want this to happen. I've missed you, a lot."

"I know ya didn't mean it to happen. By the way, this city of yours is much bigger than I remember it being when I visited back in high school."

"You're here? Now?" asked Sebastian surprised, ears perking.

"I had to see you again, even if it was over. I walked away from you. I couldn't let it end without at least giving ya the chance to walk away from me."

"Where are you?"

"I'm staying in a hostel down in the Copper District. It's cheap, but I don't need much."

"The Copper District, that's roughly seventeen blocks from where I live. Have you eaten dinner yet?"

"A little while ago. It's taken me all evenin' to get up the nerve to finally call ya."

"Give me the address, and I'll be there in twenty minutes to get you."

***

The subway ride down to the Copper District was short; he had considered walking, but the subway was the fastest way to get there. He arrived early, but Hector was already outside waiting for him. The coyote waved, and Sebastian rushed up to him. The akita wrapped himself around the coyote, tail wagging happily. The coyote's familiar scent filled his nose; he had thought he would never smell it again.

"I've missed you so much," he whispered into Hector's ear.

"I've missed ya too hun," returned Hector almost melting against Sebastian. They held each other for a bit, drawing some curious looks from passersby before they broke off. "Where's the car?" asked Hector looking up the street.

"In a garage at the apartment. It was faster to take the subway than get the car out and drive."

"Oh—" said Hector surprised. "I guess parking ain't cheap around here."

"It isn't," smiled Sebastian. "Want me to get your bag for you."

"It's not much to carry."

"Well, come on, let's get you home and get that off your shoulder," said Sebastian reaching down to clasp one of Hector's paws.

The coyote looked down and looked back up. "Ya never held my hand before in public."

Sebastian smiled, feeling the years melt away. He felt giddy, like he was back in his youth. "You want me to let go?" he said gently pulling at Hector.

"Not at all," the coyote replied.

Sebastian smiled and gently led Hector to the subway station and down to the platform. They waited for the train holding hands together. This was Hector's first time on the subway, and the coyote was awestruck by the experience. He kept his eyes closed for most of the trip so he could better feel the swaying of the train carriage.

Coming up the stairs out of the subway, Hector paused to look up at the skyscrapers. "The buildings touch the sky just like the mountains back home."

"It's a far cry from the Birch River Valley," teased Sebastian. "It's easy to get lost in the city."

"Maybe, but with you here that won't be a problem. You always know where you're going in life."

Sebastian looked up at the skyscrapers. Did he really know where he was going in life? Wasn't he lost, but just in a different way? For Hector the city was new, exciting, and different. For Sebastian, it was old and familiar. It was something you just navigated your way through, going about your business, and didn't think about. For him, the city was a place to escape from. The city didn't speak to him anymore like it had when he was just out of college. It wasn't just familiarity which colored his view, Sebastian realized looking up at the tall buildings. Life in general had lost its luster for Sebastian.

"I just live at this point Hector," he ruminated, "I'm not really going anywhere anymore."

"Well, you always seem to know what you want," said the

coyote.

Sebastian shrugged, "Confidence is part of my job. When I go into a meeting with a client, I have to look like I know what I'm talking about. If I look like I'm second guessing myself, that makes the whole company look bad."

"Well what do you want then?"

"Not sure anymore, but I'll figure it out," he said softly. "I'm happy your here though," Sebastian added squeezing Hector's hand.

The coyote smiled, his tail wagging. He led Hector to the apartment building where he lived. Sebastian waved at the doorman; once they were in the elevator, Hector turned and pressed himself against the akita.

"I've been lonely without ya," he said rubbing the front of Sebastian's pants.

Sebastian yelped, but pushed Hector's probing hand away. "The doorman has a video feed for the camera in the elevator." He leaned forward and gave Hector a quick peck. "I would rather not give him a free show."

Hector blushed a little, the insides of his ears turning pink. The elevator dinged as it reached the correct floor and the doors opened. Sebastian took Hector to his apartment, and showed him in. Hector walked into the middle of the room and did a slow sweep of the space.

"It's smaller than I thought it'd be. This is just a studio?"

"Yup," said Sebastian. "It's a large studio, but it's still a studio. Joshua and I lived here when we were together. It's been home for so long, I haven't wanted to move."

"It's definitely you, I can tell from the furniture." He strode over to the window. "It also has a good view, even if it's just of the buildings across the street."

Sebastian walked up to Hector and wrapped his paws around

the coyote as he gazed out the window. "Well, I hope you approve."

"I do," the coyote said, his wagging tail thumping against Sebastian, "cause it's yours."

"Thanks" smiled Sebastian feeling his chest warm at the thought. The feeling of having Hector in his arms felt comforting, and he almost thought he was going to melt against the coyote. He'd missed this warmth, this closeness, so much in the past month.

"Now, where were we?" said Hector slipping his hand into the top of Sebastian's pants.

Sebastian squirmed at the touch. He'd missed this for so long, but he didn't want to rush; he was going to make this last and make this special for Hector.

"I thought I was the one who was always over eager," said Sebastian slipping out of the coyote's grasp.

The coyote smirked. "You're not interested right now?"

"I didn't say that," said the akita. "I just need to finish some work first."

"Work, you're kidding me right?" said Hector, ears drooping.

The akita nodded his head. "It will be about fifteen minutes. Why don't you watch a little TV?"

Hector glared at Sebastian looking disgusted and wandered over to the couch. It pained Sebastian he had to do this, but there were some down sides to having a studio. One of those was the lack of privacy. He had dressing screens set up in front of his bed to help break up the openness of the space, but they only covered up so much. After getting Hector settled on the couch in front of the TV, he disappeared over to the bedroom area, mumbling something about needing to get a paper file. Hector just rolled his eyes and started channel flipping without really watching anything.

Digging into the bottom of his underwear drawer, he pulled

out the fishnet shirt and briefs Hector had given him. Quickly, Sebastian pulled off his shirt and slipped on the fishnet shirt. The shirt made his skin feel cool as the air flowed through his exposed fur. Sebastian then took off his pants and boxers, and slipped on the black bikini briefs. Dressed, he glanced carefully around the screen to make sure Hector hadn't seen him. Satisfied that the coyote wasn't paying attention to him, he looked at himself in the mirror.

The akita in the mirror looked out of place in his eyes. The shirt hugged his body well, and it actually looked good on him. The markings in Sebastian's fur had faded a little with age, although the black didn't seem to draw that out at least. He'd always found boys dressed up this way really hot, but he'd never wanted to wear it for himself. He'd always thought of them as being easier, looser, and more accessible. That was part of what made them sexier to Sebastian. If this was what Hector wanted though, Sebastian was going to give it to him. Finally mustering up the courage, the akita walked out from behind the dressing screen into the part of the studio he used as a living room and stood behind the couch.

"Hector," he said softly. He wanted to say something else, but he wasn't sure what to add.

"I don't see why work couldn't've waited," said Hector turning off the TV and turning around. The coyote's ears went up when he saw the way Sebastian was dressed. All the anger in Hector's face drained away as he looked the akita up and down. A soft whistle left his muzzle as he licked over his exposed fangs, "I see I got just the right size."

Sebastian blushed. "I feel a little vulnerable in this," he said while gesturing down.

"They're just clothes silly. I've seen ya walk through the house naked in front of me just fine. How is this more compromising than that?"

"I don't know. On other guys this stuff has always turned me on. A lot of the guys I meet who wore it were really easy and slutty. I was always the one in control."

The coyote tilted his head. "Sebastian, do ya really think I'm just easy and slutty?"

The akita shook his head quickly. "Only when I first met you. Once I got to know you, I realized that wasn't the case. I think the last month proves you're no pushover."

Hector smirked. "Come over here Sebastian," he said coyly.

It seemed a little odd for someone to call him to his own couch, but he obeyed quietly, his ears splaying out as he sat down.

Hector laughed at Sebastian's apprehension. "Geez, don't need to get all submissive 'bout it now. Sit with me please hun?"

Sebastian sat next to Hector who started to run his paws over the akita's broad chest, teasing at the fur underneath the fishnet shirt.

"You know that feels weird—good, but weird."

"You've done it to me before," said the coyote. "Why did you put this on now?"

Sebastian sighed. "I want you to realize I accept you for who you are. I'm not a very giving lover always. I have a bad habit of taking."

The coyote nodded solemnly in response. Sebastian slowly reached out for one of Hector's hands. "I want you to know I want more than just an easy way to get my rocks off. I want you, and I want to give you the option to 'take' me. I know you've wanted to, but I haven't let anyone since Joshua do that."

The coyote's ears perked at that statement. "I'm honored. Why'd you two split up anyway?" asked Hector.

Sebastian sighed. "It's a long story. We were just starting out in life after college, and I was trying to make a name for myself at work. We were both working long hours. Our schedules didn't really line up. I got lonely, and I ended up doing things behind his back that he eventually found out about. Joshua was livid, and it went downhill from there.

"Afterward, there was just work in my life. I didn't really have time for someone, and I didn't want to get back into something serious. There were guys I *dated*, but it never went beyond having a 'someone' to call when I needed to get off. As I got older, I wasn't getting the attention I used to get when I was younger, and cynicism set in."

"You're still hot in my book," said the coyote pulling the akita to him, wrapping himself around Sebastian.

Sebastian licked Hector on the nose. "Thanks."

Hector smiled and nuzzled the akita affectionately. "You still want to be the bottom?"

He nodded slowly. He was ready to give himself to the coyote in a way he'd not given himself to anyone since Joshua. The coyote leaned in for a kiss and started running his paws down Sebastian's sides, teasing the fur through the netting. He couldn't keep himself from squirming under the touch. Hector didn't stop though and pulled Sebastian closer to him to deepen the kiss. They had both been semi hard while they were talking, but now, Sebastian could feel himself pressing into Hector's stomach as the coyote held him.

Breaking off to pant, Hector asked, "Here or on the bed hun?"

"The bed," responded Sebastian. Pulling the coyote along, he brought him to the other side of the apartment. He jumped on the bed with his tail wagging and turned around to face the coyote. Hector unbuttoned his pants and let them drop as he slipped off his shirt. Pausing to model the black thong he had on for Sebastian, Hector slowly pulled it off and let it drop to the floor. His erection was already past his sheath as he climbing up on the bed, joining the akita.

"I love that underwear I bought ya; but ya need to take them off." He said sliding paws underneath them as he slowly worked them down. Sebastian lifted himself up making the task easier for the coyote. The akita leaned forward, and the two met in a passionate kiss; their muzzles and tongues sliding against each other.

"There is lube in the top drawer of the nightstand," said Sebastian breathlessly as he broke the kiss.

"Mmm..." mumbled the coyote as he reached for the dresser, the bed creaking as he shifted his weight to get it. Sebastian rolled over and closed his eyes bracing himself. He wanted this, but he was still nervous; he had only occasionally bottomed when he'd been with Joshua, and he could feel himself getting tense. Hector though, took it easy and slowly started to apply the lube before he gently fingered the akita.

"Ya gotta relax hun," drawled the coyote as he moved a slicked paw to stroke the akita's swelling shaft. The familiar stroking sensation relaxed Sebastian; the rhythmic caresses caused him to break out into a soft pant. Hector gently pulled his finger out of Sebastian after tracing the dog's insides. "That's a good boy," murmured the coyote. He then adjusted himself so he was pressing his firm cock tip against Sebastian. He held himself there, and when Sebastian pushed himself back a little to show him he was ready, Hector started to press his length into the akita. He didn't get greedy, and when Sebastian whimpered with Hector half way in, he stopped and held himself there.

"You okay now?" asked Hector.

"Yeah," whimpered the akita somewhere between pain and pleasure. "It's just been so long."

"Don't worry, I'll take this slow for ya." Hector pressed himself in gently, and after waiting to let Sebastian relax while he ran his paw over Sebastian's cock, he started to thrust. Each stroke was slow and gentle; deliberately made to make the akita wither in pleasure. Sebastian's tail was twitching so much Hector had to brush it out of his face a few times. The coyote settled into a slow rhythm weaving and growing into a deeper passionate flow. This was not the wild unbridled lovemaking of their previous encounters, but something much more intimate and tender.

All too soon, Hector had Sebastian gasping for breath, nearing climax. The coyote released the akita's pulsing cock as he felt Sebastian building up to his limit. "Finish yourself off for me ya overgrown puppy." He said as he moved his paw to the akita's hips continuing his passionate pace.

It took only a few strokes of Sebastian's paw before his body tensed, his back arching as he howled, each pulse of his orgasm raising the pitch for a split second. Shots of thick seed spraying down onto the comforter under him, forced out with each intense stroke of his paw. Hector gently pulled out of the akita and rested back on his haunches stroking himself, soon joining Sebastian in his orgasm and adding to the mess on the comforter. As their orgasms subsided, Sebastian fell over onto his side and curled up near the top of the bed while Hector looked on smiling.

"Ya gonna be okay hun?"

"Yeah, just really exhausted now. Let me go clean myself up. Can you pull the comforter off the bed and just put it aside. I'll wash it tomorrow," said Sebastian as he crawled off the bed. His knees felt weak, making him stumble slightly as he forced himself up.

"Sure," said Hector getting off the bed.

They both took turns cleaning up in the bathroom. There was something very domestic about this process that gave Sebastian a warm feeling. Afterward, they curled back up on the bed under the sheet. Hector nestled under Sebastian's neck, his body pressed up against the akita. When Sebastian had said he was keeping the fishnet shirt on for the night, Hector smiled and went to his bag to pull out his own fishnet shirt. They got in bed, each wearing just a fishnet shirt and nothing else. Sebastian was amused by how the shirts felt rubbing against each other when Hector nuzzled himself up against his body.

Sebastian ran his paws over Hector's side and the coyote snuggled closer to him. He smiled down at Hector and looked around his apartment. He remembered when he and Joshua had lived here. He remembered the mistakes he'd made that in the end, had cost him the relationship. He was older now, wiser now, and he didn't have to repeat those same mistakes now did he?

"Ya know I love ya?" asked Hector.

"I know," murmured Sebastian starting to drift off to sleep. He was going to make this work.

"I want ya to know, I would have come back to ya sooner, but after Joshua called me, I had to think about how I felt about you and what future there was for an us."

Sebastian sat up immediately, tossing the sheet to the side uncovering both of them. The warm relaxing glow of sex suddenly gone, replaced with anxiety and anger. "Wait, Joshua called you?"

***

"So," Joshua said as the waiter left the table with their order, "what wild thing this time has you calling me at 6:30 in the morning, asking me to meet you for lunch?"

"I figured you'd be awake, and I didn't want something to come up before I asked you to join me," said Sebastian.

"Artists aren't often awake at 6:30 in the morning Sebastian."

"Advertising executives are," the akita said smiling.

"You seem happy," said Joshua as he picked up his glass of water and sipped it studying Sebastian. "Big promotion at work?"

Sebastian shook his head. "Hector came to town to visit me

last night.

"Hector?" said the fox surprised. "I thought he ended it with you a month ago. You've been brooding on it since then."

"He did end it with me. He came to town to surprise me. He said he was unhappy with how it ended." The fox didn't say anything but regarded him cautiously. Joshua had the look of someone appraising their prey. Sebastian wasn't sure what the fox was thinking, but he proceeded anyway. "He loves me Joshua; he loves me like you loved me all those years ago, and that's something I don't want to lose again."

"Do you love Hector?" Joshua asked him softly.

Sebastian nodded.

"Can you get away from work enough to make this work? I'm happy with the life I've made for myself Sebastian, but I had to make time in my life for Reggie. It would never have worked if I didn't. He's given me so much these past ten years; I can't begin to think where I would be without him."

"Oh I know," said Sebastian, and then his voice turned icy. "Is that why you told Hector I was no good for him?"

Joshua frowned. "Beg your pardon?"

"Don't pretend I don't know what you did. You called him up after the fight we had and told him he was better off moving on with his life. Do you realize how messy that is? I have never interfered with any of your relationships like this!" growled Sebastian, lashing his tail angrily. "Where the hell did you even get his number?"

Joshua looked down at the table apparently to think before he looked up at Sebastian and met him in the eye. "I asked Sam to find it for me; he looked it up," he said softly.

"How could you sell out my happiness like this! The boy was afraid to call me after you talked to him."

The fox smiled then, his fangs showing. "I was concerned you were just using him for sex; I figured I'd enlighten him on some of your habits and your history. That's all I did. If he was looking for something more than that, I wanted to let him know he was barking up the wrong tree."

"I thought you were my friend Joshua," said Sebastian as he leaned forward to growl at the fox.

"I'm your ex-boyfriend Sebastian. I know you better than anyone else does."

"So that gives you the right to screw up my life?" said the akita incredulous. The fur at the back of his neck was standing up, the anger rolling off him and filling the intimate space of the table.

Joshua daintily reached for his water and took another sip. "I didn't expect you'd be happy about what I did."

"Then enlighten me with why you did it." Sebastian's voice was starting to get louder.

"Now, do you really have to ask me that?" said Joshua smirking.

The akita stood up. "You disgust me."

"Says he who calls me one week and says I met this awesome guy, and three or four weeks later, I find out it's over. You've done this for years," said the fox loud enough so that people started to turn their heads.

"Hector is different; Hector isn't going to be one of those guys. There is a reason I never told you I was seeing someone else!" Sebastian looked around. People were starting to stare. He pulled out a twenty dollar bill from his wallet and threw it onto the table. "Just stay out of my life Joshua," he said softer before he turned and walked right past the now confused waiter carrying two plates of food.

"Then prove me wrong!" came a final shout from the fox. He paused, wanting to turn around, but didn't. There was nothing he could say that would refute Joshua's point of view. Joshua did know Sebastian's history far too well.

Sebastian walked outside and started down the street. He

knew Joshua wasn't going to try and follow him, but he wanted to get away. He still had a good bit of time before he had to go back to work and finish up for the week. Still angry, he pulled out the cell phone from his pocket and hit the speed dial button. After two rings, Hector picked up.

"Well," the coyote drawled. "How did it go?"

"As well as I expected it to go," said Sebastian.

"Did he apologize?"

"No. There is nothing for him to apologize about. I can guess pretty well what Joshua said about me. It may be a little exaggerated, but it's all true."

There was dead air on the other end of the phone. Sebastian was pretty sure the coyote back in his apartment had gone stiff, and not in the good sense. A few seconds passed before there came a soft, almost scared reply.

"What are you going to do about it?"

"Prove that bastard wrong; I love you Hector, and I don't want my past to jeopardize our future."

"I love you too," said Hector crying a little, "but, I don't want you to hurt me."

"I can't promise I won't—but I can promise I will do everything I can not to," said Sebastian with force and determination. "I'm not the same stupid dog I was back then."

Sebastian knew what Joshua thought he was going to do, but he wasn't going to give him the satisfaction of being right. He'd wanted someone like Hector in his life for so long, yet he'd been unwilling after breaking up with Joshua to make a serious commitment, until now. It was time to turn over a new leaf. Fifteen years and Sebastian was finally moving ahead with his life again. Even an old dog like him could learn new tricks.

If our toys could talk what would they say?

Means to an End

Whyte Yoté

Look at him; just look at him, sprawled out on the bed with a copy of Tuesdays with Morrie *in his paws, whiling away his Wednesday off.*

But I know better.

I know the real Tuesdays with Morrie *is locked away in a suitcase in the closet. His wife doesn't have the key, but he does. Because what's also in that suitcase is a dust jacket for* Fifty Shades of Red, *the new bestseller, according to the papers. I know this because Brook and his wife Maxine have talked about it.*

I also know that because Brook's reading it right now. He switched the covers right in front of me. He's done a lot in front of me over the years. You might have seen me around.

My name's Mush, and I'm a vindictive son of a bitch. Or, I would be, if I were alive. As fate would have it, I was made in China. I have the tags to prove it, even after all these years.

I also have a hole under my tail. But I'll get to that later.

So there he lies with that book in his face. He's reading about this business-fox who lures big, masculine males to his house and turns the tables on them by revealing how dominant he is. It's horribly written, according to critics, but that hasn't stopped half a million people from grabbing it off the shelves. It's for everyone—for females, because they get a kick out of seeing two guys getting it on, and males, because if they buy the book for their women they'll get more action in the sack.

And then there's Brook, who bought it for himself, because he's the one who gets a kick out of it. Well, more than a kick at least when the house is empty for more than an hour. Any less and he hops on the internet for some videos … of foxes. Any longer than an hour and he invites over a fox. It's always the same thing with Brook; always has been, ever since he was a kid.

I remember the look on his face when he opened my box on that Christmas morning back in 1973. Disappointment. "I wanted a fox," he'd said. No matter that I was a husky just like him. We could've been best buds. But in my opinion we've never been more than acquaintances, especially after what he did to me.

Why am I still around? Because I have a hole under my tail, that's why. But, like I said, I'll get to that later.

You'd think I'd get bored up here on top of the entertainment center in the bedroom, but you'd be wrong. I'm the master of my domain, lord of all I survey, from the edge of the computer desk to the corner of the closet that's barely visible if the doors are open and the blinds up. And boy, do I see a lot. Some of the best stuff happens in here, and it's a good thing my mouth doesn't move from its endless grin, because I have things to say.

You don't miss much of anything if you can't blink.

It doesn't take him long before his paw's wandering downward over his jeans. If he were serious about it, though, he'd be naked, but Max is out shopping with the two kids who aren't yet in college, and that'll take a few hours at least. Brook likes to make sure she texts him when she's on her way home. She never misses a single one, dutiful wife that she is. Little does she know she's complicit in her own husband's infidelity. Then again, it's Brook having his boys over that's the big part of the adultery.

Why didn't he find a nice top fox and settle down? He wanted the damn kids.

Don't get me wrong; he's a great father, from what I've seen. I was supposed to be the hand-me-down from kid to kid, but I only lasted a couple years with Shelly, the eldest. She was two when the internet invaded the house, and all of a sudden Brook found a whole new world of foxes outside of magazines and the occasional secondhand pulp fiction. He could store images on floppies. And he could hide the floppies almost anywhere.

Guess who "anywhere" happened to be? That's why I have a hole under my tail.

I'm not sure you understand how it feels. *Rape* isn't a word that should be used lightly, but I think it applies here. No consent, just violation—purely being taken advantage of. Sure, you could say it was only a few stitches and some polyfill, but he slit me a tailhole. He shoved a disk up there, and every time he wanted to entertain himself he would just...take it out again, save some pictures, and shove it back.

Sure, I can't sense pain. Not physically anyway, but *you* have someone stick their paw up into your stuffing every day and see how you feel. Raped, that's how you'd feel.

The doorbell rings, and he's off the bed in a flash, throwing the book into the suitcase and bounding down the stairs. A moment later there's pleasantries at the door. Two male voices. One of them is a fox, I just know it.

Fucking foxes.

***

It wasn't so bad, once you warmed up to me. I lay in the toy box for three years, forgotten, until you opened it up looking for a lost Matchbox car. You forgot about the car when you saw me and exclaimed, in a way that surprised the hell out of me, that you'd missed me so much. It wasn't like I was gone. I was a toy. In the toy box. You weren't the brightest pup.

After that I was your constant bedtime companion, warmed by your breath and body, privy to your deepest thoughts and desires. Most were ordinary, a few were fantastical, and by the time you hit puberty I knew way more than I ever wanted to know. Like a vet from Vietnam, you had to be there, man. I've seen things. It's a miracle I made it all the way to '95 unscathed, if a bit over-cuddled.

Those first few years were wonderful. I got to watch you grow from a gangly nine-year-old into a solid, sporty twelve-year-old. Most nights you held me to sleep, and sometimes, when you'd had too much Mountain Dew or just gotten through biking around the neighborhood with your friends, you would talk to me as if I could hear you. And I could Brook, I could hear everything.

If I'd been able to talk, I might have reassured you that it was normal to feel the things you were feeling when you watched the 1980 Olympics and couldn't take your eyes off Dean Wilson as he swam for the gold. You were old enough to know what your body was doing, but your dad throwing the Growing Up Canid book on your pillow with a note didn't help much, did it? Sure, you read it and understood it (you were thirteen, for God's sake) but you asked me the questions instead of asking your parents. Because it wasn't about girls.

I guess you could say you played it safe. On the surface, at least. Now look where you are.

He brings the fox in by the paw, practically dragging him down as they sit on the bed. He's got this look on his muzzle like he didn't sign up for this. "Nice place," is all he can say.

"Thanks."

"I kind of...expected something different, from what you were like in chat," says the fox, his eyes jerking around everywhere but at Brook. Then he looks at Brook, and Brook looks away. Real suave, that one.

"I never lied," says the husky, and that's probably true. Brook tends to leave out important details, like his marriage and kids. He's perfected the art of dodging, judging by what I've overheard from his Skyping.

Poor fox. The guy can't be more than twenty, twenty-two at the max. Still college material, young and virile and nervous as hell now that he knows the odds the husky's playing. Some of 'em get off on that we-might-get-caught thing, but this one's skittish. Might take some extra convincing. Brook knows how to get what he wants. He takes the fox's paw and looks deep into his eyes. Cue the sappy music.

"Hey, man, I don't wanna be part of some love triangle, okay?" The fox's tail thrashes uneasily on the bed. "It was cool and all, talking to you, but this family shit gets in the way, y'know?"

Brook doesn't know, though, because the family's never gotten in the way. He's a master philanderer, worthy of the soap operas Max watches when she's home alone and finds a spare minute to catch a show here in the bedroom with me. I see it all. Well, I hear it all, since I can't see the screen.

"There's no triangle, Stace," he says smoothly, exerting his two-decades-plus of experience. It must be hard asking foxes half his age to go top on him. Some are naturals. Others he has to pay to play. All I'm saying is, so far, no one's walked away.

"I've done this before," Stace says. "Guy's wife walked in on us. I never ran so fast in my life, and she still got claws in me."

Brook isn't deterred. His ears remain as perky as ever, blissfully ignorant of consequences. Under all that coolness, I know he's barely able to contain himself, the fear and the thrill overriding what little common sense he possesses. He was always one to act first without thinking. Plenty of scabs and broken bones over the years can attest to that.

"I've got her trained, guy." Smarm oozes from the husky's lips as he slips his paw behind the fox's head. He's used to trepidation, not resistance. I can almost see the gears turning in his head. But a well-placed kiss seals the deal, because apparently foxes can't stop once they've started. This Craigslist thing really works people up.

Before things can progress, Brook peels himself away and sits down at the desk, clicking away at keys while the fox named Stace watches with a pouty face. Making sure the little red light is on, the husky gets up and pulls me down from the shelf. I hate this part.

I don't care what you say about me not being able to feel pain. When he sticks his paw under my tail and roots around my filling for his USB drive, it's not pleasant. It's like someone rearranging your intestines. With the drive plugged in and the camera recording, it's time for Brook to do his thing.

These are the times I wish I could blink. It's not that I don't like it, but that I'm incapable of reacting to it. What happens, happens and I can't unsee it. I have forty years of stuff stored somewhere inside of me. I wonder where it all goes.

But the guys on the bed are nothing I haven't seen before. He knows it can't last forever. I know it's only a matter of time. And I have all the time in the world, from where I stand.

***

I remember that day, in 1985, when you came home from high school and told me all about Rory.

"Miranda was a bore anyway," you said, dismissing her like an empty plastic bottle. Never mind how she'd let you do whatever you wanted in bed. You were never one for the standard stuff, and Miranda was as standard as they came. She was a fox, sure, but she was a girl. And I'd had enough pillow-talk education already to know exactly what got you riled up. And it wasn't her. "I broke up with her." You started crying. I started soaking up the tears.

"I knew he was gay," you said. I nodded in theory because you wanted me to nod, though I didn't know what the hell you were talking about. His name was Rory. He was a fox, a plain old red fox, which made you automatically interested. He was on the football team, a wide receiver. A skinny, fast thing. Rumor had it he was gay too.

"He didn't deny it either when I asked him. I thought I could at least make a friend." And then you told me how you two went to that diner after class and shared an order of fries. You had something in common (liking guys), you could vent to each other (finding nice guys), and then suddenly he was flirting ("Wanna do guy stuff?"). But he implied one thing, you wanted the opposite, and he walked out. "He said he was too proud a fox to be dominant. It wasn't his place in the world." And you bawled your eyes out on my back.

I could've told you that was the reaction you'd get. At least, back then. Homonormativity, you complained. Times have changed, and roles reversed. It's progress, baby, and far be it from you to stand in its way.

Besides, once you met Max, none of that mattered anymore. I wondered how long it would be before you cracked, but you lasted a long time before you brought the first fox home. Then again, I can only see what goes on in front of me. Maybe you didn't last long at all. Maybe you never stopped.

You still managed to fuck three kids out of her, so kudos for that.

***

"Oh, fuck, she never texted me!" Brook jumps out of bed, out of the afterglow cuddle, away from the fox's naked back, and fishes around in his jeans. "Fucking silent mode! Get up!" Like russet lightning, Stace is on his feet and scrambling into his pants, stuffing his bikini briefs into a pocket to save time, looking hilarious.

"Ohshitohshitohshit," the fox panics in a frantic whisper. "You fucking lied, dude, what the fuck?"

Brook shoots him a glance that would freeze lava. His only regret is being caught, not fooling around. I'd be laughing if I weren't stitched into a permanent smile. Max and the kids are down in the kitchen, putting groceries away by the sound of it. Will she come upstairs and find her husband pantsless with a fox boy in their bedroom? I don't need a remote for this kind of show.

"Brook, we're back!" she calls over the voices of their kids.

"Down in a minute!" he calls back, throwing Stace's shirt at the fox's face and nearly causing him to fall. While the fox scrambles Brook runs to the en-suite and comes back with a bottle of NeutraScent, applying more than enough to erase all traces of their indiscretions. "Wolf Christ, get your shirt on."

Stace looks dumbstruck. If only he knew how Brook's mind worked, he'd be able to understand. It would piss him off, but at least he'd know better than to come back. He seems to be an honest enough kid that this stuff bothers him so much. I wish him well; maybe he's learned a lesson.

"You're a coworker, we had some files to go over, you brought them to me instead of making me come to the office, okay?" Brook maintains his paw's presence squarely in the center of the fox's back, pushing him out of the bedroom. Stace's indignant assents die off as they get to the top of the stairs. Then someone comes back. It's the husky.

"Fuckin' bitch," he growls, bending over the computer. After clicking the mouse harder than he needs to, and trying to type the same thing in three times, he rips the USB drive out of the tower and tosses it up to my shelf. I can't reach out to catch it, but it lands on my paw anyway. It's not very secure, though, held against my fake fur by its own tiny mass. Brook doesn't even look at it when he storms back out into the hallway to greet Max, who's mounted the stairs to ask him who the jittery fox was she met at the front door.

I don't hear that conversation, but I know Brook'll have no trouble convincing her as easily as he can convince himself.

***

It's hard to believe how you thought the internet would never amount to anything. I have to admit, though, neither did I, at the time. We didn't know any better, but I'd venture to guess I picked up on it more than you did. Viewing the world from the same position for years at a time, you pick up on changes because you're unchangeable. You live in the moment, you're not likely to notice all those moments congealing into evolution.

The day you brought home the good ol' Compaq I was as fascinated as you and Max at the piece of cutting-edge technology that would improve your lives and put the world at your fingertips. Five hundred whole megabytes, remember? How could you possibly fill up all that space? Nowadays the jump drive you threw so carelessly onto my paw holds a hundred gigs of your other side. Just saying.

Max wanted to put it in the kitchen, so it would be central to the house. You wanted to put it in the den so you could do bills. By the time you both agreed to set it up in the bedroom, you two were so exasperated that she left for the afternoon and let you deal with the plugs and cables.

And like a man, you threw away the instructions and struggled with the thing for twenty minutes before digging them back out of the trash. And then you found out it was all color-coded.

Not long after, the modem fired up—I bet that sound would

still get you excited if you heard it now—and you were clicking away. That first week or so was all about learning how to navigate cyberspace, but the next time Max was away you got to clicking so fast I could see the lights and colors flashing across the white under your muzzle.

Of course, you didn't have to hide anything. You were alone, or so you thought. I saw it all because I can't close these pieces of plastic I have for eyes. It's not like I'm not into it. I'm not, not into it either. I don't have morals like you, because morals lead to decisions. I can't make decisions, being inanimate. I just watch.

I didn't expect you to cry, though. You only did it once, but it was enough for me to see past the shell of arousal into the gooey center of shame you can't let anyone see.

Because I couldn't talk back.

You would do that a lot after finishing, basking in the glow of your own endorphins, until you realized where you were and what you did. Most of the time you would clear your history and close the browser because things were that easy back then. But that one day, you broke down. You held your head in your paws and cried like a pup, great heaving sobs, the likes of which I hadn't seen from you since your voice changed.

Then you looked up at me with your tearstained face and your bloodshot eyes and launched yourself out of your chair, grabbing me and throwing the both of us to the bed.

"I'm sorry," you moaned into my neck, over and over again. "I'm sorry, I don't know what's wrong!" Sure, your pants were still off, but that didn't matter much at the time. With you in your moment of weakness and self-loathing, my job was to be cuddly and comforting. Eventually you calmed down enough to blow your nose and talk to the ceiling. At least that's where you were staring; I knew you were addressing me.

"What am I gonna do?" you asked, and repeated. "What am I

gonna do?" I didn't have any wisdom to impart back them, and even now there isn't a damn thing I can do to help you. Not only because I can't talk, but because it's entertaining—dare I say fun—to watch your life spiral down into its own black hole.

Also because of what you did next.

You stopped crying, snorted back a wad of snot, and got a strange look on your face. You looked deep into my eyes, like you had done on countless flashlight-in-the-sheet-tent reading adventures after curfew. Your muzzle quirked on one side. And then you went to the desk to root around feverishly.

When you came back to me I could see the Swiss army knife in your paw, the side of its blade an arc of bright chrome. And I was scared, I think, if you could call it that. Any time you get a blade near a stuffed animal, what is it supposed to think? Then again, I've never conversed with one.

Muttering to yourself about keeping safe and normal, you turned me around and pressed me to the bed. I don't know which was worse: not being able to see what was going on, or feeling my stitches snapped one by one until your fingers had pried apart a four-inch gash under my tail. No, it didn't hurt. Yes, I can be sewn up. But I can't forgive you.

"She'll freak if she finds this stuff," you said, pulling polyfill from me to make room. That feeling of my rear being collapsed and deflated is not something I'll ever forget.

You went to the desk and frantically clicked away at the mouse and keyboard for ten minutes that might as well have been forever. One more click and you sighed to yourself, chuckling. "Genius," you said. "Can't believe I thought of it." The bed leaned under your weight as you knelt and pulled me backwards. The floppy slid neatly into the hole you'd made, suspended between my back and belly. You giggled while you placed me back on the entertainment center, not a trace of guilt in your eyes for what you'd done to me.

I can't forgive that, either.

***

Sometimes, things happen for a reason. Sometimes they happen because someone makes them happen. And sometimes you can't tell the difference.

So I'll just say the jump drive fell off my paw. It seems plausible, given how precariously Brook left it sitting there, on the verge of going over. Could've happened anytime between dinner last night and just now, when Max is bringing the vacuum in to do a little housecleaning.

After seventeen careful years of stuffing porn inside me, he flies too close to the fire and leaves an ember glowing right in front of me. It doesn't even seem like that long, come to think of it. I'm a vindictive son of a bitch, but I'm patient. I have to be. I don't have a choice.

I thought for sure that Brook would race back up to the bedroom as soon as he could to put the drive away, but he stayed downstairs after seeing Stace out and selling Max his lie. He stayed down there for dinner, and television after that. The kids went to bed. The parents came up around ten. They made love. And that was that.

When the husky did his morning routine, I waited for him to stop, look at me and quickly correct his mistake, but he left for work without ever giving me a second glance. Seems he was trying so hard to keep up appearances that he not only convinced Max of his dealings with Stace, but also himself.

Max is a creature of purpose. Every Thursday she vacuums the house from top to bottom, starting with the master bedroom. So when I heard her open the closet down the hallway, the drive decided to fall, caroming off the television two shelves below me and skittering under the bed skirt. One can hope she'll be thorough in her cleaning.

She comes in with her iPod plugged into her ears, humming some old tune from the seventies most likely. Decked out in blouse and capris and a pink bandana on her head, she passes for less than her forty years. Brook doesn't deserve her.

Swaying her hips to the music I can't hear, she unravels the cord and puts the plug into the socket. The thing whirs to life, and she dances around the room with it, like a star with her partner. From the end table to one meticulously-folded hospital corner, she goes up and back in rows, bringing up the pile where they tread it down every day, stopping at the foot of the bed to empty the first of ten or so canisters of shed fur and dust.

I can't see the jump drive from where I am, but it's got to be right under the edge of the skirt. If she doesn't step on it, or if she kicks it further in, it could be years before anyone notices. The panic on Brook's face when he can't locate his treasure trove would be consolation enough, even if he does end up finding it.

But Max rounds the corner, her curly tail leading the way backwards, wagging as she goes row by row, setting things to rights. For a second it doesn't look like she'll get under the bed, but she takes a few steps back and plunges in. I pray to whatever god looks favorably upon stuffed animals and hold my metaphorical breath until a horrendous clattering startles her into dropping the machine, shrieking. She runs over to the wall and yanks the plug. To my joy, the vacuum spits the drive out with its dying breath.

Max kneels next to the machine and picks up the drive, working it around in her fingers. "Christ, Brook, give me a heart attack!" she complains to the empty room. Standing, she inspects it. Aside from a healthy number of fresh scratches, it's intact. "What the hell is this doing under the bed? He must have lost it." Then she puts it in her pocket and goes back to vacuuming, leaving me disappointed and kind of pissed at her, that she didn't find it suspicious in the least.

The rest of the bedroom gets swept without further incident. I find myself hoping she confronts him later on with the drive. Maybe he'll confess to the whole thing, breaking down and begging at her feet. More likely, he'll just thank her for the drive and hide it again. That she may inadvertently contribute to her husband's affair is ironic, but still sad.

She comes back in, though, digging around in her pants until the drive is out again, just in time for her to turn on the tower and jam it in. Bluish-white glow brightens her face as she does what needs doing to open the desktop or whatever it is computers do these days.

"He's gonna kill me. I know he's gonna kill me if he finds out." But even as she's saying it, I can tell she's assuring herself she's doing the right thing. I don't know what she expects to find, or suspects of Brook, but chalk it down to women's intuition. Curiosity killed the cat, but I don't know if the same applies to canines.

It's hard not to feel sorry for her when the sound comes on and the first voice is Stace's asking Brook about what he wants and how much. Max leans in first, squinting at the screen, and gasps as she realizes what's going on. I have to give her credit for watching the first five minutes before clicking ahead because she doesn't need any more convincing. The paw to the mouth. Trembling in the chair. Claws furrowing the compacted sawdust of the cheap Walmart desk. And at last, a whispered, "Oh, my God" when she hears her own voice calling from the entryway, sending the males into a panic.

She sits there for a very long time, stiff and quiet, her paws worrying themselves in her lap. I liken it to the day she learned her aunt had been killed by a drunk driver. There are no words to match the well of emotions. And this is coming from a plush husky who can't feel much of anything. But I watch.

I can't help but feel like I'd be smiling right now.

Max takes three deep breaths and lets out a scream so loud and so primal that you'd swear she was fit to be tied to a team and pull a sled. Tendons stand out on her neck, her hackles poof, and she smacks the desk hard enough to topple the monitor over. Then, equally amazingly, a sense of peace comes over her. She once again looks like a suburban mother of three, collected and proper in her modern hairstyle and attire.

"Fuck this shit," she says and, with an unnerving smoothness, stands, pulls the drive out of its socket and drops it into her blouse pocket.

If anything could be said about how she spent the rest of her afternoon, you could say she cleaned the house with a vengeance.

***

Things are changing. They are not obvious things, but I can tell all the same. Brook and Max are not the same couple they were when they were married. They're not the same they were four days ago, the day that will live in infamy (in my own mind, at least) as Huskygate.

I have to give Max credit for grace under pressure. Any lesser woman would have crumbled under the knowledge of a disloyal husband who subs for foxes, of all species. But Maxine Waters, wife of Brooklyn Waters, will not go down without a fight. Of the numerous phone calls she made over the weekend, I couldn't hear much, but I could tell by the excitement in her voice that shit's about to go down one way or another.

Brook, for his part, has been every bit the model husband, exhibiting a kind of Ward Cleaveresque behavior that's freaked out the kids. This would normally be cause for concern, but since Max is hiding some facts of her own she plays along. If I didn't know both sides of this story, it would be downright disturbing. It still kind of is.

An hour after Brook leaves for work the doorbell rings. I hear Max answer in a voice an octave higher than normal, cheery in a creepy kind of way. Two sets of feet come up the stairs and down the hallway into the bedroom.

"Okay, well, this is it," she says, encompassing the space with her gesture. Her tail is a metronome. The fat beaver in overalls next to her looks around appraisingly.

"This the room you want bugged?" he asks in a tone that suggests he's done this before. Max winces, but regains her Stepfordness quickly. "If you want to call it that, yes."

"Because that's what we do, ma'am," the beaver says, stepping forward to look around the space. "It's a private investigation company. We do the spy thing." He puts his paws in his pockets, obviously pleased with himself.

"Spying is kind of a strong word," Max says, rubbing her chin. The ghost of a grin lightens her face. "I like it. Gonna get that motherfucker."

The beaver double-takes and looks back at her. "Ma'am?"

Max ignores him and starts going around the room, looking at lamps and knickknacks. "Oh, nothing. Not like you'd need to know anyway."

"It's not my business, t'be honest," says the guy, shifting his tool belt around his prodigious waist.

"My husband is fond of foxes." Max says it with all the offhandedness of a weather report. "Male foxes. He likes for them to tell him what to do. And then punish him anyway." She doesn't see the beaver blush brightly, nor hear him clearing his throat.

He swallows and says, "I'm sorry about that, Mrs. Waters."

"Don't be," says the husky, throwing her paws up and coming

back over to the beaver. I almost expect her to start talking to him in a sultry voice, dragging a claw from one side of his chest to the other. But this is real life, not harlequin romance. "I already know he's done it in here, and I can prove it. But I want to catch him in the act. I want him to twist in the fuckin' wind." The room gets twenty degrees colder.

Several seconds go by wherein I expect the beaver to just bolt while the bolting's good. Instead, he looks around, his eyes landing on me. "What about that husky?"

Max follows his pointing finger, stares at me for a second, and I recognize the flash in her eyes: revelation.

"Oh," she chuckles. "Oh, that's perfect." Mr. Beaver's already taking things out of his tool belt and setting them on the bed. Up I go, and down again, until my muzzle and hers are almost touching. "It's about time you came in handy. Huh?" She looks down, then back up. She turns me around and lifts my tail. "Oh, God dammit!"

"M-maybe I should leave," says the beaver, eyeing Max warily. "This seems like a touchy situation."

But Max laughs at him, shaking my rear end in front of his face. "He was storing his porn in this. It hasn't moved in years, and it was right there. I wonder how long he's been doing it. How long will it take to install the camera?" Now I'm dangling upside-down, held by the tail, piecing together what they're about to do to me.

"Fifteen minutes, tops." Pulling a pocket knife from a pouch on his belt, Mr. Beaver takes me from the leering Max and holds me by my neck. "His mouth is black already, so I suggest we put the cam in there. It only needs a quarter-inch hole to work. They make 'em small nowadays."

"Great," Max says, growing excited. "Can I help?"

"Sure, if you want. Hold him while I cut the hole." She does just that, keeping me still while he digs around the center of my permanently-open muzzle until the material slices open. This is nothing like what Brook did to my tail. I'm looking forward to it, actually.

"So, where does the power come from?"

Mr. Beaver picks up a cylinder the size of a stubby pencil with two wires coming out one end. Each is attached to a small black box. "One of these is a USB memory hub. That's where it gets recorded. The other is a battery, good for ten hours. You get the remote, so you can turn it on whenever. Charges on the wall when you're done. Pretty simple setup."

"You got that right," says Max, holding me up to rub snouts with her. "We're gonna catch him, and we're gonna make him pay, aren't we?" Her childish tone is starting to disturb me. The beaver seems disturbed already.

"Well, here," he says, "let's get him outfitted so you can get right on that, okay?" He no longer wants to be here, and I can't blame him. But I do. I want to see Brook squirm, and I'm honored to be the tool that catches him.

"Okay, yeah," the husky murmurs breathlessly, and her craze is a little contagious. She holds my dead, plastic eyes while the beaver flips my tail out of the way, a cold fire burning in the icy blue. "Make him pay."

I hardly feel the beaver's fist moving through my innards and poking the tip of the camera out the back of my throat, or his fingers as he works to secure the wires and boxes inside my body without making it look like I've been tampered with. When he takes his paw out the stitches back there burst open with a sickening rip, like a death knell. This may be my last purpose in life.

But I kind of enjoy the thought of getting back at Brook for stuffing shit in me by getting stuffed full of more shit. It's like a circle, coming back around on itself.

"I almost feel sorry for the little guy. He coulda made a good toy," says the beaver.

"I never liked it anyway," says Max, but I don't care. I have a job to do. "Neither did my husband. He always preferred foxes, he said."

"So you mentioned, ma'am." Putting me back on the shelf, little bits of fluff freeing themselves from my hole, the beaver hands a small fob to Max. "Top button. Try 'er out. Channel one on your tube, there." I hear a burst of static below me, and the guy changes the channel while Max pushes the button on her fob. My polyfill comes alive and crackles with an energy I can't describe. Maybe elation would compare on the scale of real feelings. It fills me with a warmth I've never felt before, probably because I've never been crammed full of electronics.

But that's okay.

Max reaches up and adjusts my head, watching the TV screen until she's satisfied with the picture. Then she turns and hugs the surprised beaver, who wastes little time in returning it. A little bit never hurt anyone. While he writes his invoice, the husky comes up to me and pats me between my permanently-perky ears, her smirk never faltering even when she whispers to me, never mind the insanity of the words: "Now, you be my good little boy and catch Daddy like I know you will, okay?"

Like I said, I'm a vindictive son of a bitch.

Careful what you play for.

COMPETITIVE NATURE

Zantal

Morton couldn't decide whether he loved or hated Friday nights at The Watering Hole. The rest of the week, it was a well-mannered habitat, as the name implied. It was frequented by some of the best billiards talent in the area, and that was starting to include himself, though he'd brush it off if someone mentioned it. But the atmosphere changed when the weekend came, and to-day was no exception. The place was overrun with Greeks—and not the chisel-chested Adonis type Morton might have preferred to look at, but cocky fraternity jocks and their accompanying girls. The upshot was that it was easy money for the regulars, though Morton never found this particularly sporting; the frat boys seemed to consider a point of pride for their bets to outweigh their skill.

Nevertheless, it'd been a hard week for the collegiate crocodile, and he hadn't fed his addiction recently, so here he was, being the predator, preying on the weak—well, the weak at pool and mon-etary restraint, anyway. He would be catching a glance at some of the handsome guys, but Friday nights were pretty fruitless … literally. There were too many males looking for easy female tail for it to be worthwhile. Weekends were particularly bad for the slow, methodical hunting Morton relished.

Instead, Morton was enjoying slightly vindictive pleasure in playing against and watching the reactions of a toned tiger in a leather jacket. His competitor was accompanied by a lioness who

161

was an unknowing accomplice, returning back with a couple of drinks that Morton knew wouldn't help the big cat. Not that it mattered at this point. A slight but toothy smile crossed his scaled maw as the ball he'd aimed at dropped into the pocket with quiet ease, sealing the game.

That turned into an eye roll as Morton caught the lioness quietly whispering to the male, "Don't worry baby, I'll clean up your balls." He wondered if she might clean out his wallet too, with those fancy drinks, before trying to force himself not to be too cynical just because they were so normal, so predictable. The crocodile collected his winnings and headed to the bar, chuckling a bit to himself. He was glad his confidence had paid off; he'd forgotten to bring cash tonight.

A few moments later, the still-smiling reptile returned to the pool area with a bratwurst and garlic fries, swishing past the tables a few of his friends inhabited. He cheered a couple of them on, harassed one or two with a good-natured grin, and finally stopped at another regular's table, finding a seat near its edge to eat.

A particular stranger caught the crocodile's attention as he surveyed the room. Morton had watched him play a few shots earlier while waiting on the tiger, memorable because he seemed to be one of the few here tonight that were mostly sober. The tan gazelle now leaned against the wall not too far from the reptile, idly watching a game with a couple of friends. He seemed happy but a little bored, and after a few moments, Morton convinced himself to try and start a conversation. Before long, the two friends left to go somewhere else in the bar, and the crocodile slipped over to the gazelle.

"Let me guess … DD?"

It took a moment for it to register on the gazelle's face, and then he chuckled shyly, seeming a bit surprised "Yeah, designated driver … I hope I wasn't that obvious."

Morton realized the other male was blushing a bit, and replied "Me too. Don't worry; I just hang out here a lot, and tonight everyone else is making it pretty easy to tell who's driving." He took a bite of his bratwurst, chewed, and swallowed. "You must practice somewhere else though; I haven't seen you here before."

"Oh, I play a fair amount. My friends like this place, 'The Shooter', across town; that's usually where we end up."

Morton could see the gazelle's small tail flicking timidly. The reptile smiled disarmingly "Ah; I know of that place." He took another bite and let the mammal continue, every now and then letting his eyes dart to look at the rest of the gazelle. He was cute and lanky, but it was difficult to tell what lay below the clothing. Historically most gazelles were fairly toned, though, owing to their ancestry.

The gazelle's chuckle interrupted his thoughts. "It's funny, my apartment is actually right around the corner from here, but some of my friends live over there."

"Ah, sure. I like this place," Morton continued, "it's not too far from campus, and the players are usually pretty good during the week."

"I guess I should have figured you went to State, too."

"Yeah, I think it's pretty common in this part of town. I'm Morton by the way," he said, offering his scaled palm to the other male.

"Kevin," the gazelle replied, and his soft-furred paw joined the crocodile's.

"Well, would you like to get a game started when I'm done with this bratwurst? It'd be nice to have a little more competitive match." Morton smiled a little wider and glanced momentarily toward the tiger he'd recently dispatched.

"What're the stakes?" the furred male replied.

"Well, we're both driving, so we can't do it for drinks. I already got dinner, and I only like to do cash bets with those I don't know." He chuckled and paused briefly in thought. "How about this: if you win, I'll come to The Shooter next week for a rematch, and if I win you come here." He paused and added "And, winner of that game buys dinner."

The gazelle thought for a few seconds. "Okay; you're on," he said with a smile.

"Alright, let me go wash my hands; I'll be right back." The crocodile said, excited at the upturn in his evening and the chance to play an experienced but unknown player.

It was the start of one of the more rousing matches in Morton's recent memory. He could tell his tan-furred opponent was talented, and the crocodile needed to use a number of his tricks and tactics—placing balls behind his opponent's, knocking away the gazelle's balls, and generally using more complex, drawn-out strategies—to pursue victory. It was far more interesting than the average game. Quietly, confidently, he stalked each of the balls, forcing them into the pockets.

In the end, the methodical, scaled one pulled off the win. When they shook over it, the gazelle looked him confidently right in the eyes and asked, "Best two out of three?"

"Sure," Morton replied, still a bit high on his hard-fought win. This was a heck of a lot more fun than anything else the bar had to offer.

The next game, though uniquely its own, went much the same as the first—a slow, strategic pursuit, a very enjoyable back-and-forth, and the crocodile finished first. Afterward, they chatted for a bit about school and the city before parting amicably to reconvene with their friends, the promise of the rematch in the back of their minds.

***

And so began an ongoing competition. Each week, they'd meet in one of the two bars and play. Afterward, they'd converse over dinner, learning a bit more about each other. Kevin was from the suburbs, while Morton had lived near the city his whole life, but it turned out both had plenty of interesting stories of their friends' and families' antics. The loser would pay for dinner and go to the other's bar the next week.

It took a few weeks before the gazelle won, but Morton knew it was inevitable; they were too closely matched for him to always come out on top. The crocodile was actually glad it had happened; he'd been feeling a bit bad about the gazelle always having to buy dinner, so he was glad to repay that. But, his competitive nature would never have let it happen intentionally.

As the weeks and games passed, and the crocodile and gazelle continued trading places as winners, Morton noticed they were both definitely improving. Each played against a different group of competitors in their "home" bar. When they came back together, it was a tacit exchange of knowledge and skill. Their two styles were merging as they discovered new tricks from each other, both becoming more talented.

Along with the rivalry and friendship, the crocodile had also noticed another feeling developing over the weeks. This feeling was a bit more concerning, confusing, and hidden. Maybe it was predatory instinct, maybe it was lust, or maybe it was even something more. Whatever it was that was developing, the gazelle's presence would sometimes make his heart race, and he found himself desiring the gazelle's company more and more often.

He had a perfect stimulus to stoke the fires, too. Every week, he'd get to see that tan-furred sprite bent over the table, focusing on the game and oblivious to the wandering eyes of the crocodile. Those reptilian eyes had started studying each and every detail of the mammal's rump: the way that short tail barely hid the objects of lust, the way his fur grew thinner, and no doubt softer, toward his inner thighs, and the way he sometimes spread his legs to lower his body for a particularly difficult shot.

Morton would also sometimes steal glimpses of the furred male's front when Kevin would stand back up to survey the table. The reptile was more toned than most gazelle—including his new friend—but thin lines from pecs and other musculature were visible through the light-brown fur. Morton found the understated yet still powerful body of his prey astonishingly attractive.

There were reasons to keep his lust hidden, however. In the modern world, though traditional species roles were no more, there was still tension and expectations. Whether the bottom was male or female, Morton knew some predators saw it as a sign of weakness to be topped by lower members of their long-ago ancestors' food chain. Likewise, prey would worry of overly-domineering, uncaring predators.

He didn't share these antiquated views, though; each year fewer did, and it was more common in the older generations. More problematic was a factor Morton knew was not unique to him; he had a good friendship and competition going that he didn't want to mess up. Trying to take the relationship further could risk what they already had. For now, the social risk prevented him from pursuing his desires.

Morton successfully kept his feelings in check in public, where he began to see more of his friend. They enjoyed a friendly wave when they occasionally ran across one another on campus, and they even managed to grab lunch together a couple of times. Kevin introduced him to a few of his friends, and vice versa.

One day in his English class, his professor had mentioned that the word "frenemy" was being added to the Oxford dictionary. Morton could think of no better description of their relations.

Competitors on the table, friendly everywhere else. He couldn't help but wonder if there was a word for when you mixed friend, enemy, lust … even love. "Complicated" maybe.

There was a moment Morton slipped a little, when the two ran into each other in the school's gym locker room one day. When he saw that handsome male bent over putting on his shoes, the reptile decided to get his first feel of those soft rump cheeks that begged to be cupped in his paws. He gave the other male a gentle smack right across the two globes as he walked past, a gesture others would attribute to a typical predator jokingly picking on a prey. Little did they know the crocodile's grin was because he'd gotten to feel that ass.

Of course, Morton hadn't expected Kevin to walk past when he was kneeled down putting on his own shoes and "accidentally" smack his snout with his tail. It left the crocodile spitting a bit from the feel of hair in his maw, smiling from the playful retaliation, and trying to hide a bit of a blush. Morton shrugged it off, though, knowing he couldn't win this time; Kevin was heading for the track. Even though he was in shape, there was simply no way for the crocodile to keep up with a gazelle's running. Likewise, he knew the buck would never have accepted a challenge on the weight machines.

Well, maybe he could still win … the crocodile let his mind drift a bit as he got on a treadmill. His imagination switched to himself, ripping off the gazelle's towel as they entered the shower area. The crocodilian maw would meet Kevin's, stifling his yelp of surprise, and he would press him into a shower stall, closing the door behind him with his tail.

He'd take the naked, shivering buck right there, lifting one of his furred legs so Morton could slip his warm shaft between the gap, aiming it for the male's fleshy entrance. Suddenly, the crocodile realized that back in real life, his slit had begun to bulge somewhat, and he quickly turned his thoughts elsewhere. He also chastised himself a bit; Kevin was his rival, yet he was obsessing about the softness of his groin fur.

For better or for worse, the reptile didn't run into Kevin again. He finished his workout and headed home. Morton focused on homework for one class, then studied for another, successfully keeping sex out of his thoughts until it was time to head to bed. He brushed his teeth and slid between the sheets, and—like any male with an object of lust—the crocodile allowed his thoughts to turn to it.

He imagined standing in the bedroom, naked, his hardness hanging in the air while Kevin lay on the bed, showing off for him. Morton thought of how he'd long to slowly stroke his bullhood in full view of the gazelle as the cute, sexy buck before him looked over his shoulder and flicked his tail. The scaled male dreamed of how cute Kevin would look, bent over in some tighty-whities that left nothing to the imagination, and how erotic it would be to rip through them with his claws, revealing the gazelle's private parts.

No, he thought, his visions turning naughtier, *make them panties*. The reptile's cock twitched a bit in his paw as he squeezed the head gently and thought of the buck's sexy, sizable balls pushing against pink fabric, their shape clearly outlined. That cute furred male would blush as he showed off for the reptile, being displayed in such a feminine way.

"Why don't you slip those off, Kevin?" the scaled beast commanded more than asked in his fantasy. The imagined version of the gazelle shyly brought his legs together and gripped the edge of the pink, too-small underwear, slipping them down his legs and completely exposing himself to the crocodile. Back in the real world, Morton was breathing heavily, touching himself in all the right spots as he thought of Kevin's short tail flipping back and forth, teasing him with much-too-short glimpses of the fuzzy orbs, the throbbing shaft hanging below, and the tight ring of his entrance.

"Oh, Kevin," he moaned, not caring that the words actually slipped out of his maw in the real world in a breathless whisper. In his mind he had crossed the distance to the bed and was rubbing against the naked object of his lust, sliding his dripping tip along the ever-so-soft and pliable globes of his friend's rump. "Mmm … feel that? That's what you want, isn't it? My thick cock slipping inside you, pleasuring your most intimate spots … show me you want it; raise that … oh, yeah." He growled as the imaginary gazelle panted for the crocodile and flicked his small furry tail upward, letting Morton see everything he wanted.

The reptile knew he was close when he imagined the buck shyly turning, a smile on his face as he panted softly. "Yes," the imagined buck whispered, pausing when their eyes met. "Take me," the gazelle gasped, moving shyly to kiss the crocodile's cheek. Pre squirted in Morton's clawtips back in the real world.

He could almost feel how the furred, naked male would be trembling in anticipation. Kevin would tense up, and the reptile would stroke his chest, calming him as the gazelle got his first feel of the croc tip. Slowly, he'd feel that ring expand and slip deeper into that warmth …

"Ah! Ah! Yesssss!" Morton could take no more and moaned aloud. Thick spurts of musk splashed onto belly scales, his paw wrapped around the middle of his shaft while it throbbed. The crocodile felt a warm wetness land near his neck, and soon he could tell there was more of it on his underscales than any time in recent memory …

"Yesssss …" No other thoughts crossed his mind as he drifted into the ecstasy of afterglow, and from there into the soft caress of happy sleep.

***

Over the next few weeks, despite his restraint in public, Morton found the gazelle in his fantasies more and more often. Something about it, whether it was the closeness of the two friends, the unrealized desire, or something more, just made everything feel better, made the croc cum faster, harder, and more.

Of course, the reptile began to wonder what the other male's persuasions might be, and he tried to be more observant at the bar. He started to watch when particularly showy females walked past, catching most eyes in the bar … but never Kevin's. Of course, it was possible he was simply shy or focused on the game, but Morton had a glimmer of hope. And one day, a toned otter boy that Morton would describe as fairly handsome was at the pool table next to them, and he could have sworn he saw Kevin steal a few glances at him.

But most important to the crocodile, Morton began to cast his eyes upward just a bit, keeping his head still, when he lined up shots. And what he thought he noticed was the gazelle looking over his body.

The reptile was careful not to let himself set expectations too high; he knew his desires could cloud his thinking. He doubted that he was that lucky—that the buck felt the same way he did— but it seemed he was either carefully sizing up the crocodile's shots or the crocodile's body. These new observations began to turn Morton's pursuit into one that properly fit his style.

Another new element was also coming into play. The two had chatted about drinks one night; they'd never had more than one each when they were together. It turned out that neither minded getting a bit tipsy from time to time, and they had decided that they'd have add that to their games every once in a while.

Despite what some claimed, drinking seemed to decrease skill.

So, each time one of them scored a ball, he would have to take a half shot. It was an effective way to balance the game, and at the end of the night, the loser paid for the drinks.

An important side-effect of those nights was that the reptile needed to sleep over at the buck's, or vice-versa; neither were in shape to drive. On top of that, Kevin didn't have a crocodile-sized couch. However, he did have a queen-sized bed. Which he'd offered to share with the scaled male.

"I trust you," Kevin had said nonchalantly. Oh, if he only knew …

The first couple times they did this, about a month and a half between them, Morton won the games, and afterward they simply headed to bed. Nothing remarkable transpired. The third time was a night Morton would never forget.

They arrived back at Kevin's apartment, stumbling a bit, and started getting ready for bed. As usual, the reptile had brought his toothbrush and a change of clothes. He used both, then left the bathroom so the gazelle could take his shower. He slipped into the bed, breathing in and quietly savoring the scent of his prey.

Morton had gotten quite comfortable, when a few minutes later an urgent need to pee hit him. He'd forgotten to, and after a few seconds, it became more apparent that it couldn't wait. Dashing to the apartment's sole bathroom, he hesitated, then opened the door. A cloud of steam rushed over the crocodile's scales, surrounding him with pleasurable warmth. He heard startled movement in the shower, and Kevin asking "Morton? What's going on?"

"Sorry bud; had to pee; couldn't wait." The reptile issued a sigh of relief as he achieved his goal, then reassured the gazelle, "Don't worry; I can't see anything with all that steam." But the truth was, he could see something that demanded all his attention. Through the frosted glass and steam, he could still make out the gazelle's body, complete with a prominent, pink, erect length.

It was just like he'd heard, just like he'd dared to imagine: long, straight, and thin. It had to reach almost to his chest. And from Kevin's quick breathing, the reptile suspected the other male had been pleasuring himself. Just before he'd walked through the door, Kevin's paws must have been rubbing over that length, the same length the crocodile longed for, longed to feel, to squeeze, to rub in all the right ways to make the buck gasp and moan in pleasure …

The scaled male knew that he couldn't resist; he had to find some way to watch the rest of the show. What lay before his eyes was one of the single most erotic and attractive things he'd ever seen, and he hadn't even seen the best action yet. Thinking quickly, he knew the buck's visibility into the bathroom wouldn't be great. But he needed an excuse in case he got caught … Looking around, his heart racing, he spotted a pair of his boxers he'd left on the floor. Perfect. Now, he just had to fool the gazelle into continuing.

When he finished peeing, he opened the door, then closed it again without leaving. He stood near it, hoping through the fog his dark green scales would blend with the brown shade of the door. If they didn't, he'd have to think fast to explain this.

"Morton?" echoed through the fog. The crocodile's heart raced, and he stood frozen in place. A few seconds later, the gazelle began to move again. It looked to Morton like he was washing his back and arms. Sure enough, the furred, erect male had gone back to his shower.

Morton slowly, quietly let out the breath he'd been holding, and he began to wonder if he'd startled the gazelle enough that he'd stopped pawing off. He mentally willed, begged the other male to renew his erotic stroking, and after a short delay, his heart jumped when he saw the buck's paw move to the base of that long shaft, then slip down its length toward the tip.

Only in his imagination could the crocodile see the veins on the cock and the way water droplets were swept off the length as

172

the paw slid over it, slid from where it met the gazelle's handsome body to the thin, tapered tip, wicking away a clear droplet of pre. Only in his imagination could he see that chest flex with each pleasured breath and the way Kevin's maw hung open in pleasure.

What was clearly seen by the crocodile, though, was that the male gazelle's paw rubbed up and down that sensitive flesh, and when the other paw joined it, it gripped at the base, right where he imagined the shaft met his body. Kevin leaned back, and Morton heard a soft smack of wet fur contact the wall, the gazelle leaning against it as his paws continued to touch his pleasure spots. The croc had seen those supple paws work a pool cue—how it slid between the digits—and now they were working a much more tender, sensitive pole …

Morton began to hear soft, gentle moans accompany each "thrust" the buck's paws replicated on his own maleness. While the crocodile watched the object of his desire teasing the most sensitive areas of his body, the understated soundtrack of the buck's pleasure would be forever etched into his brain, memories of the ultimate eroticism he saw. Oh, how he would have driven the gazelle wild if those were his paws on the furred male. Morton would have been determined to earn more of those gasps of pleasure than he could count, to make the male moan even louder from previously unknown heights of pleasure …

As his eyes took in every movement they could see, it occurred to Morton that the gazelle's lower paw was almost certainly slamming back into his sheath and body. Combined with the heated wetness of the shower water cascading over the buck's shaft, each "thrust" must have felt like he was hilting into something so slippery and warm … *Definitely slippery*, the crocodile thought, as he saw the paw move to the side of the shower, and then he heard the sound of a bottle being squeezed.

As if that weren't enough to drive Morton mad with lust, he

watched as—after the bottle squeeze—the gazelle under the hot stream of water moved the paw around to his rump and leaned forward from the wall. The reptile was nearly drooling at this point, basking in Kevin's unintentional erotic display. After only a brief moment of teasing himself, the furred male straightened a bit, and Morton heard hooves clatter gently. Then, the gazelle sighed, one of effort and pleasure. A couple of seconds later, he gave another happy grunt, and realization hit the croc: he was now watching firsthand as the other male fingered himself.

Morton took a slow, deep whiff, and his nostrils were overwhelmed with a thick steam that warmed his insides and made him feel refreshed. Then, as the scaly beast exhaled, he could barely keep himself from emitting a low purr. He'd found that hint of the buck's musk, the scent of his friend's arousal. It made his own cock jump in its scaled enclosure, which he rewarded with an idle claw touch.

The glass separated him from all the details he wanted to know so badly. The crocodile longed to glimpse the details of that lengthy maleness, to watch the heavy veins throb in time with the buck's proud breeding tool. He wanted to see each contraction of that ballsack, and the reptile imagined what it would feel like to have his own paw wrapped around the weighty lumps in their soft-furred, sensitive sack, rubbing them gently to make the gazelle squirm with arousal.

Most of all, Morton wanted to see how the other male was using his fingers on those two pleasure centers. He wanted to watch how Kevin's paw squeezed his own tip, and how it rubbed the opening at the end of his fleshy spear. He wanted to gaze at the pre strands between the furred fingers. His thoughts turned to the gazelle's other paw. What direction were those soft fingertips? And how many? He almost squealed with need as he envisioned the cute black ring of muscle, its wrinkles disappearing when it tensed around the fingers. The croc dreamed of watching it be spread open so the needy male could touch himself inside, touch himself right where it felt good … and of how the lube would make it slippery inside the buck.

Morton could hear just fine, and that was torture. He could hear the way Kevin was moaning softly every few moments, and he could only conjecture if that was accompanied by a dribble of precum, or a gentle wiggle of his paw digits inside the buck's cute rump, or a flicker of that oh-so-small tail that would do so little to cover the male's private parts from the crocodile's slitted, inquisitive eyes.

The crocodile would've been pawing off furiously if he hadn't been in the same room as Kevin. Morton could feel wetness in his previously-clean underwear as he rubbed his erect, throbbing crocodile shaft through the cloth. The scaled being knew after his escape he would have to find a way to paw off, even if it meant grinding desperately against the sheets, pretending to be asleep until the sexy buck who tortured him began his quiet snoring.

Kevin's breaths were coming harder and faster now, bringing a smile to the maw of the lust-wild reptile. *That's it, my hot gazelle, let yourself go*, he thought, dreaming of saying it breathlessly into the furred male's ear. *Go on,* cum, *sexy!* he mentally urged, dreaming of the other male tensing and giving in as he said that. *Give it all up for me …*

Morton had thought the quiet moans were hot, but they were nothing compared to the loud gasps of erotic pleasure that soon filled the bathroom. He could see the shaft of the gazelle actually visibly jump, twitching in the other male's paws, and he just barely caught a glimpse of a white blob spurting into the waters. The crocodile felt a shiver run through his whole body. Oh, how he longed to be in there, smelling the male's essence and feeling its sticky yet slick texture as the gazelle lost himself to passion.

Oh, to hold the other male's body as his prey lost all thought, succumbing to the pleasure and moaning so loudly.

Mmm, my hot gazelle … The reptilian male smiled, envisioning his own finale. The thoughts filled both his groin and mind with warm feelings. Penetrating his prey, his enemy, his lover with his pink crocodilian shaft, claiming the other male as his own. The image shifted to quick, shallow thrusts hilted deep inside the gazelle, so close to his release. *Ah … g-gonna mark you, Kevin; mark you as mine.*

Morton … do it … make me yours. The reptile dreamed of holding the other male, groaning in pleasure as he started to fill him with warm seed, hilted deep and pumping it all inside.

Kevin's actual shuddering gasps were coming to an end, and the gazelle stumbled forward as his climax entered its last few spurts. Much as the crocodile yearned to stay behind and see the sensual, no doubt copious mess his friend had made all over the shower, he knew this was his last chance for escape. While the gazelle was still reeling from his orgasm, Morton oh-so-quietly opened the door, slipped out, and closed it back as silently as he could.

With the state the gazelle was in and the shower water still flowing over his body, Morton knew he was probably safe. Well, safe except that his desires must have increased tenfold. The crocodile slipped back under the covers, lying in wait and pretending to sleep. A few minutes later his friend joined him, hooves clattering as he stumbled to the bed. Morton knew it wasn't the alcohol. Minutes passed, the silence striking compared to the action just moments before. The reptile lay, his whole scaly body throbbing with arousal.

The crocodile was still, listening to his friend's breath slowing into what he knew would be the deep sleep of afterglow. Even keeping his own breathing slow, Morton picked up a familiar scent: the gazelle's musk. He knew Kevin was tired; he must not have cleaned it all up. It wasn't surprising he'd miss a spot with how much he must have shot, with how powerfully that lengthy rod had twitched as Morton looked on.

He forced himself not to move, the minutes dragging on. The crocodile lay, taunted by his friend's close, naked, musky body, anticipating what he would get to do but knowing he had to wait. The images, real and imaginary, of the buck next to him that ran through his head did little to ease the wait, but they did make every moment of pent up desire so much sweeter.

Finally, a few minutes after the handsome gazelle had begun softly snoring, Morton could wait no longer, and he made his move. A scaled paw very gently touched his friend's soft underside, gradually increasing its contact until it was slowly finding its way lower and lower on Kevin's warm, furred body. It didn't take long before he found a spot of rough, matted fur.

As he rubbed his paw slowly over his friend's dried musk, a naughty thought crossed the crocodile's mind. How far would he be willing to go? Aroused and already feeling daring from the night's success, the reptile's paw digits moved a bit, pressing his friend's fur a bit and seeing if it would wake him up.

When the gazelle didn't move, Morton's head slowly disappeared under the covers. Carefully, slowly, he shifted his body until he was on all fours, leaning over the spot he had found. The crocodile male's tongue slowly flicked out, a shiver of excitement running through him as he touched it to the rough, dried seed, wetting it and suckling gently.

It was his first taste of herbivore seed, and it was stronger than he expected, but Morton considered the taste a nice surprise. It was earthy, a little sweet like the fruit Kevin ate, but most of all, it was overtly sexual, and overtly male. His facial scales flushed a bit as his tongue softly licked at the fur, wetting it and slurping the musk into his maw, until he'd gotten all of it, leaving the buck's underside moist.

How far, Morton? How far will you go? he asked himself, as his long snout pressed to the tip of the buck's sheath and inhaled the delicious aroma. He was now drunk on sexual excitement too, the combined effects of arousal and alcohol making him daring, willing to pursue his desires.

One lick, he told himself, before he slipped his tongue into the other male's warmth. *Just let me taste it right from the source.*

Warm, smooth, and tight. Keeping his tongue in the sheath of his friend took more force than he'd have thought, the flesh squeezing around it. And it tasted distinctly—if less powerfully— of the same musk he'd just suckled off of the buck's fur. Morton flicked his tongue around in circles in the warm, moist grip, all inhibitions gone as he savored the erotic feeling. He wasn't sure how many moments had passed when he finally managed to pull his tongue away from the slick, squeezing, smooth insides and the taste of the male's essence that he greedily savored.

It had been a battle to stop, but the crocodile knew he'd reached the point where he wanted to go no further until his friend was conscious and looking on lustfully, his soft voice encouraging the scaled male to keep arousing him further, driving both to higher levels of passion …

And Morton knew he'd have no trouble releasing himself. His paw wrapped around his thick crocodile maleness even before he'd moved back to his side of the bed. The croc found himself already dripping pre, gasping softly as he relished the taste of the other male that filled his maw. He stayed on all fours, and the reptile's memories vividly reminded him of watching the buck finger himself to release in the shower … of leaning over the buck and slipping his tongue into the male's warm sheath … of his fantasies of pressing his cock deep inside the buck, breeding that tight warm tunnel, or even feeling that long cock slipping deep into his own scaled body …

The crocodile had to stuff a pillow in his maw and bite hard to prevent a loud moan, almost a roar from the strength of his orgasm. His cock twitched forcefully in his paw, pumping its gift onto the sheets under him in spurt after spurt. Finally, it slowed to dribbling pulses. Collapsing onto his side, the croc panted in the afterglow. Morton ran his paw through the load he had splattered on the sheets, idly making a musky spot as his mind sank into the depths of sleep, all the while drinking in the blended scent of the two males' musk.

***

The crocodile awoke to the sound of a running sink in the bathroom, and he blinked his eyes open in the sunlight. His thoughts of the night before quickly turned into a rush of adrenaline as Morton noticed the dried seed on his paw. He gripped the covers, quickly pulling them off to check for evidence of his shameless behavior. He was relieved to discover that the pattern on the sheets hid it well. The only spot Morton could find was high enough it could be explained away by drool, and the smell should have faded before the morning came.

Morton was quieter than usual that morning, as if to make up for his risky, lust-fueled actions the night before. Before long, he drove home, and all day long he tried to keep his mind on homework instead of the incredibly sensual experiences he'd had. He wasn't very good at it, though; by the time the evening rolled around, he'd already pawed to the memories twice, and even licked up the seed imagining it was his competitor's.

As the days passed, there was no doubt Morton was in a hard place. Expressing himself—his true thoughts—to the gazelle would be difficult. It would put a friendship and progress in his hobby at risk, but his most ominous worry was the fear of rejection. For now, he could dream about the other male's sexy body, what they'd do together. If he tried and failed, that fantasy would be shattered, and there was no guarantee it would haunt him any less.

But deep down, Morton vowed to himself that he wouldn't let these longings go unspoken. They were simply too vivid, too deep to be suppressed, even if it meant pushing himself to overcome his fear. He wasn't the sort to let this pass him by, to hem and haw waiting for the perfect moment, the perfect way, and never being honest.

The reptile knew, actually, what it felt like to never make good on his desires. In his first year of high school, an anole on the basketball team had caught his eye. They'd struck up a conversation and become fast friends. He didn't get much court time, but Morton had enjoyed watching him. Secretly, he'd dreamed of getting inside that lithe male's shorts, and showing him what other male reptiles were capable of—what a crocodile felt like on the inside and outside.

The lizard was smart, shy, friendly; all very sexy attributes to Morton. But Morton had never gotten up the nerve to make it anything more than a good friendship, and the shy anole never made a move either. So the crocodile had been left to wonder what could have happened with the other male, what pleasures they could have enjoyed in each other's scales if only he'd made a move.

Even the lust for that lizard didn't compare to Morton's feelings now, though, or how hard he came even the second and third time that day when he dreamed of that tan fur. Morton made a promise to himself: he was not going to let nerves overcome him. He would force himself to accept reality and seize it for all its potential, whether it led to joy or heartbreak.

Inevitability didn't make it any easier, though. It was another two months before the crocodile could get some private time with Kevin, during the next one of their drinking nights. The pool hall was too public of a place for that conversation, but unfortunately when they got back, the two males were fairly tipsy. Morton had lost but was happy he'd gotten to pay for things; both males were still in a jovial mood. It hardly seemed like the time for an honest, serious conversation.

As the crocodile slipped into the covers next to the gazelle, he wondered if he'd have a chance to broach the topic before he left. He began to rationalize that maybe he shouldn't, that it would spoil the fun. *No,* he told himself, pushing aside nervousness, *I will tell him before I leave, or I will meet up with him this week. I will not let it go on longer.*

When he woke first, Morton felt it was a good thing; he could set the stage. He opened the fridge and set about preparing some bacon and eggs, idly running through what he might say in his head. The anticipation wasn't helping; he almost wished he could just get it over with.

Finally, the gazelle opened his eyes, and looked toward the kitchen. "Mmm … that smells wonderful," he said.

Morton smiled back. "Thanks. It's almost ready, too."

He watched as the cute furred male stretched and slowly walked to the bathroom, and Morton waited patiently for the other male to finish up and join him for the conversation that would define what they were to each other. Minutes filled with suspense passed, until the gazelle finally arrived in the kitchen, and the idle small talk began.

Morton responded cheerfully to the furred male's comments, but his mind was focused now; he waited for the right break in the conversation. His heart racing, he grabbed the reins and steered them into the dark, not sure of what he'd find, but he had to find out.

"Kevin, there's something I've been meaning to tell you." There were only a few phrases that could follow that, and Morton's plan was no exception.

"It's something only my closest friends know. Not because I'm ashamed of it. It's just not really been a topic that's come up. But, Kevin, I prefer males 'that way.' They're what I lust for, and what I want as a mate."

The gazelle smiled back at him. "Morton, I'm glad you didn't mind telling me that. I hope you wouldn't think that'd matter to me," he said.

"Kevin, there's a reason I'm telling you that." Morton took a breath and forced himself to continue. "I have a crush on you, Kevin. No, more than a crush, that sounds childish. I want you, Kevin, as more than a friend."

That brought a little more surprise to the gazelle's face. Meanwhile all Morton could think was that he was screwing it up. He'd gone out of order; it wasn't the plan. He was supposed to try and figure out the gazelle's feelings before admitting his own … but he had to keep going now, had to make the best of it. "Kevin, I want you to be honest with me. I want to know what you like. And I want to know … if you want what I want."

Morton wasn't sure if he'd be able to hear the gazelle's response with the way blood thundered through his head. He second-guessed himself a hundred ways—he shouldn't have done this, it was too soon—yet he felt a vast wave of relief, from having finally stopped holding back his desires, whether he'd get to experience them or not.

The crocodile's paws were shaking. He sincerely hoped Kevin wouldn't notice …

"Morton, you were honest with me. And I really, really appreciate that. So, I guess I need to do the same." Morton braced for the worst, the rejection he'd feared, but maybe it wouldn't be so bad. He seemed to be taking it well …

The gazelle sighed gently. "Morton … almost since the day we met, I've noticed how sexy your scales were." At this, Kevin actually heard a happy, small chirp of surprise from the crocodile, which brought a smile to his face. "I … I've been wanting you 'that way', as more than a friend, for … to be honest, months. But, I never thought I'd get the guts to ask." He looked down at his morning tea, then found the strength for one more sentence. "Morton …" He looked away shyly. "It would really make me happy if … if you and I were, well, together … sexually, and even in a relationship."

A happy silence fell over the two for a moment, finally broken the only way it could be "I … don't know what to say." Morton said. "I'm … just glad I don't have to hold this in." After another pause, confidence surged in Morton, and a wide, sincere smile spread across his scaly muzzle.

"Come here, you sexy piece of buck ass." He grinned, feeling on the verge of tears just from the geyser of emotion inside him, though his pride wouldn't let him. The gazelle walked around the table and pressed against the crocodile, rubbing his soft belly fur against the scales of the other's body as they embraced.

A few moments passed before each copped a feel of the other, then nervously chuckled even though they were no longer off limits. "I … it feels like I got so much weight off of my chest." the crocodile said happily.

"I'm glad you took care of that for me, Morton—well, for us. I don't know if I could have done what you did." the gazelle replied. "I didn't want to risk you."

They sat there silently for a little longer, each enjoying the other's warmth for a few more moments. Finally, Kevin slipped out of the reptile's arms and swished his tail as he walked toward the couch. "What say we enjoy a couple cartoons before you have to go?" he asked Morton.

"Sure," was the instant reply.

It felt a little odd to go from such a mature discussion to a reminder of his childhood, but both were things they could enjoy together. Morton leaned his head against his new boyfriend's shoulder, relishing the touch of the fur that his muzzle rested upon. He lay in a dreamlike state, idly watching the TV but mainly just enjoying the happiness their company brought him—and the feeling of relief from succeeding where he'd been so nervous.

He had to wonder whether the gazelle was feeling it too, and judging by the soft smile he wore, it was the same for him. Gingerly, the reptile's paw moved to scratch the other male's furred chest. The effort and risk had been worth it.

The next half an hour passed in their idle chatter. A few smiling comments were made about how nice it felt, but no serious discussion. Finally, the gazelle broached a topic that Morton had actually been curious about but too satisfied to bring up.

"So … when will we get some … ah, alone time together? And um … who … erm … tops?" He smiled in a way the crocodile hadn't seen before, but it was clearly cheekier than usual. The question was certainly more brazen than Morton had grown to expect. He had to wonder what sort of images were going through the gazelle's imagination, as a few crept into his own.

"I don't know," the reptile began, "I think we're both switches." The gazelle nodded meekly. A brief silence followed, each holding back explicit sexual thoughts. "Well," Morton continued, "we could do it the same way we decide other things."

"You mean pool?"

Morton nodded. The furred male looked pensive, then said, "Not a bad idea. We'll both be pretty busy until our next match anyway." He paused, then grinned. "Why not? That'd be fun. There really isn't a better way to decide."

A bit of a blush swept over the crocodile. He'd only been half-serious when suggesting it, but the gazelle was right. *Why not, indeed.* He smiled back at the gazelle that was now truly and properly his. "You're on."

They lay together for a few moments, before the gazelle leaned and whispered deviously to the crocodile. "Next time, we'll head back to my apartment, but not because we can't drive. Because one of us is going to be feeling his cute tailhole getting teased open, and the other one is going to be the one doing it." This vocal naughtiness from his buck was unexpected and arousing … they both blushed and grinned, excitement and anticipation running through them.

An hour later, the crocodile sadly had to leave his new boyfriend to meet up with some other students for a group project. They had an almost stereotypical awkward-goodbye moment on the doorstep until Morton decided to fix it. He pushed through their hesitation, and they enjoyed a few quick kisses and the best hug the reptile had ever shared.

The project felt unremarkable, a lackluster event compared to the time he'd just spent with his gazelle, but he knew it had to be done—they were evaluated by their other groupmates. He'd almost decided to call in sick before a furred paw had smacked him right in the rump, his boyfriend telling him to go ahead, that he'd still be available when Morton was finished.

Indeed, later that evening it was clear the buck also longed for the company of his crocodile, calling him and inviting him over for a movie. And, oh, how they snuggled, the body of the reptile wriggling as he practically pressure-fused his scales into the soft, warm fur of his gazelle. Sure, Morton had ended up as the small spoon, but his pride was comforted by reason. The buck was a big, fuzzy blanket, and the crocodile wanted to be wrapped in it, not the other way around. But, he'd have to make sure to be the big spoon next time.

The week wore on, and mild excitement hovered in the back of his mind. Each day was a pleasant surprise when he got out of bed and remembered it all, adding a charge of nervousness yet excitement to his day. By Wednesday he was counting the days; there weren't a lot left. Three days. Three days from now, he'd be in that bed, laying—or getting laid by—the stud his mind and body yearned for.

By the time Friday arrived, Morton's stomach was filled with butterflies. He drove to the pool hall and parked by the gazelle's apartment, remembering what he'd said about why he wouldn't be driving home tonight. He entered The Shooter and saw his opponent—also the object of his feelings and lust—standing across the room. Kevin was slowly shifting from hoof to hoof, making it plain that he was nervous like Morton and similarly ready for the challenge.

Few words were spoken between the two, each knowing what lay at stake, but the game wasn't without a fun kickoff. "My balls are going to win tonight." Kevin grinned, looking daringly into Morton's eyes.

"Your ass is mine." The crocodile replied, and so it began.

It was probably the most mentally-charged game he'd ever played. Morton wasn't the sort of player to get intimidated or let distractions influence his game, but the context of this game was impossible to ignore. He cursed himself as he missed an easy shot, celebrating internally when he saw the gazelle do the same. Usually he could deconstruct games with little effort, but nothing about this game seemed simple to the crocodile. Adrenaline was running as hot now as other fluids would be later that night.

Even in the tense atmosphere, Morton took advantage of their new openness to be less hidden about eyeing the furred male, and he noticed Kevin doing the same to him. He assumed the other male was also envisioning how it would feel to be in either position in the bed that night, and how this would decide which of those experiences each would feel.

Each shot felt momentous with the concentration and effort put into it. Before too long, though, the crocodile had only two balls remaining to win. Kevin had three, but then he expertly put away two of them. It was down to the last ball, but it was a tough shot, one Kevin didn't make. The scaled male sized up the table, breathing carefully to calm himself down. He lined up, made a smooth stroke, and missed.

The resulting shot was neither easy nor hard for the gazelle. With all the tension in the air, there would be more than enough potential for the crocodile to redeem himself if the buck missed. But he wouldn't get that chance, not tonight. The skilled, furred paws of the gazelle nudged the cue ball just right. The reptile watched as it struck its target gracefully, and the eight ball dropped quietly into the right pocket. He knew both of their hearts were racing even more now, as they knew what was to come in the initiation of their relationship and their experiments with each other's bodies.

It was hardly a disappointment to Morton. He wanted to give himself to his male, to feel their bodies joined and Kevin deep inside him. The crocodile would have admitted as much to the gazelle, but the competitive part of him still held on, even if his body would be rewarded regardless …

"Best 2 out of 3?" he couldn't help but ask.

The gazelle smiled and leaned toward him, speaking in hushed tones so no one else could hear. "No, sexy reptile. I want you all to myself. I've earned the rights to fill your body tonight, to make you breathless with pleasure … and I intend to take full advantage of it." The sensual words hanging in the air, Kevin leaned just a little more—looking to anyone else in the bar like he were whispering—and snuck a kiss on the reptile's scales, his warm breath teasing them.

They walked out of the pool hall, Morton blushing deeply enough that it was visible even through his dark green scales. He knew where they would be going, what it would entail; all his fantasies lay ahead of them. The crocodile's heart pounded in nervousness and anticipation, and he knew that his buck—it was so nice to really call Kevin that now, "his buck"—was feeling the same way.

Morton took initiative and gently wrapped his scaly paw around the gazelle's, adding a touch of romance and breaking the shyness.

"You thinking about it?" Kevin asked. The gazelle's own slight blush made it clear that he was.

"How could I not be?"

"Yeah. I guess it's going to be one heck of a night," the buck said, a smile stretching across his face.

That was a pretty big understatement, Morton thought. But how could one describe in words the feelings that would be shared? The anticipation of getting to know each other intimately? There simply was no way, and so they'd do it with words, noises, and most of all touch, in the physical expression of their passion.

Teasing words turned into a meaningful silence for the rest of their short walk. Their minds were both filled with the pleasure of their company and anticipation of the moments to come.

When they got to Kevin's door, the gazelle smiled that naughty smile Morton had only seen him use this past week, and he slipped the key in and out, in and out of the lock, mimicking a pair of rutting animals. Morton gave him a slightly incredulous look, then rumbled softly and leaned on the furred male, gently pressing him against the door. The key turned in the lock, and the pair slipped inside.

As soon as the door was closed, the buck wrapped his arms around the crocodile, pulling him against his warm coat of underfur. Their noses were just inches apart. "You're mine, croc, and you know it. I'm going to penetrate that sexy scaled body of yours, and you'll love every second of it, and you'll beg for more whe— mmmf." The gazelle was cut off by the reptile's maw moving over his own and kissing him right on the lips.

When they separated, Kevin had to take a deep breath before he continued. "Giving up my own essence inside you …" the hot breath brushed over Morton's facial scales as the other male whispered the erotic words, making his heart pound even faster.

A deep purr radiated from the crocodile, a low internal bellow of arousal as he pressed back into the gazelle. Kevin's dirty words had achieved their intended purpose, driving him to new levels of excitement "Good … that way we can compare with how much of my seed you drip next time …" Morton purred, eyeing the buck to watch him blush.

The long, scaled muzzle of the reptile nuzzled against the soft facial fur of the gazelle, and his thick tongue gently licked through it. Strong arms pulled the furred male just a little closer as his maw opened, bringing the two into their first deep kiss. Gently the crocodile's tongue stroked along and then around the buck's, the intimate touch of their two sensitive fleshes making them both breathe even harder.

Fur met scale below the passionate connection of their lips, their two bodies grinding against each other as they strived to be even closer. A strong scaled paw found its way to the back of Kevin's neck, holding him into the kiss as it deepened. Both had their eyes closed in passion, the feel of their tongues and their bodies all they needed to know.

Whether it was one long kiss or multiple connected ones was

difficult to tell, but it wasn't long before the reptile's claws were gently scratching the bare fur under Kevin's shirt, sending waves of sensation through him, followed by a slow tease of the mammalian nipples. The supple, furred paws that found their way up Morton's own torso had no fleshy nubs to play with, but his soft underscales were vulnerable, highly sensitive to touch. Especially in the scale gaps, which Kevin apparently had no difficulty discovering could be stimulating, erogenous places.

Soon, both males were huffing and gasping each time their lips separated, and the shirts—after some slightly comical difficulty with Kevin's horns—became a forgotten pile on the floor. Warm scales pressed tightly to soft fur, the crocodile's rumbles reverberating through them both.

Their kiss could have lasted forever and neither would have complained, but the electricity it left in their bodies compelled them to keep moving. Even so, it was difficult for Morton to pull back from the kiss. When he did, he flicked on the light switch behind him so he could look at the sexy gazelle. Their furred and the scaled muzzles were connected by a strand, evidence of the sensual act.

For a moment they both stood shyly, before Kevin ground his hips against the crocodile's again. "I feel that bulge in your slit Morton." He spoke softly as his furred groin teased against it. "Come on, let it out … you know you want to." The gazelle purred, a set of skilled fingers slipping down the front of the crocodile's shorts, inside his boxers, to rub directly on the tender areas near the male's slit, and even touch that sensitive gap.

"Kevin!" The crocodile gasped, the feel of the other male's paws there shooting pleasure up his body.

"That's it Morton … good croc … come on out into my paw."

"Mmf … oh … Kevin, yes," was the only thing that came out of Morton's maw while the sensations flowed through him, his muscles tensing as he ground his body forward into the sensual rubs. The crocodilian slit parted quickly under the attention, short moans issuing from his scaled mouth as the gazelle's fingers danced over his opening, teasing the sensitive area. Soon Morton's moist tip had pressed through the slit, and Kevin's warm paw quickly grasped and stroked over it. From there it was a matter of seconds before the full maleness of the crocodile pressed out and slipped into the other male's grip.

A grin spread across the gazelle's face as he said, "Good to see you're just as sensitive there as the internet said you'd be."

The dumbfounded reptile smiled back, impressed but too out of breath and busy riding the pleasure to respond. But Kevin soon slipped his paws out of the other male's shorts, wordlessly turned, and slowly walked into the bedroom. That cute rump was like Morton's personal pied piper, and he eagerly followed. As the croc entered, it was remarkable how different the room felt, knowing what they were here for and what would take place.

Kevin grabbed a bottle of lube from the dresser, driving home how real the erotic act that filled their minds was about to become. He grinned again and rummaged, before pulling a pink pair of panties out of the dresser. "Why don't you put these on?" Kevin asked, smile still wide as he met the croc's gaze and then tossed them to him.

Morton blushed as his memories rushed back to his visions of the buck in the submissive role, when he'd imagined Kevin moaning that he wanted the crocodile to take advantage of his cute, barely protected rump. Morton knew he couldn't deny his buck of something he found so incredibly arousing himself. He knew it was his turn to show off and display his body so it was nearly begging the buck to penetrate it.

The crocodile's first task, though, was to remove his constricting shorts. Stepping back to the wall, Morton leaned against it and arched his scaled hips forward, bringing his paw to outline the obvious bulge the gazelle had created. He squeezed the bulbous tip once, then undid the clasp and the zipper, letting the front of the shorts slide open. All it took was one more thrust, and the even more detailed outline of the boxer-clad shaft pressed into the open. The bulge from the reptile's maleness was damp from the crocodile's slit fluid.

"Mmm …" Kevin murmured at the striptease, looking on as the crocodile met his lover's eyes and licked his lips. Then the reptile turned and bent, showing off the curves of his rump while he teased his underwear down. The tip of Morton's hardness was visible between his legs, and it became the rest of his pink, exotic shaft as the garment was removed. Slowly, a strand of precum stretched between his cock head and the underwear until it broke soundlessly. Still bent over, the crocodile's tail swayed and curled like a serpent, but his entrance stayed covered while he stepped out of the clothing and into the panties.

One leg and then the other stepped into the feminine fabric, and then his paws slid it upward. The crocodile was sure he'd never blushed more in his life as it stretched over his rump and erection, barely able to contain the two. The fabric was velvety soft as it rubbed across sensitive places, adding to the taboo but erotic sensations. It tightly encased his most naughty bits, yet did nothing to hide them. Quite the opposite—the panties highlighted the mismatch between the underwear and the male parts inside.

And, much as he hated to admit it, the silky fabric felt good against his scales. Unbidden, Morton began to enact the scene he'd dreamed of, doing his best to drive the gazelle's lust even higher, to give him the most erotic show he could imagine. The reptile leaned over the bed, and he could feel the tight fabric stretching across his rump. He looked over his shoulder sensually, making eye contact with the buck as Morton lifted one leg, then the other onto the bed and stretched out on it, grinding his front on the covers.

The scaled male rolled over onto his back, separating his legs a bit as he arched into the air, pressing his hard shaft into the fabric that confined it. Leaning his head up a bit, Morton watched the gazelle's reaction as he lewdly showed off his scales. The furred male's paws were groping his own nether regions, touching himself as his eyes stayed focused on the reptile's body and his seductive display. A lengthy bulge there was becoming more and more visible, the soft digits running along its underside.

Morton's face was hot, flush with embarrassment and arousal, but he knew at this point they'd both let out all their stops. From here on out it was pure lust and passion, and both would do everything they could think to increase the excitement of the other.

Slowly the crocodile rolled onto his paws and knees, stretching out the most erotic way he knew how, assuming the position of a croc bottoming for another. He knew it was tantalizing, his body practically begging for it, even before he curled that thick scale-ridged tail back on itself and slipped the tip through the waistband of the panties. Morton turned his head to meet the gazelle's gaze, watching his reaction as the tail deftly, slowly slipped the underwear off of his rump, momentarily baring his soft hind scales and exposing his stiff, softly throbbing maleness.

The pink garment was slipped back up his legs after that quick glimpse, the thick, muscular tail of the crocodile swaying seductively above the pink cloth covering his sensitive areas. The competitive croc wasn't about to limit his display to a submissive role, though. "Just think, Kevin, it won't be long before you get to feel my thick tail pushing its way inside you." The crocodile grinned, watching the surprised but happy blush form on the buck's face from the teasing.

It didn't take the gazelle long to reply as he approached the bed and climbed onto the crocodile. The warmth was remarkable, enveloping Morton as the gazelle's arms wrapped around his chest. And there was the impressive bulge that pressed insistently against his scales through the layers of fabric, and Morton yearned to see it in full detail.

"Mmm … tonight, though, I'll get to feel it in my paws as I gently pull it upward, revealing my crocodile there for the taking." Morton felt his heart jump, more from how Kevin had called him *his* crocodile than from the very arousing image the gazelle described.

The gazelle slowly rolled Morton over onto his back and lay down over him. The touch of the two soft, warm undersides, scale meshed with fur, sent shivers through both of them. Pressed together, the quiet romance was like adding gasoline to the fire. Both males stared into the other's eyes, and each could feel the other's heart thumping in excitement.

A peck on the lips became gentle nuzzles, and the crocodile's paws found their way under his gazelle's clothing to cup and squeeze needily at the furred rump cheeks underneath. When he felt Kevin's soft paws do the same to him, skillfully working their way between the panties and the sheets, Morton moaned quietly and arched up into the gazelle. Feeling the gazelle kneading the silky underwear into his scaly behind emphasized the forbidden garment he wore, one he'd never admit outside the bedroom but that added to his lust.

"Mmf … I've longed for this …" The crocodile gasped, sliding his paws from Kevin's warm behind to the tented front, where he began to unfasten the clasps of his belt and jeans. Visions of what he'd imagined the buck's shaft would be like raced through his head; he was about to learn.

"Yes," Kevin panted in response, "me too …" A shiver ran through the gazelle, and his haunches thrust forward as the jeans slipped down, partially freeing his maleness. Morton teased his paw along the underside, feeling the heat and firmness of his mate's member, and he saw how the length stretched the fabric enough that the underwear's waistband stood out a few inches from that toned furry stomach. His buck panted with need the whole time, and the crocodile had never seen a male look sexier in briefs.

Morton could only stand that tease for a few seconds, though, before his paws greedily rubbed down to where the top of the briefs hung in midair, and he peeled it forward and over that tip, revealing his buck's most male parts to him in full detail for the first time. A sizeable amount of pink flesh was out of his sheath, and it quickly extended to the gazelle's full length now that the confines had been removed.

A thin and tapered tip, just like he'd read about, bobbed in the air with the gazelle's heartbeat. Morton could see tiny veins along the shaft gently pulsing in the same rhythm. Every part of it outside the sheath was a surprisingly smooth pink color, no spots or lines. The sheer length, the one part he'd seen fairly clearly even in the shower, was even more striking up close. If their girth were as impressive as their lengths, gazelles would have been reserved for size queens, but thankfully, it seemed tractable.

Under it all hung a pair of dark-colored, heavy external balls, each almost as large as the pool balls they played with regularly. The sack was just tight enough to show off their shapes but still look pliable. Seeing them, Morton knew neither of them would have any trouble soaking the other's insides with male fluids.

"You think we can fit all of that inside me?" Morton said with a smile, his paw stroking the gazelle's cheek. He didn't look particularly worried.

"Mmf … all of it and a full load of cum, too, croc … but there's only one way to find out …" Kevin leaned forward and placed a gentle kiss on the crocodile's nose, and Morton felt his scaly paw gripped by the gazelle's, the furred fingers gently rubbing his own. The mammal guided the reptile's paw to his shaft, placing it on the long, thin, warm length.

Slowly, Morton rubbed his scaled palm down the gazelle's fleshy shaft. He squeezed it gently and found it harder than expected, and he began rotating his paw slightly as it slipped over the maleness. The reptile could feel it twitch a bit in his grip, obviously pleasured by the touch and squeezes he offered. Kevin moaned a bit as he asked, "Similar to what you've fantasized about croc?"

The crocodile blushed as the gazelle mentioned his previously secret desires. He hesitated, and his gazelle reassured him. "Oh, I know, my sexy reptile. Don't think I haven't made my sheets sticky thinking about you." Kevin shyly looked away but was too far into the action to stop. Despite their physical contact, it still felt so naughty, so arousing to admit his attractions. He blushed deeper as he continued. "Your scales are even smoother on your underside that I'd ever imagined. And your … um … cockhead." He stared deep into the sheets, unable to meet the crocodile's gaze. "I can't stop looking at it; it's even more exotic than they described online."

A brief sex-charged silence filled the room after the buck's admissions, punctuated with quiet moans. Both were enjoying the pleasures of close contact, the crocodile continuing to rub his paw slowly up Kevin's shaft to its tip. Once there, he began to squeeze and slip over the sensitive areas, indescribably aroused by how he was rubbing the gazelle's real, live erection.

Kevin slowly began to thrust his hips, sliding his cock through the softly ridged scales of Morton's paws, the reptile feeling the buck's tip press into and through his squeezing pawtips. The crocodile returned a shy admission of his own. "Kevin, I … I stayed behind that night when you were in the shower. I saw you paw off.

It … it was my fapping material for weeks."

The gazelle issued a happy grunt and replied "Hah, I should have known. Mmm … Morton, your paws are heaven …" His voice trailed off, but his hips didn't.

The crocodile grinned widely and there was a brief pause before he responded, feeling his face flush, "Well, wait until you feel my insides."

The buck must have decided he'd had enough teasing, because he sighed, clearly in deep pleasure, but pulled his hips back from the crocodile's paws that massaged his penis so wonderfully. The scaled male looked down at the lengthy shaft that twitched above his body. "I knew how big you were from the shower, but feeling it, seeing it up close …"

"Morton," the gazelle panted as he gazed down at his male crocodile, "look how far it's going to go inside you …"

Morton looked where the gazelle was staring, at the shaft his paws had been massaging, noticing how it reached from his entrance almost to the base of his chest. There were no words to describe it; he was so unsure what it would be like, but he swelled with an intense desire to feel it, experience it. The reptile simply moaned, "Kevin …"

The croc saw the gazelle open the lube and hold it above his scaled paws, and he knew the foreplay was over. Morton cupped them to catch it, and the cold slick liquid squirted into his paws. Lewd slurping sounds filled the air as he rubbed them together, warming it, then put his paws back on his mate's warm length. Massaging his hands along the fleshy spire that was soon to penetrate him, he coated the other male's penis with the slick fluid that would help it slip inside him. The knowledge of what the lube meant burned in his already overloaded brain.

Slowly, the gazelle pulled back from the reptile's paws, hooking his fingertips under the panties and tugging them down the scaled groin, working them over his crocodile's pink, throbbing shaft. Once Morton's intimate parts were fully bared, the furred male pulled the feminine garment down and off of his body. With a grin, the buck noticed a large wet spot on the front of the panties, from his mate's pre and slit fluid. Then, those scaled legs were teased apart, leaving the crocodile feeling excited to be truly exposed to his lover … and to have his mate's slick shaft being positioned to slip inside his naked scales …

"Oh, did the internet tell you how much we cum?" Kevin asked and paused briefly to see the crocodile's reaction. "Our big, full balls aren't just for show." The gazelle rubbed one paw slowly over his orbs, shifting the heavy contents of his sack. "But why bother telling you more …" he grinned, "when I can just let you feel it inside you."

For the brief moments while that shaft rubbed against the croc's scales, hunting for its target, Morton thought back to all of those jerkoff sessions. He'd imagined the buck underneath him, the feel of Kevin's soft fur in his scaled claws while Morton rubbed his thick length against the thighs of the other male. He'd envisioned leaving trails of pre across the gazelle's pelt as he made the other blush and pant with desire.

But now the real thing was here, and the roles were reversed, and it was still so much more than the croc could imagine. Heat and need filling his body, he was ready for passionate lovemaking with the gazelle … his gazelle. Blushing, overcoming his pride, Morton relaxed and gave himself to this buck. *His* buck.

"I love you."

It had slipped out, but nevertheless rang true. Morton may have hidden it from himself, especially from the buck, for months, but that never changed the fact, never made it any less true. But the crocodile was chilled by what he'd said, knowing that saying such things too flippantly could ruin a relationship. He was left wondering whether he'd screwed up his greatest fantasy, and desperately hoping the gazelle shared the feeling.

Inside, the questions began. Had they gotten this far and now he would ruin their friendship? Was it just sex and lust; had he gone too far? Would he, so close to fulfilling his desires, see them yanked from his grasp?

He waited in silence. The crocodile thought his heart had been pounding before; this was a new level. No answer came to his ears. Instead, the gazelle lifted Morton's hips and lined up. His tapered warm tip pressed against the sensitive scales that guarded the crocodile's entrance. But the only thought in Morton's brain was, *Did he hear me?*

The grip on the crocodile's legs tightened, and the pressure on his tailhole grew. Kevin leaned over, placing his head next to the crocodile's, resting it on his shoulder. Finally, he kissed the scaled cheek and whispered to his crocodile. "Of course I love you, Morton. Otherwise I wouldn't be here … holding your sexy scaly legs apart … pressing my length against your cute hole … preparing to mate your hot body …"

Morton shivered as happiness washed through him, relief and a warmth that made it feel as if his body were a furnace. And that feeling coursed through him as the crocodile and gazelle's bodies joined for the first time. A soft gasp of surprise and moan of emotion slipped from the crocodile's jaw as he felt his ring stretched around the thin tip of his buck … his lover.

The reptile could only guess how tight his insides must feel, from the way even that thin tip felt large as it spread him for the taking. A soft-furred paw was now stroking his chest soothingly, and Morton realized it was just how he'd fantasized, except that he was the one taking a fleshy length under his tail. He willed himself to relax, letting his boyfriend control their movements.

"You okay, love?"

Love. Morton shivered. "Yes. Just … full. And a lot more to go." He grimaced and smiled.

"Don't worry, croc. I'll make sure you love every inch I press inside you." Gently but firmly those hips pushed forward, and Morton could feel new parts slipping into his body, knowing more had entered. His scaled legs were rubbed by Kevin's paws, teasing them just a little bit further apart before Morton felt the haunches pull back slightly then thrust forward, and suddenly enough was in him to reach that pleasure spot.

"Kevin!" the crocodile half-gasped, half-purred.

"Did I reach that spot?" The gazelle asked, grinning down at the reptile.

"Yesss …" was the hissed reply, Morton's clawed paws gripping the sheets and tearing them a bit.

"Good. Now just think of all the rest you have left to go. It's going to press and rub on it … and slowly the thickness and pleasure will grow …" Kevin must have particularly savored the sight of his maleness entering his croc, because he stared at where his cock disappeared into the crocodile's entrance for a few seconds, gently working his shaft forward and back.

Morton's legs wrapped gently around Kevin's torso, a subtle sign of his pleasure as his penetration continued. There were more obvious signs too, like how his maleness jutted from his slit—a throbbing, pink, moist spire—or how he moaned softly when another firm push filled his tailhole with just a little more of the buck's slippery, firm shaft.

A soft squish could be heard as Kevin pulled back and humped again into the crocodile, slipping just a little deeper. The gazelle was still barely inside the tight scaly body, but finally enough where he could begin the thrusting that would drive both of them wild and help work Morton's tightness open even faster. When Kevin pulled out a bit, he leaned over and met the other male's maw in a gentle kiss.

The two exchanged moans between their lips even as their tongues rubbed against each other. Only a short time later, the gazelle broke the kiss and began to lick down the reptiles chin, lapping at the soft scales underneath. The feeling of the gentle licks on the underside of his chin made Morton wriggle his head back and forth. This rocked his body a bit, leading to a softly spoken "yes" from both as the tight tailring tensed slightly, and the shaft pressing against the crocodile's prostate moved a bit inside him.

Kevin moved back and just lay his head next to Morton's, and his hot breath tickled the side of the scaly maw. The reptile felt him slip out just a bit, and then another thrust as the gazelle fed another inch into the crocodile's body. With it came a loud moan from the reptile, a tightening in his passage, and a single drop of clear pre right on the tip of his maleness.

The gazelle looked down, grinning as he reached toward the other male's exposed, neglected hardness. That soft paw surrounded the head, rubbing its finger tips across each sensitive part and smearing the pre over it as lube. The sensation made Morton tense around the length inside him and forced an even stronger gasp from his lungs as Kevin simultaneously electrified both of his pleasure centers.

More of the gazelle's cock disappeared into the crocodile as the thrusts continued, sending waves of pleasure into Morton's body. He felt the buck's paw leave his hardness, and he arched, his legs tightening around the gazelle's haunches as the crocodile lightly humped the air. That led to even more moaning as it moved the maleness inside him, shifting how the buck's shaft pressed against his spot. Panting heavily, Morton looked up and saw the gazelle gazing at the scales of his lover, admiring his form as they joined together.

The silky touch of his lover's paws began to caress the crocodile's rump cheeks, rubbing over the sensitive globes and cupping their scaled forms. A shy, happy rumble came from inside the reptile, deepening when the gazelle's paws teased those tender masses apart, exposing Morton's body even more completely to his lover.

The crocodile's blush and arousal only grew as he looked down and got a better view of the hard shaft spreading him open … and how much there was left to go. It was such a sexually raw, yet romantic vision: watching his buck as those furred hips tensed, seeing and feeling at the same time as he pushed that lengthy cock deeper inside of him. All of his body yielded, welcomed, loved every second of the buck's advances, every inch of his sweet penetration.

Panting from his intense arousal, Kevin leaned back and rested a bit. Morton looked on curiously, then felt the bottle of lube pressed into his paw once again. The crocodile looked back in surprise when he realized the lewd implication, and he gingerly began to spread the squirted lube on his paws. Once they were coated, he reached between his legs to where the buck's maleness joined his entrance, wrapping his paws around it.

Morton heard a soft moan from above as he slipped his paws up the exposed shaft, feeling the heat radiating from the other male's spear. He reached up until his paws felt the sheath of the other male, then rubbed with care, spreading lube over every part of his mate's pride that was still outside his body. As he rubbed his paws back down the shaft, Morton couldn't resist going all the way down and feeling his own tight ring, stretched around the maleness of his lover.

The crocodile lay back, his paws still covered with lube, noticing he'd become more relaxed, and his tailhole had adjusted to his lover's advances. A few seconds later, when Kevin pulled out slowly for the next thrust, Morton felt a small emptiness inside. He wanted it back; his tightness longed for the feel of the other male, and the crocodile moaned when it was delivered. His relaxation was helping it drive even deeper. As the gazelle pressed more into him, the length continued to slide against his special spot, sending jolts of pleasure through the reptile.

Each thrust made progress now, the crocodile's tailring more accepting, and the added slipperiness letting the buck press more inside him. Morton was quivering in pleasure as his body was filled so exquisitely by the gazelle, the reptile's paws tearing through the sheets in passion and even scratching the mattress underneath. "Kevin … ah, so good …"

Soon, the gazelle's speed and force began to increase, making Morton's chest heave as the pleasure grew ever more intense. He knew the buck must feel it, too, as more inches slid deep into the scales of his lover. His thick tail wrapped around the gazelle in passion, tugging the furred body against his own. A few more rocks of Kevin's hips were all they needed for Morton to feel a softness against his overly-stretched, sensitive tailring, and he knew he'd taken the gazelle's full length—that the buck's sheath was pressed against him.

The male reptile panted, the feeling of pride barely registering through the euphoria of his prostate, the new feeling of being so full, and the warmth of his lover's body that pressed against his. But when he looked down, the knowledge that those inches he'd seen outside of him, the ones he'd lubed up with his own paws, were now deep inside his scales; it added to the most erotic situation he'd ever been in.

Kevin hadn't quite finished taking the crocodile, though. He gave three last, strong thrusts, each punctuated by a deep huff, and Morton felt the final, hidden part of the buck's spire slide into him. The soft groin fur of his gazelle was now flush with his scales, and the croc knew that his tight entrance had pushed back the sheath to take the last few inches. Morton felt his mate pause, fully embedded inside him.

As they held still for a moment, Morton also registered two warm objects resting between where his legs were separated so the buck could mate him. It only took a second for him to realize the buck's heavy balls were now resting on his scaled rump cheeks, yet another reminder the gazelle had fully penetrated him.

Kevin leaned down against his croc, breathing both hard and fast. Both were overwhelmed with absolute mental and physical bliss. The gazelle planted sloppy, quick kisses all along Morton's maw, and the crocodile's paws reached up to feel his lover's body. Every inch of gazelle that touched him, inside and out, was warm from the arousal and exertion, and the whole body of his buck trembled. The furred form above him rose and fell with labored breaths, while the crocodile's digits traced each and every detail of his body.

Morton rubbed his hands over the magnificent horns of the creature above him, feeling their ribbed shape and smooth texture, gingerly fingering the sharp tips. He stroked them lovingly as he waited for the buck to catch his breath, all the while basking in the feel of such deep stimulation. A gentle whisper came from his scaled maw. "You're beautiful," he said in a deep voice, watching how it made the gazelle shy even in their compromising position.

Kevin responded with a softly-spoken, "humph," but it earned the crocodile a gentle kiss on his cheek. Then the gazelle was ready to lift his hips again, drawing sudden gasps of pleasure from them both. The following thrusts were neither graceful nor methodic, but they were absolute euphoria for both of them. It wouldn't be a full night of pleasure. It was their first time together, and the insertion had already worked them up to incredible states of arousal. But, they were determined to enjoy every second they could squeeze from their mating, every last shuddering, gasping thrust.

Now that the buck was hilted, the trademark sounds of sex

began. The smack of furred hips and scaly thighs filled the room, as Kevin pushed again and again as deeply into the crocodile as he could go. The buck's full balls echoed their bodies, making a softer slap as they hit Morton's rump after each thrust. Heavy breathing, gasps, and moans were interrupted by cries of, "yes!" "Morton!" "Kevin!" and "so good …" But perhaps the most lust-inducing sounds for the croc were the slick squishing and slurping of the wet flesh sliding in and out of him. Over and over again, the crocodile's body was filled with buck cock, pressing into him as deeply as any ever would and spreading the gazelle's mating fluids inside him.

The pre that Morton knew was likely being spilt inside him was mirrored by his own shaft, which was already beginning to drip the clear, warm fluid. Their two bodies ground the upturned shaft between them as the full penetration continued; it rubbed trails of the sticky fluid into the stomach fur above it and occasionally dripped onto the scales below. The crocodile could actually feel Kevin's long shaft forcing it out of him as it pushed over and over again against his gland in their mating.

"Rrrh …" Kevin groaned lowly, about as close to a growl as an herbivore could. "You feel so good inside, your warmth around … all of it." With a deep thrust, the buck wiggled his hips and stayed hilted, savoring the sensation of his full maleness being inside the hot grip of the crocodile's insides. "Much warmer than I expected a cold blood …" his words trailed off.

"Good," the crocodile said between deep, huffed breaths that made it clear how much pleasure he felt. "All of it … so full, so good. I'll be your predator, your prey. Come back … anytime …"

Through it all, the scaled paws had continued to rub the warm, soft body of his lover. Now they traced along his neck, gently bringing the buck's maw down to his own, where he pushed their lips together. That kiss quickly turned into a messy, almost desperate make out session, both males gasping and moaning into it, all while trying to keep the kiss locked and their tongues lapping against each other. It was erratic, passionate, and chaotic, and it added to the slurping sounds already in the air.

For a while, Morton savored the gazelle's thrusts and focused on the kiss, letting the gazelle's hips and maleness push him closer to the inevitable climax. Before much longer, though, his shaft began to feel needy from all the stimulation. Unable to resist, Morton reached down and started to paw his bullhood, adding to the shared stimulation and the slick sounds. He gasped into their kiss as he found a tempo that matched the rhythmic pressure on his prostate to the timing of his rubs on the bulbous tip of his crocodile maleness.

"You know ... I'm going to compete ... next time." Morton squeezed out between overwhelming moments of pleasure.

It took a few seconds to register, and the buck gave him a slightly quizzical look and a distracted, "Hrm?"

"How much ... erf ... you pre, when I'm ..." Morton gasped, "on top, how much seed I fill you with ..." Even as he said this, the croc's hind legs were still pulling the gazelle closer, still clearly enjoying every inch of the buck inside him. But his pride and predatory nature compelled him to make sure the buck knew he wasn't just going to lay down and take it. Well ... not *every* time.

"As I feed you pleasure ... when you start to get close, keep you ..." In the midst of sex, the moans that interrupted their conversation seemed perfectly normal. "Keep you right on the edge, at the best feelings. Make you moan ... h-have you tell me what you want ... make you plead for it as I mate you ..."

Even as a shiver ran through the gazelle at how undeniably *hot* that sounded, Kevin's own competitive nature wouldn't let Morton take full control. Spurred on by the teasing and rivalry, the gazelle's thrusts started to come more powerfully and twice as quickly. He went faster and harder, until he saw the scaled male under him close his eyes and drop his toothy maw open in pleasure. The bliss was evident on the buck's face too, with heavy, open-mouthed gasps …

"Are you my bull crocodile?" the buck purred against the reptile, making his own intentions clear.

A moment's hesitation, and then, "Yes … oh, yes … I … I'm yours," the crocodile gasped out, giving in. His feelings for the buck and the waves of intense, raw pleasure that rolled through him overtook the need for competition.

Morton was biting his lip from the pleasure now, his shaft and his hand coated with fluids forced from him in pleasurable spurts by the lengthy maleness inside. Soon, he knew, it would be white, and there would be much more of it …

Kevin leaned over the reptile, admiring the sensual sight beneath him before he raggedly gasped out, "I … I'm close, crocodile." The gazelle's paw reached for the dripping length of the other male, closing around it and slipping over its head, pumping it and making sure to squeeze the dripping head each time.

"Ah! Just … shut up and breed me!" Morton panted as the feeling of the other male milking his shaft just added to the already overwhelming sensations. He closed his eyes and let the pleasure of the thrusts flow through him.

"What do you want, Morton?" the gazelle gasped in a husky, lustful voice.

"Ah! … Ah, your cum Kevin! D-Do it, cum inside me! Please!" He moaned, overcome with passion, so close to release and the completion of their mating, needing it so badly …

The gazelle's moan became a shout, and the crocodile's bellow shook the apartment as they climaxed together, the first time together, their first coupling as lovers. Morton could actually feel Kevin's hot cum squirting like a fountain inside him, and he almost couldn't believe how far in him the gazelle's warm seed was … or how much was filling him. The lengthy shaft twitched inside him as it pumped its warm, sticky gift from the gazelle's balls, through the reptile's tight entrance, down the buck's maleness, and deep into the crocodile.

Morton's own maleness was splashing his mess in full view of them both. He'd been too distracted to see the first few shots, but the evidence on them showed multiple spurts of semen had made it to their chests. Even now, rope after warm, viscous rope was splattered between them. The crocodile couldn't remember ever having cum this hard. Both were surprised at how the crocodile's orgasm so completely soaked their two stomachs, caking fur and scale with the results of their passion.

They collapsed together into the bed, all feelings, thoughts, and sensations pushed from their minds except for the warmth of the one next to them. Their arms and legs wrapped around each other, as did the flexible length of the crocodile's tail, the spent and happy pair holding each other tightly. The crocodile didn't know how long it took the gazelle to finally pull out from inside him, but when he looked down, he was still a little amazed just how much flesh had been inside, drowning him in pleasure and lust. He also knew that he'd be in for a very erotic morning of leaking the buck's sperm, judging by how much of that long shaft was coated in the gazelle's cum, which he'd so copiously given and the croc's body now held inside.

They fell asleep in each other's arms, together, complete. They had been enemies in competition. Now, united, they stood as enemies to others. Enemies of cultural history, tradition, species, roles. Proof of just how good it felt, how good it was to blaze their own path alongside one another.

Chess is more fun when it involves real lives.

BODYJACK

Kandrel

"I have a game for you to play, my precious pet—my pretty girl."

His voice was in my head through the open connection, as clear as if he were standing next to me. It was deep and commanding, the type of baritone belonging only to the greatest of villains. I would have been compelled to obey that voice, even if it hadn't been leading me to everything I wanted. Just hearing it gave me a warm rush—partly because his voice always sent tingles up my spine, and partly because I knew that tonight would be a special night.

"I'm looking forward to it, Master." Some masters preferred that their pets not talk. Mine wasn't one of them. He wanted to hear everything I wanted to say. He said it helped him get to know me better and to craft his experiences more accurately to my tastes. It was true that he found ways to please me—and by extension, himself—better over these last few months, but I secretly believed that he wanted to hear me praise him. He gave me enough reason to.

I shut out the world around me and let him come. First it was a trickle, like hands closing over mine to guide their movements. Then sensation spread to my arms, and legs. Slowly, he took control from me, leaving me just a passive rider in my own body, with him the pilot. My hand lifted from the compad, and the glowing outline around where my palm and fingers had been faded from brilliant blue to purple, then disappeared altogether.

211

I felt him gazing out from my eyes. He looked down at my attire—he always liked to make sure I'd followed his instructions to the letter for one of our nights—and rewarded me with a rush of pleasure and approval. "So charming. So unique! You will be the star tonight. Do you like this look, girl? Come, my pet, tell me what you think." The words were formed by my lips, but they weren't mine. All that was left to me was a little corner of my own brain where I could observe. As my pilot, only he could hear me when I crowed my appreciation for his taste.

He was right; I was striking. The pristine white suit he had instructed me to wear contrasted starkly with my black fur. It'd taken an hour of brushing beforehand to ensure that no stray wisps of shed panther-fuzz would ruin the effect. It'd been worth it. The rosettes in my pelt veritably glowed with a blue that was darker black than black, and the white suit gleamed so brilliantly bright. It was a style of feminine curves backed by the masculine cut of the suit in a gender defying blend that somehow managed to arrive somewhere near center.

My hands—his hands—tugged my suit straight. With a confident stride my legs weren't quite accustomed to, he strode out into the night.

2:00 A.M. was as bright as day, ersatz sunlight glaring down from holographic signs containing smiling people performing questionable acts with overpriced products. Master ignored them; I ignored them. Advertisements hung motionless in the sky, suspended like replacement stars that lit our way as he walked to the first checkpoint.

Identity checked—I was clean. Bored officers shined a laser off of my retinas and ran hands perfunctorily over my body. My credit chip beeped against their terminal—hard earned money exchanged for four hours outside my designated district. If I overstayed my welcome, they'd come looking.

Second checkpoint was fifteen minutes walk. The officers here carried guns and their frisking would have been indecent and illegal if it had taken place outside of the security zone. It was double the charge for city center. I couldn't have afforded it myself, but Master paid the bills tonight. I probably wouldn't have even cleared past security, but Master must have pulled some strings.

They asked my destination, and I responded, "The Crown Royal." The guard's eyebrows lifted incredulously. It was a surprise to me too. That was upscale, even for Master. The Crown was the go-to for everyone who was anyone, and off limits to anyone who was no one. The officer glanced at me, doubt in his eyes. A girl from two districts out with an invite to the Crown? He shrugged. It wasn't his job to wonder—just to confirm identity and record for later use.

With my suit rumpled from over-inquisitive fingers and my pockets lighter, Master straightened my jacket and strode into the deep chasms between the skyscrapers. Buildings in my home district were squat little affairs; the best they could ever do was sprawl. These buildings in city center, though, loomed. I could barely see the reflection of neon off of the smog clouds far above for the steel and glass that crowded about me like a towering cage.

"Here we are, my pet. A private party, and we're invited. That is, I'm invited, as long as I'm you. We're going to be the stars of the show tonight, my precious. Are you ready to give your best performance? I know I am." His whispers were musical, a song of eager anticipation.

What little of my mind I still owned tried in vain to discover his motives. Stars of the show? What did he have planned that was going to thrust us into the spotlight? This was the hardest part of our nights—the not knowing. The wondering what was in store for the body I was so intimately attached to.

There was a smartly dressed footman by the hotel door, standing just below a small security camera that focused on me as soon as I came within twenty paces. Master canted my head and gave him a warm smile, then pushed my thumb against the ID plate next to the wide double doors. The city was dirty (as Master had been so quick to show me on our outings,) but the street front of the soaring Crown Royal was immaculately clean, scrubbed, and bleached, until its color actually resembled bare concrete.

The doors gave a muted 'beep', then slid aside. Master had taken me to the Crown Royal once before—there had been this slinky ferret Master fancied—but the open atrium that rose all the way up the hotels eighteen floors still managed to impress on second viewing. Green plants (a rare sight in the city) draped from pots hovering midair in the atrium making a surreal rainforest. Above it all, holographic emitters painted a night sky on the roof that held a billion stars.

"You seem surprised, my pet. Tell me, what makes your heart race when we step into this artificial dream?"

It's the stars, Master.

I felt him smile with my mouth. "One day you will travel outside the city. By hover or by jet, you will fly above the smog cover and see the stars for yourself."

But you won't be with me.

"This is true, but you will still have seen them even with my absence." He walked me to the nearby elevator. Even before his confident stride took him within five feet, the elevator sensed his presence and the doors started to slide open. "Do not gape at this pale reflection, pet. It's not worthy of your praise. The stars, they are much more grand when they fill the sky from horizon to horizon.

"Look, my pet. Forget those fake stars and see what I see out in the city. See it out there, lit in neon and ultraviolet and amber streetlights? There are eighty-three districts in this hellhole of a city, pet, did you know that? Not many do. The city is larger than most old nations. Can you guess how many of them any one average 'citizen' may travel to?"

He waited for me. I knew the answer by heart. He told me this every time he took me to the center. *Four.*

"Four. Four measly collections of squat little shacks, trying to eke out a sad little existence on careful rations. I've shown you the center of it all, the splendor of the Aerie Bridge, the flying arches of the Atomic Reserve, the marvelous jungle here in Crown Heights. Isn't it beautiful?"

Yes. My heart yearned for the green jungle with the stars twinkling overhead, fake as it might be.

"Shouldn't everyone be able to see the marvels that their own blood and sweat has bought? Yes? You are special, pet. You and half of point-one percent have the honor of seeing it in person. Everyone else is locked away behind the district walls."

Inside, the elevator accepted my thumbprint again, and rose into the green jungle speckled with stars. A small camera whirred behind me as it brought me into focus. Master ignored it. "You must do me a favor tonight, my pet, my beautiful plaything."

Anything for you Master.

"You must turn off your safeword. It would be dangerous if used tonight."

It was a strange request. I had never used my safeword on Master, even when things became more than I thought I could handle. I knew it'd be the end of the evening, and perhaps even an end to Master's visits. Any momentary discomfort was worth the price for his continued attentions. *I would never use my safeword with you, Master.*

"Pet." It was an admonition. I could hear the steel in his voice— my voice.

It elicited the response he wanted. Almost instinctively, I acquiesced. It was a little mental switch, a fail-safe built into the jacking rig that had cost most of my life savings to have implanted. It meant that I could—when absolutely necessary—kill the transmission. My body would be my own again, instantaneously. It wasn't meant to be turned off, but I could. And at Master's command, I did.

"Very good pet. Now, the evening's plans can truly begin."

We rose above the greenery then passed through even the layer of stars. The glass tinted to black, or perhaps there was simply nothing outside to see. Then it 'dinged', and the doors slid open.

I exited onto the hotel's roof. I immediately felt a rush of adrenaline, quickly stifled by Master's control. I could see the whole city fall away below. The retaining walls on all sides of the rooftop seemed too short, too flimsy. In the private little corner of my own mind, I felt a thrill of fear.

"None of that, girl. We have a show to put on, and I won't have you distracting me with your inadequacies." He whispered through a smile. Around us, I found that the cultural elite had gathered. For the first time at one of Master's little fetes, I recognized some faces. There was Albert Hall, the city mayor. Rushcliff, the commissioner stood at his side, short and fat in a suit that did little to restrain the muskrat's girth. Representative DeLancey, the slimy fox that stole the election was chortling at something one of the other two had said.

Master had never dabbled in politics. In fact, he despised it. "It's one big shell game, and all that's at stake is the lives and livelihood of all the people they're representing. Politics is the worst kept lie that everyone knows is a sham, yet every election day the brainwashed poor shamble out of their boxes to put their print on yet another social contract, signing even more of their soulless little lives away to the cultural elite." His own words. If I'd had control, my pelt would be crawling.

"Patience, my pet." He murmured, only for me. "The night holds enough excitement for all nine of your lives, if you're patient enough for the climb before the fall."

Albert Hall glanced my way, and to my surprise, I was recognized. "Ah! And here's tonight's hostess, the beautiful Demosthenes. Gentlemen, make room for the most brilliant firebrand of our time."

DeLancey held out his hand, and I shook it. Rushcliff stood aside to make room for me. I smiled a little insidious grin, and I could feel Master's pleasure bubbling beneath the surface. Demosthenes? What had he done? I recognized the name—anyone who kept an eye on recent events would. She was a piranha in the goldfish pond of political media. Her daily feed had been picked up by every local news site. I knew the name even though I'd never read one of her columns. Everyone knew that name. Hell, most likely half of the big-wigs here could trace their recent political success—or the failure of their opponents—to her. Demosthenes? Me?

"Good evening, gentlemen. Thank you for accepting my invitation. I assure you, you'll find what I have to say most exhilarating." My lips curled in a demure little smile, showing teeth.

"It had better. Some of us should be working." Rushcliffe scowled. It seemed to be the sole expression that suited his face.

"Patience, Mr. Commissioner. It will all be over soon. In fact, I do believe it's time for the festivities to start."

Master walked me to the edge of the rooftop. Around me, names and titles began to creep in to identify the faces. Jackal, tall and sharp, that was Governor Henries. Short female deer with a permanent look of panic on her face, that's the secretary of the treasury Ms. Catherine. This was the creme-de-la-creme of modern politics, the puppeteers that pulled the strings and danced the little wooden feet, and they were all here apparently at my behest.

"Ladies and gentlemen of New City, gaze down upon what your leadership has brought!" The words were clear and practiced from my throat. I felt like the ringmaster, with all these politicians my performing animals in their little cliques—circled together like rings at a circus. I was certainly dressed for the part, resplendent in my white suit and midnight fur. I was a mirror-image, the inverse of them.

They all gazed up at me, dozens of pairs of wide and intelligent eyes. I felt Master smiling—the game had begun. "Look down into your streets. Can you see them all looking up at you—your voters, your constituents, your responsibility, and the source of your power? Look around you and see what you've given them."

My arms spread wide, encompassing them, and the New City. They smiled up at me. Someone clapped, then another joined, and another. They all knew the game had begun too, though somehow I doubted any of them were playing from the same deck as Master.

"I've watched you all so closely; some more closely than others." I spared a mean little smile for someone in the crowd, and there was a giddy laughter that spread like a whisper. Was that the justice secretary? The face on the warthog was familiar. "Some of you I've even helped to get where you are now, because I thought you deserved it."

Helped? Master, you hate these people. What are you talking about?

"But you've all achieved more than I could have imagined. Look out on the city you've had such a hand in creating. The district safety act!"

The act that limited where citizens could travel, depending on their earnings. There was a cheer from the crowd.

"The clean skies bill!"

Corporate factories could purchase the sky above their factory, as if the smog they created would stay only in that one small patch of air. There was another cheer, especially from the director of the city natural trust and his cadre.

"The Safe Streets initiative!"

Empowering the police to arrest and incarcerate anyone they deemed dangerous. The cheer that erupted momentarily drowned out my speech.

"I've invited you all here tonight because I, Demosthenes, who have spent my life dedicated to the city and its well-being, have finally reached my verdict."

There was a response from the crowd, but it was confused. As was I. *Verdict?*

"The city is ailing, and you—are its disease."

Moments passed as the announcement slowly seeped into the politicians and their lackeys. Then the cheers turned to complaints. I wondered—had Demosthenes been a shadow puppet with the cultural elite dancing to Master's music? Master turned me to face the sheer drop, hundreds of feet down to the pristine and manicured pavement outside the crown. "You had all the tools to craft a utopia your people, and this—this is the splendor you create? I stand here ashamed of the land entrusted to your care."

"You crazy bitch, this is utop—"

"This is a jail!" I cut him off.

Master turned me back to face them, teetering on the edge of the building. I felt the vague touch of fear as gusts of wind played with my suit. *Too close, Master!* He ignored me.

"And you can point that fat little finger of yours no further than the mirror, Mister Mayor." The fat ursine face, so full of vinegar and hatred, puffed and gasped like a fish out of water. "This isn't the promised land, you collection of cowards. Gaze down on the little piece of hell you've made. Your petty and selfish reign ends tonight; the great devourer you've crafted has arrived to consume you all."

A general chorus of disagreement and anger started to rise. *Master, we're between a rock and a hard place. This game you're playing, this is suicide!*

"No, my beautiful pet, it's the start of something much grander than that." He whispered only to me. He turned my head to the sky, blackness reflecting the wasted light of the city below. I could feel their eyes burning into my back. Master hadn't just taunted them, he'd flat-out threatened them. Oh god, had any of them come to the party armed?

Master closed my eyes, and lifted my hands to cover them. At any moment, I expected to hear the retort of their gun firing, to feel the incendiary slugs boiling their way through me, to smell the stench of my own flesh cooking. *Master! What have you done? I—*

And the sky was filled with light.

I could see it even through my closed eyelids and the hands covering them. It was warm on my pelt like momentary sunlight. The light flowed across me, so solid I could feel it seeping like liquid through the seams of my suit. I'd never stood in light so intense.

Then sound rippled my fur, a thunder that brought wind with it and left everything silent behind it. The first bang of thunder so loud that I felt it more than heard it. After just a second of vicious sound, my hearing disappeared entirely. From then on, I just felt the waves of vibrations ripple through me as I stood statue-still.

There was a scratchy feeling to the connection with Master. *Connection terminated.* Then it was just me; alone inside my own body, and I felt panic. *Master? Master, are you there?* The jack rig didn't respond. I pulled my hands away as the light started to clear, and then opened my eyes. A spot in the sky glowed behind the greenish clouds like a second, poisonous sun. It was just me; alone, standing here uninhabited, and it made me feel naked. More than naked; I'd been naked in front of crowds before, but as long as Master was there with me, I was always safe, content in knowing it wasn't me, it was my Master.

Then the jack rig responded. *Executing script. Control restricted.* It wasn't like Master, not quite, but who else could it be? A script? This must have been set into my rig from earlier in the night. Master had planned for this, and now his plan was coming together. It didn't feel quite right, but it felt close enough. Master spun me, and looked over the gathered crowd holding their eyes and ears, pitiful little squirming lumps on the ground, all pretense of dignity and pride evaporated. Mouths were open, probably shouting or screaming, but all I could hear was a soft ringing that was slowly getting louder.

And I could hear Master. Maybe it was some part of the jacking rig, or perhaps it was because I could feel my own mouth forming the words for me, but when he spoke, I had no trouble understanding. "Thank you, my precious pet, I could not have done this without you." I walked down among the writhing politicians and took the gun from Commissioner Rushcliffe. Master held it confidently in my hand, and I felt only the slightest recoil as he pushed the muzzle against Rushcliffe's cranium and fired.

I watched fur and skin and muscle peel back from beneath the shot. The exposed bone charred and crackled. There wasn't much of the commissioner's head left when his body flopped lifeless to the rooftop. Master didn't spare him a second glance, because the second pull of the trigger was for Mayor Hall. Then the next for DeLancey. Three, four, six, ten, one by one, Master made his way efficiently through the group. By the fifteenth, my hearing had recovered enough that I could hear the *pop* as the small handgun fired, and by the time all thirty-four bullets in the clip had been expended, I could hear the sizzling of flesh as Master dispatched the minister of agriculture. What little I still owned of my mind had crawled into my corner, watching the effortless execution with numb shock.

This wasn't my game. It had always been about pushing limits, sure, but it had never been intended to hurt anyone. *Cupcake Apocalypse!* I screamed it inside my mind. Nothing happened. Of course nothing happened. I'd switched off the safeword. Stupid, stupid, stupid girl. Fall in love with Master, trust him to handle you right, and you get burned again. If my eyes had been mine, I would have cried.

The gun fell from my hand as Master lost interest in it. Silently and efficiently, Master turned me towards the edge of the building. He'd shown me that he was a dancer, when he'd used my legs to waltz and foxtrot. It was almost like dancing as he brought me to a break-neck sprint. With a grace of a diver, Master threw me from the roof of the Crown Royale.

Program terminated. And my limbs were all mine, free to flail as I screamed in freefall.

***

I had a roommate who got a jacking rig, Sarah. Sarah was a worker girl, just like me, but she'd had a big payout from a mark, and spent it all to get a jack rig. Within the first month of recovering, she not only paid her rent early for the first time, but she also paid the back-rent that I'd been 'lending' continually for the last half a year. I'd been so angry that she'd spent all the money she'd earned on that jack rig instead of paying me what she owed, but by the end of the month I was jealous. At the end of the second month, I borrowed enough from her to get a rig of my own.

By the time I'd recovered from the surgery, she was rich. At least, she was what we'd consider rich, able to afford her own place at the top of Aerie Heights, the tallest high-rise in our otherwise squat and squashed district. I didn't hear from her more than four or five times over the next year as I started to pick up jackers of my own.

By the next time I heard about her, Sarah was dead. It wasn't a big story, so it's a wonder I caught it at all. See, even all the money in the world couldn't make Sarah a smart girl. A jacker that'd hired her had climbed up to the top of a tower in city center with a wingsuit and a parachute. Why she didn't safeword out as soon as she saw the skydiving gear—Well, as I said, she was stupid. Maybe fifteen years ago you could have flown from the top of the Locke tower and arrived on the ground with nothing but a stiff fine and a night in jail. Not anymore.

They found her body in pieces. The jacking rig in her—and in me—was a good part stainless steel—ferrous. The magnetic webs that held all those 'floating' advertisements and decorations in place so high and prominent in the night sky had torn her to bits. She'd never even made it far enough to open the parachute.

I never imagined I'd end up like Sarah, but it began to sink in as the world seemed to move so slowly around me as I drifted from the top of the Crown Royale, I knew I'd never see the ground again. It was a strange feeling, an awkward, detached feeling, like the loss of a pet. I felt the tug, oh, that was unmistakable, the magnets had me. It felt like a harness, arresting my fall and lifting me unkindly towards an ad for a soft drink.

The steel grip on my insides faded, and I began to tumble. The massive sign pirouetted once, then began to fall with me. It was almost graceful the way gravity stole over me and the sign, making us dance to its irresistible music. Another magnet tugged me sideways into its field in short, sharp jerks that made me feel ill, then it too failed.

At the very end, I must have fallen fifty stories, but by the time

I hit the ground, it was as if I'd leaped down no more than a flight of stairs. With my head-over heels tumble, I collapsed amid the rubble of the monstrous signs that had preceded me in the fall. Bruised, scared, and in shock, I stood from the rubble. If nothing else, I was alive.

Around me, alarms sounded sporadically. When I'd walked here only twenty minutes ago, displays had shone in all of the windows, showing news, and silent shows, and more advertisements. Now, those few screens that were still functional were only showing static. Every storefront was either in lock-down, or had failed halfway through the process. Steel webs had drawn over gaudy display windows, guarding precious possessions.

Above the erratic alarms, I could hear people: two million packed into the city center district alone, those that weren't awake yet would be soon. The yelling, shouting, and crying droned together into one horrifying sound. All at once, I wanted to flee, fight, and curl into a ball and hide.

But I couldn't do any of that. I wouldn't be free for long if anyone upstairs had survived. Had survived? Of course they had. Master had been efficient, but there had been only thirty-four bullets, and there were at least fifty up there on the roof, counting the serving staff and assorted bodyguards. Worse, Master clearly hadn't intended me to survive. That hurt most of all. I guess over the last months I'd grown used to being used. Even as what I'd been made to do had horrified me, it hadn't been *me*. What I'd done wasn't as horrible as what Master had done.

Why, Master? Hadn't I been good enough for you? Had I disappointed you somehow? Was I not everything you'd—

Stop it. He didn't deserve my worry anymore, and standing here in the ruined street was what stupid Sarah would have done. No, I needed to hide. I wasn't exactly familiar with downtown, but this wasn't the first time Master had brought me here. Whether he'd intended to or not, my memory immediately gave me a address: eighth and harbor, in a little alley behind the Italian fast-food— the key hidden in the mail slot.

My feet carried me, automatically, as if I'd had a jacker. There only real outward appearance of trouble downtown was that it was darker—much darker than normal. Without the overhead signs and neon billboards and video and holo feeds in the windows, the night was just that: night. I stumbled as much as I walked, with fallen signs cluttering the road. What should have been a quick five minute walk dragged into a quarter of an hour as I picked my way between piles of rubble. On sixth and harbor, I found a lithe greyhound in police clothes banging his radio angrily on the roof of his car. I decided not to tempt fate and made my way around.

The key was still where Master had me leave it. Inside, it looked like no one had so much as opened the door since I'd last been there. Thinking about it, maybe no one had. Safe. As if ushered in by that thought, I barely had time to close the door before what I'd seen—what I'd done—crashed in like an unwanted guest. It'd never been like this before. It'd always been someone else.

But I could still remember the soft gust of hot wind as I watched the fur smolder and skin peel back, just disappearing beneath my fingers like the touch of some angry mythical god. I could still smell the smoky reek of burnt flesh in my pelt, sunk into my suit, hanging over me like a guilty cloud.

Off came the suit; on went the shower. I rinsed and scrubbed until all I could smell was lilac fur shampoo. Then I stood under the water until I told myself I couldn't even remember the smell anymore. I was lying, but I was good at lying to myself.

How could I not have seen it? Isn't that what I'm supposed to be asking myself now? No, I couldn't have. I didn't even know Master's name. He was just an anonymous at the far end of the line. He was the puppet master that pulled all my strings, and

I'd never even asked where he lived. But then, that was my job. Anonymity was what paid me until I was the richest whore in the district. If asking questions had been my modus operandi, I might have been smarter, but I'd also be broke.

That bond of trust was supposed to go both ways, though, and as I stood under the hot spray, the guilt slowly seeped away with the water, leaving just anger. I'd been played with and thrown away like a toy in the hands of a petulant child. For money? No, money couldn't buy what Master had done with me. I didn't feel guilty, I felt used and scared. The police would hunt me down. You didn't run from the police, at least not for long.

So now I was living on borrowed time. Thanks, Master. Every minute—every second was precious now, and I wasn't about to waste it. I jabbed at the touch-sensitive controls on the shower and the hot spray stopped. I didn't need to think about 'what next'. I wasn't going to be brave. Brave implied that there was something to lose, and Master had taken that away from me. As soon as the power came back up and order was restored, I'd be number one on the police's hit list. Nothing that happened now could be worse than what would happen once I was caught. Nothing to lose so nothing to fear, right? That wasn't bravery that was logic.

But I'd need more than bravery, logic, or courage to actually achieve something. For that, I'd need skill and experience, both things I was in desperately short supply of. But who said I needed to use my own? Every apartment had a compad, especially here in city center. It only took a few seconds to hop online. I had the inklings of a plan, but I couldn't do it alone. I needed friends, and failing that, I needed a jacker.

Body looking for Soul. No payment requested, but must have net tracking/hacking skills.

The site was called "In2U", and I was no stranger to it. In the right forums, I was the highlight, but I wasn't using those today.

My lifestyle was bleeding edge, too technologically advanced to even be illegal yet. It would be, of course. The room I watched now was filled with the more difficult fringe types, the ones that couldn't pay their way into my normal room unless they broke in the hard way. In other words, they were exactly what I needed.

After a few instantaneous responses-bots, which I ignored-the real responses started to roll in. Names, ages, offers of currency, measurements (height and otherwise) as if any of that mattered.

Serious about the tracking and hacking. First one to break into my compad and put an image of a llama on my screen gets in.

Silence again for a few seconds. Some of the offers immediately withdrew. One cheeky fellow by the name of "Gh0stInYourShell" managed to put an image of a yak into the chat window. Not good enough.

I counted down the seconds. Everyone online seemed to fancy themselves some elite net god, but the reality was that few of them could code themselves out of a paper bag, let alone crack an old connection. Ten, twenty seconds, then a minute went by. Hope slowly faded.

Then a new thumbnail appeared on my desktop. I brought it up, and it brought a smile to my face. It was a fuzzy llama with its tongue out, and a hastily added caption said "Llama delivery service. -BodyRaider"

Sure enough, I had a message from BodyRaider, blinking in my chat window. I laid my palm against the compad, and a thin beeping in my ear told me voice chat was enabled.

"Get it?"

I ran my fingers over the pad, the burn of anticipation tingling down my spine. "Got it."

"Good. What's the rules?"

"Twenty minutes, in exchange you hunt someone down and leave the trail for me."

"How much access?"

That's what they called it now. 'Access'. It was just another name for the thing I'd been selling since I was old enough to run away to the city. I hesitated, but not for long. It wasn't being brave; I just had nothing more to lose.

"Full access, but can't leave the apt."

There was a pause on his end. "Anything interesting in the apt?"

"Who needs what's in the apartment when you'll have me? Trust me, you won't be disappointed."

"Deal." It seemed like the equivalent of a shrug. He probably would have accepted no matter the details. Full access for free didn't come along every day.

I put my hand on the compad and opened the connection. Most of the hardware was inside me, or on the other side at BodyRaider's place, but it needed the compad to make the connection. Once that was established, though, I felt him arrive.

It was like slipping into sleep, a comfortable, detached sleep, but staying awake to experience every second of it. Muscle by muscle, inch by inch, his will took over where mine disappeared. I retreated to the safe little corner of my mind. All of my senses stayed alert and active—I could hear and smell and see as if it were me—but the will wasn't mine anymore. It was BodyRaider.

"Oh, oh my." My mouth formed the words. My hands dropped to my belly and started to caress my body. It was a ritual that every new jacker seemed to follow. He gazed down at my body and saw me for the first time with my own eyes. Sleek black fur, still slightly damp from the shower and gloriously naked, apparently met his approval. "Whoah. I didn't expect..." His thoughts were uncharitable. I knew what he'd been expecting: fat or disfigured, or ugly or scarred. Pretty girls like me weren't desperate, so we were expensive even for the simplest "access." But I wasn't today, because I was desperate.

Fingers tweaked at interesting places, and a hand roamed over my chest, measuring the rest of my features. I could feel his surprise and pleasure. I had other motives tonight, but even distracted as I was I couldn't help feeding off his excitement. As much as I craved to simply throw it all away and enjoy it, though, that wasn't what I was here for tonight.

Business first, BodyRaider. I made the mental equivalent of a tap on the shoulder. If he misbehaved, I could just safeword out and find another. If I posted my picture, I'd probably have them lining up in the channel.

"Just Andy." .

Okay, Andy. Up until an hour ago, I had a jacker that I need to locate. Can you do that?

He chewed my lip nervously. "Probably. He must owe you a lot if your willing to give full access to chase him right now. Did you guys get knocked offline by that electrical storm earlier?"

Storm? If he thought that whatever Master had done earlier was a storm, he has to be buried in someone's basement somewhere. Bless the nerds in dark closets; they were my best customers.

Something like that.

Andy pulled my limbs into a flurry of activity. The first few bits I recognized. He pressed my wrist to the compad and started diagnostic mode in my jacking rig. It was a simple thing to extract the first part of the trail—that I could have done myself.

Then it began to get complicated. Numbers and portions of words flashed onto the compad's screen and disappeared just as quickly as Andy dismissed them. Every once in a while, I caught the snippet of a location. There I saw the Crown Royal, and here I saw a secure checkpoint (access denied). There were other city names, too, Ulster Point and Darmitty, both of which were hundreds of miles away.

In my private corner of my mind, I had the sudden ghost of

fear. What if Master was in another city entirely? It'd never occurred to me, but why not? Everything was global these days. If he was, my little mission ended here. There was no way I could travel, that'd require permits and authorization. I might as well call the police and hand myself—

"Got him." Andy brought up a map and searched for an address. It was local! My panic waned, replaced with a feeling of accomplishment.

Okay, tell me all about him.

"Hey, I found him for you, that doesn't mean—"

How do I know you didn't just make up an address?

Andy paused, then with a renewed sense of purpose the compad screen started to flicker again. This time, it glowed with snippets of personal information. It was a chaotic medley, too confused to be talking about one person. Architect, soldier, businessman, free-thinker and radical, politician, doctor, psychotherapist, cybernetics engineer and, for some reason, daycare nurse. These couldn't all be Master, but at the top of every one, the same picture appeared.

It was my very first view of Master—the hand behind the puppet—and any doubt was replaced with certainty. He was a tiger, regal and handsome, with a savage, feral grin that managed to show more teeth than smile. Immediately, my mind filled in the details. He'd have a deep, throaty voice that purred and growled in equal measures. I could hear so many of our conversations echoing from out of that smiling mouth, attach so many of his eccentric mannerisms to that personable but dangerous face.

"Well, I don't know how many of these are real, but that's him alright."

No doubt about that, Andy. That's...

Words—or thoughts—failed me. Master was stunning. No amount of personal grievances could still the way my breath caught in my throat when I looked at just his picture. Could I do this? Could I take revenge on this; this Adonis among cats?

Then I remembered the smell. I remembered the way I walked between them, executing them without so much as a thought for the life I was ending. I remembered how I'd been used, then thrown away.

"I hope you can get him to pay. He looks like a tough customer."
You have no idea.

From my peripheral vision, I took note of the time.

Twenty minutes start now, Andy. Full access. You earned it. Remember, no leaving the apartment.

My tongue licked along my lips, and the flush of arousal immediately made the room feel slightly too hot. It wasn't my arousal—it was Andy's—but there's only so far you can distance yourself from your body. It wasn't mine to begin with, but by the time Andy had started to drag my hands over my front and down between my legs, it had become mine too.

And really, wasn't this part of why I was in this profession in the first place? All the regular girls, they'll tell you it's just a job. They'll insist it's just good money, and that it's no different than stocking shelves or flipping burgers, but they'd be lying. The girls that didn't get this, this slow and steady burn of pleasure from being *used*, they went out and did exactly what the axiom stated, they stocked shelves and flipped burgers. It wasn't just the money, it was the sex, and the adrenaline, and the control (or lack of) it brought with it. So by the time Andy began to really get into the feeling (and subsequently, into me), I wanted it as strongly as he did.

I expected a full-on rush into eroticism, hands down and fingers everywhere, but it seems Andy wasn't the type. Almost at a leisurely pace he tapped at the compad. In moments, I saw an image of myself. Ah, so I was to be a show. Secretly, I was pleased.

I was proud of my body, and any inhibitions about showing it off had melted away under months under Master's control.

With the compad's built-in camera focused and my naked body well-framed in its view, Andy stepped me back gazed into the lens. "Hey Andy, I've got a special show just for you, big boy." Ugh, typical porno-writing. I didn't interfere, though. This was his fantasy, and he'd earned it.

He pulled my arms down over my chest, and fingers pushed up under my breasts to accentuate them. One pushed up towards my muzzle, and he ran my tongue slowly over my aureola, then swiped it directly over my nipple. My tongue was raspy, and I could feel it tugging at my skin as it passed. My mouth closed, and I could feel sharp pricks from my canines as he dug them into the sensitive flesh.

He had me purring. It was an autonomic reaction like breathing and blinking, and it startled him. He stopped momentarily, and the purring stopped with it. He must not have been a cat. When he started again, the purring doubled, as if he was intentionally overdoing it for effect. As if? No, he was. I could feel his arousal, fed down to me through the jacking rig, as the rumbling purrs filled the compad's audio buffer. You like that, Andy? I can purr for you.

He dragged a chair over towards the compad and put one leg up on it. I knew he was intentionally letting it build slowly, but I could feel him getting close to that point, where foreplay and teasing just isn't enough anymore. He wanted to see everything—to feel it all, but I knew someone with a romantic streak when I felt them. He wouldn't want to just to dive in, he needed to let it grow until he was ready.

So even with my leg up and slit clearly in plain view, his fingers still only barely grazed around my mons. Index and middle finger spread to either side, just squeezing at my lips. I let myself ride the wave of his arousal. I needed it after tonight. He wasn't the best I'd ever had jacked in. The way he dragged my fingers was just a little too fast, and when he squeezed, it pinched just a bit. He was a little rough for being gentle, but I'd learned long ago that 'good' didn't have to mean 'best'.

It wasn't until after five minutes of rubbing and caressing that I felt my fingers pushed in between my lips. Knuckles dragged inside as he slid them deep. He'd spent so long rubbing and caressing that I was aching for it by the time I felt the first touch to my sensitive flesh, and the sensation of digits spreading me open was almost electric.

He spread my legs for the camera. He wanted to be able to see in the recording every little wet twist of fingers on my flesh. I could tell by the way he moved how my body worked him. I knew he found me gorgeous. He'd be reliving this over and over in his buried little basement for years to come.

Go ahead, Andy. Make it a show to remember.

It worked to stoke the flames. He made me moan, and then the fingers twisted. Oh, it felt good when my claws touched just there, a hard and sharp little tickle contrasted with the short fuzz of my fingers, against the silky smooth flesh.

How I'd been looking forward to this all night, the sensation, like a charge, building, threatening at any moment to spill over. It's what I'd been waiting for since Master had jacked in. Since...

The sudden darkening of thoughts seemed to seep through to Andy, because he faltered. The fingers pulled out with an audible slurp. Immediately I quashed the memories of the explosion, then of the gun and the smell of flesh burning. Okay, so maybe not immediately, but quickly enough to hide it from Andy.

No, no, keep going.

In an attempt to make the move seem natural, he had me smile at the camera and spread my slit wide open for his inspection. In the display of the compad I could see myself in miniature, leaning back against the rickety chair with legs wide apart and displayed lewdly. It wouldn't the first time I'd been on show, and not by far the most intimate one I'd given. For a regular paying jacker, this would have just been the opening to a good night. Or for Master …

No. I wouldn't go there again. I kept my thoughts neutral as I just enjoyed the sensations as my fingers dove in and started to stroke and prod again. Minutes passed as Andy enjoyed my body, and for my part, I simply relaxed into the pleasurable stupor of being a passenger in my own body. I rode his excitement like a roller coaster. I had no control over where the tracks took me, but what a ride it was as Andy took me over the top of the hill, then down the other side.

He had me shivering, and I could hear myself purring for the camera. My hands were slick with juices, and I could feel short fur tug at my insides as my fingers slurped free. I was panting, but rather than rest and enjoy the afterglow, he pushed my fingers in again, aiming for round two.

Andy

He was too deep into it. He wasn't paying attention, or maybe he was intentionally ignoring me.

Andy, your time is up.

I felt him beg: a wave of hopeful sorrow that ran through my body like a shock. He didn't want it to end. I was no stranger to the sensation, so gently—as gently as I could while still being forceful—I let him know that 'no' wasn't an option.

Andy, your time is up and I have someone I need to find.

"Hh, okay." He breathed heavily, and one wet hand tapped at the compad, ending the transmission. I didn't want to have to safeword him out, but I would have. With a rush, the feeling of control returned. Slightly shaky and in need of another quick shower, I dashed to the bathroom.

Garbed in my white suit and back out in the city streets, the anarchy had grown worse—not better. The sky was bathed in the pre-dawn glow of the thick smog that was ever-present over our heads. It made everything seem even darker than deep night. Busted cars and bikes had joined the rubble on the street, and no matter where I looked, I could see at least one fire somewhere.

The crowds on the street looked less than savory. A lot of them were confused innocents. They were easy to spot—they were the ones wandering around looking lost and dazed. The others, though, I could tell they were gangs. Many of them were of similar predator species. I passed a group of wolves, each with their own functional bike. I saw a group of weasels and martens on foot but carrying firearms. There were looters, too, usually on their own rather than in a group. Once in a while, a vehicle would pass by, glutted on stolen goods and dodging drunkenly through the rubble.

The address Andy had found was another district over. By foot, it should have only been five minutes to the district gate, but rubble and dangerous crowds made it fifteen. When I arrived, I cursed myself for thinking it'd be that easy. Of course the district gate was down. Heavily armed soldiers with twitchy trigger fingers were facing down an angry mob. If their sensors didn't work—and after that blast earlier, they wouldn't—no one was going through. The rules were the rules.

Even so, I approached, hoping to find a way through. An eye-bot sank in front of me, and a sharp flash momentarily blinded me. Looking up, I saw swarms of them, little cameras on magnetic disks dodging nimbly like insects. Every once in a while, one would descend to the crowd, take a picture, then ascend before they could be caught again. Everyone was marked, tracked, and watched.

I heard a beep. My eye-bot must have seen something it liked, because it quickly ascended, and a light went off. Angry red and blue lit the crowd around me, and like the rest of them, I scattered. All the gate guards needed was a wanted criminal to be in the crowd. Thin slivers of gunfire echoed off of the looming buildings, and cries went up from the quickly fleeing masses.

I made it to an alleyway where a coffee shop stood half-open, so I ducked inside. Everything worth having had been stolen, even the paper cups and plastic holders. Just like everywhere else, though, there were compads. Every table had one, set into the tabletop. I found one that hadn't been defaced and slapped my hand against it. Time was not a commodity I had in abundance.

Body looking for soul. No payment—must be good at city running. Pain shared, so if you suck, you get hurt.

This time, I didn't wait for proof. Within ten seconds I had private messages from five would-be runners. I chose one with a monicker I liked, "L3ap", and without any further discussion, sent him the connect code.

Moments later, I felt him arrive. He looked around in disbelief. "Holy shit."

Yeah, it's a mess. You ready to run?

He shook my head to clear the fug of the hasty jack. Then he looked down at me. Hands rubbed over my front, grabbing my tits and squeezing. "Holy shit!"

Okay, enough freaking out there, L3ap. I'm in trouble and you're going to run me out of this.

"First, what's the terms."

Full access, twenty minutes once we get to the destination.

He breathed heavily, then nodded. "Right. What've you got? Mugger? Pimp you owe money?"

I ignored his rude assumptions. *District police and a swarm of eye-bots, and I need to make it into the next district. You game, or do*

I need to find another jacker?

That stopped him. "Holy shit. You serious?"

Deadly.

Unexpectedly, I felt him start to smile. "Damn, girl, you should have said so. I would'a done this for free!"

Does that mean you won't take the terms?

"And miss out on this gorgeous body of yours? Not a chance."

Red and blue lights shone through the cracked and half-shielded window of the coffee shop, and a thin wail started up. L3eap's nerves sprung into action, and I launched myself at the employee-only door. Its feeble lock didn't even slow me down.

In the front of the shop, we could hear footsteps. No doubt who that would be. L3ap threw open the rear entry, then ignored it entirely and ran back into the miniature kitchen. As one of the police examined the alley the rear entrance opened onto, L3ap silently slid the kitchen window open. Grasping the window frame, he slipped me through the window.

My feet never touched the ground on the other side. L3eap caught a pipe that ran up the side of the building and pulled me flush to the wall. Hand-over-hand I started to climb. First floor, second, third—by the fifth, I was just above the eye-bot swarm, and could see them milling about midair in the distance. By the eighth, the muscles of my arm were starting to complain. We drew level with the district wall, eight stories high and topped with thick bars. Above them, thin holograms lit the sky displaying clearly the end of 'downtown'.

"Good thing you're in shape, girl. This'd be torture if you were some fat bitch." I would have ground my teeth if I'd had control of my jaws. As it was, I made no comment, because he was good. In fact, he was damn good. He threw me from wall to window ledge, and then launched me fearlessly into a sheer climb using nothing but a drainage pipe and a bit of external electrical tubing.

How are you planning to get into the next district from up here?

He pulled me up to another ledge. By my count, this was the thirteenth floor. "Do you ask magicians how they're about to do their next trick, too?" He looked over the district wall at the buildings beyond. They were nearly as dignified and towering as those here in city center. Between the wall I clung to and the building on the far side of the divide, the glowing blue district wall looked like nothing more than a river flowing through a canyon. In a way, it was rather pretty. It was lost on L3ap, though, who was measuring distances with my eyes. With no further explanation, he threw me bodily out over empty space.

It was the second time that evening that I'd felt the dizzying sense of weightlessness. Gravity reached up to claim its wayward child, and the world spun towards me at a dizzying rate. Arms flung wide like a bird; I felt the wind cushioning me, whistling past my ears. It would have been liberating, if it wasn't also so fucking terrifying.

The fall must have been no more than a few seconds, though it felt like a miniature eternity. My hands caught one of the steel bars suspended above the district wall. I swung below, and the centripetal force threatened to tear my limbs from their sockets. Gravity and momentum sucked down at me for excruciating moments as the skyline swung uncertainly around me.

Then L3ap curled, and my feet pushed off the bar, using my redirected momentum to launch me at the building on the far side of the district line. At the apex of my arc, the staggered ledge of an intermediary rooftop appeared beneath my feet, and L3ap rolled. Twice, three times I felt the brutal tar and concrete batter my shoulder blades and back, then the world stopped spinning.

I uncurled, and stared up at the starless city sky. I could still see the remnants of angry green flitting in between clouds, where Master's little 'present' remained to play hell with the skyscape. I felt a giddy rush—not mine, but L3ap's.

"WOO!" The cry hurt my throat. He picked me up and dusted off my battered and torn clothes. L3ap then swung me over the side of the rooftop and started the descent. We were on the ground in just minutes. The wall deposited us in an alleyway, but I could see light and flickering fire just beyond in the street, along with shouting and someone singing loudly and badly.

"Holy shit, I made it!"

Rational thought stopped for a moment.

I assumed you'd done that before.

"Of course I have. Twice. First time, I broke both legs, second time I went through a closed window and cut up my arms."

You reckless son of a bitch! I should boot your lying ass out just for—

"For getting you safe and sound to the next district?"

He had me there. Dammit, he was a rude asshole, but here I was, exactly where I needed to be. I didn't want to give it to him, but he'd earned it.

Twenty minutes starts now, fly-boy.

"Shit, yeah!" He ran me out towards the street, towards the fire and shouting.

Not that way, idiot!

"Full access, bitch. Pay up or kick me out, but you know you owe me."

I didn't bother to respond, but I seethed in my safe little haven in my own mind. How dare he, with my body? After so many times out with jackers, I thought I'd finally seen the last of that impulse, but L3ap brought it out with a passion. I felt powerless, trapped in my own body—trapped by my own goddamn sense of fairness that told me I owed this prick. I felt helpless.

And that alone was enough to bring the rush of arousal back with such a force that it embarrassed me, and even that fed it further. It was a self-sustaining spiral that dragged me back down into willingness. No, not willingness, eagerness. I wanted it, I needed it so physically that I'm sure even my jacker could feel it leaking out.

In the street just around the corner were no less than a dozen canids. A few I could identify—husky and dalmatian and terrier. Some were dragging expensive electronics out of a smashed store-front, others were drinking around a car that'd been set alight. They were shouting at each other, but there were smiles on their faces and the way they held their tails and ears. No, this wasn't a group, this was a gang.

But the rest of the dogs didn't grab my attention like their leader did. I could feel the authority and ownership of the gang nearly dripping from the jackal. Lean and rangy like most jackals I'd met, he still had an aura of cool command that those poisonous politicians I'd executed earlier would be jealous of. He was the one who was singing, though maybe not as badly as the echoing alley had made it out to be. He had a clear accent, one that even the song couldn't cover. He was standing on top of a car's hood, almost like a conductor in front of an orchestra.

I didn't make it more than five steps from the alley before one of them noticed me. "Heya, pussy! Looking for some warm milk?"

Some of them turned from their looting and carousing to face me. Cat-calls and lewd suggestions echoed strangely off of the dark storefronts.

"Pretty kitty, got some salami for you!"

"Hey ba—"

L3ap cut them off mid-taunt. I pointed at the leader, and he hopped down from the car hood.

"You." I was walking quickly, but instinct and excitement had my tail twitching high.

"Yeah, bascha, you want something."

"Yes." I pushed him back across the hood of the car, and his gang let out surprised whoops and laughs around me. "You."

L3ap was at less than a minute of full access used, and already he had my hand tearing at the jackal's jeans. The jackal held his hands up, but my jacker wasn't having any disagreement. Not that the jackal was disagreeing, but he did let out a grunt of pain as my claws shredded the waistline of his pants and caught on his belt.

I didn't often use my claws for the ripping and tearing they were made for, but they served perfectly well in removing his denim jeans in a single tug. They fell away in long strips.

"Whoah, bascha, careful with the—"

"Shut up" I growled at him as I crawled up onto the hood of the car, straddling his pinned hips. More cat-calls emerged from the gang around me, and I could smell them. Dogs were shameless about their arousal, broadcasting their scent at just the slightest provocation. I breathed it in like perfume.

The gang leader tried to push himself up to his elbows, but I shook his shoulders and slammed him back down against the car hood.

"Come on, puppy, can't you show me what you got?" L3ap ground my hips down against his, and through the shredded fabric, I could feel him pulse in response. I dragged claws down his jacket as he growled up at me. There we go, he was starting to get into the act.

"Too much for you to handle, boss? We can take 'er if you can't!" One wolfhound had his cock out and was swinging it in the smoky city air. Laughs echoed from around us.

"Put your little toy away, boy! Can't you see the lady's found a real man?" The gang leader gripped my hips and tugged at my suit pants. L3ap lifted my hips and wriggled efficiently—in just moments he'd shed the inhibiting fabric, and when I sat back I felt hot flesh throbbing against me. The jackal rolled his hips. He was no stranger to the show either, and now that he appeared to be on more familiar ground, I felt his claws catch at my fur and pull.

There was no foreplay. This wasn't the place for teasing and romance. I lifted my hips, he lifted himself with two fingers, and when I sat back down, it was with a wet squelch and the rush of skin against skin as he slid up into me.

Even with L3ap in control, I couldn't restrain the hot groan of pleasure as the rubbery flesh stretched me wide. I'd had dogs before. They were always a bit floppy when they first went in, but that was a blessing given their size. I was built for other cats, and while they had passion, they didn't have that thick, throbbing girth that filled me out until it hurt. Cats didn't make it so wet that everything felt slick and velvety. And when I rolled my hips against his sheath, I felt the last thing that cat guys lacked—that gorgeously hot bulb of flesh at the very base that ballooned out as I stroked.

I almost forgot the crowd in the sensation of the hard rutting, but they hadn't forgotten me. Cats were generally fairly private, but for dogs, it was a pack thing. I felt hands drag around my waist, and fingers tugged at my tail and below. They all wanted a good view of the show.

The jackal yapped and barked. He leaned to the side and snapped at the over-bold gang-members, but with me riding his hips he couldn't reach far enough to scare them off. Someone else's flesh pressed against my side and left a wet imprint. Then someone else snarled and bit him. A squabble broke out to my right, and I didn't care. It was a whole different world than I knew, down here on the street with the gang, but here with L3ap riding me, it was exactly where I wanted to be.

I clawed at the jackal, and he bit my arm. I squeezed my hips, and he ground his knot up against my slit. This wasn't smooth lovemaking, it was a rough, feral hump down with a gang that was just one scarce step removed from beasts. No one talked—they were all speaking a language more native than English.

There was an explosion somewhere else in the city, and overhead I heard the whining of eye-bots. No one even bothered to look. The jackal growled beneath me, and I felt him throb. He was coming. L3ap clawed at his chest, and the squirming as the jackal writhed under me was enough to bring me off as well. One of the gang members let out a whoop; another laughed.

"Heya girl, got room for another?"

"Or two?"

I planted my feet against the hood of the car and started to stand. I couldn't, not immediately. The jackal had tied, and his hips raised as I lifted him bodily from the hood just by the force of his tie. He yelped and whined beneath me, and even L3ap winced in pain. It didn't stop him, though. Another harsh tug, and the thick bulb pulled from me, dropping the jackal's ass back to the car.

The gang crowded in around me, but I ignored them. Hips were thrust at me, but one set of brandished claws and a smile full of sharp teeth quickly deterred them. For a gang, they were awfully timid. I collected my suit pants, and without a backwards glance, I prowled off towards an alley. I could feel the remnants of the jackal's excitement starting to run down my leg.

That's it, L3ap. Time's up.

"Good run, eh? You're fine, you know. Look me up when you need a soul again and—"

Not a chance. Out, now before I kick you. It lacked vitriol, though. He was crass, rude, disrespectful, and only interested in his own pleasure, and maybe that's why he'd been such a great time. He could tell, too. I felt a caress of his smug confidence as a parting gift as he disconnected. With him gone, I hid behind a dumpster to clean and make myself presentable.

When I found it, Master's building was opulent, as high-class and ostentatious as anything I remember seeing in city center. The doorman had fled, leaving the door unguarded. Even though the glass had been bullet-proof, it wasn't car-proof. One still sat as a crumpled hulk in the middle of otherwise obvious decadence.

Everything that wasn't bolted down had taken a leave of absence, but quality couldn't be stolen from the mirror-smooth marble and curved, ergonomic lack of corners. The entire atrium was a masterpiece of glass and steel and carbon fiber. I saw indentations and cracks where statues and sculptures had fallen, probably suspended mid-air in the air above, but even without them it was beautiful. Master would be upstairs, but I had something I needed to do first. Around the back of the main desk was light from a screen. The atrium may have been a mess, but the power was still on. Behind the desk was a monitor with security feeds, a spilled coffee, and my goal: a compad.

The lift was out, so I used the stairs. I had to pause on the twenty-third floor to catch my breath, and again on the thirty-eighth. The stairwell terminated at the forty-fourth and emptied into an elaborate foyer. The locks in the stairwell had been modern swipe-locks that had all malfunctioned, but the front door of Master's suite was locked by an ancient and complex tumbler with numbers etched into the front. I didn't need to guess.

"There are eighty-three districts in this hellhole of a city, pet, did you know that? Not many do. The city is larger than most old nations. Can you guess how many of them any one average 'citizen' may travel to? Four. Four measly collections of squat little shacks, trying to eke out a sad little existence on careful rations. I've shown you the center of it all, the splendor of the Aerie Bridge, the flying arches of the Atomic Reserve, the marvelous jungle of the Crown Heights. Wasn't it beautiful? Shouldn't everyone be able to see the marvels that their own blood and sweat has bought? Yes? You are special, pet. You and half of

point-one percent have the honor of seeing it in person. Everyone else is locked away behind the district walls."

I'd heard it so many times that it wasn't just a recollection—it was muscle memory. I had no doubts when I spun the tumblers to eight-three-four-zero-five. The last digit let out a soft click, and the door swung open.

The first room was palatial. It must have occupied the next four stories upwards just to contain the huge window that gazed out into the city. As I started to take in the details, it occurred to me that it was the only room. Amenities of luxurious life were scattered almost at random across the smooth hardwood floor. Against one wall was a stainless steel kitchen, obviously used but immaculately cleaned. Further on was a tiled section with no walls where shower heads on long stalks sprouted from the floor and aimed towards drains. Near the towering window was a huge nest-like bed, with pillows and cushions strewn liberally about.

In the center of the room stood what could only be described as the media center. Holoscreens and old-fashioned TVs sat interspersed with overstuffed couches and equally bloated chairs. Sprawled across two of the couches was Master, the headset and wires from his jacking rig still nearby. He was large, larger than the pictures of him could have done justice. Stretched out as he was, he sprawled to fill the room that two normal people would occupy put head-to-toe.

I had planned to be stealthy, but I couldn't have anticipated the soft chime that sounded when I first stepped foot into the room. With a rush of motion, Master spun to his feet. It was a movement composed of orange and black, so fluid that he didn't seem to occupy any of the intermediate space between the couch and where he now stood. Incongruously, he leaned on a cane he'd fetched from the side of the sofa. He seemed at once both frail and deadly.

For the first time, I got a good look at my Master. The stripes just seemed to accentuate his gorgeous body, all eight or nine or however-many-feet tall he was. They crawled over his lanky musculature and crept around arms that were as thick as my thighs and thighs that were as thick as my waist. They only ended in the deep creamy white of his belly and lower.

And oh yes, I could see lower, oh so lusciously lower. He was gloriously naked, and I felt the natural reaction to such a prime specimen of feline form seep in.

We stared at each other. Remember what he'd done, I forced myself. Remember the smell. Remember the way he'd broken my trust. He'd used my hand to kill, then he'd thrown me from the top of the Crown Royal. Those weren't the actions of a loving master.

"Pet." His aggressive stance slowly melted as realization spread across his features. "I..."

I filled the silence where he stumbled in surprise. "I live. You've failed."

"Not all the way." He slowly relaxed, and a smile crept onto his face. "But I must say it's the happiest I have ever been to fail. Pet, you astound me!"

With one arm stretched out, he limped towards me, the clack-clacking of his cane echoing in the cavernous room. With a careful and bullet-fast punch to his gut, I dropped him where he stood and stepped back.

"You used me, you son of a bitch."

He coughed and held his gut, kneeling and looking up at me. That cocky grin still adorned his muzzle. "So there is bite to your bark, pet. The kitty has claws. You never cease to impress me." He pushed himself back to his feet. "And yes, I used you. You, who sold herself body and soul to me, begging to be used."

"Not for that!"

"May the hammer choose which nail it hits? You sold your will to the highest bidder. Don't blame yourself, pet. It was my will that created this new dawn for our city."

"Don't try and hide it behind your stupid philosophy. It was my hand that pulled the trigger, my eyes that watched them—" I choked on the next words. I could still smell the flesh searing beneath the barrel of my gun. "Watched them die."

"No, my pet." He walked toward me, but I dropped back into a fighting pose, and he stopped. "Don't you dare shed a tear for them. They engineered their own demise. You were simply the hand chosen to deliver their sentence."

"I am not an executioner! Nor am I a judge or jury, and don't you dare call me an assassin. This is your personal crazy fucking crusade, not some social justice. Didn't you consider what it would do to me."

His gaze fell, and he turned his head to gaze out of the window into the false dawn. Was that pain I saw on his face? Sorrow?

"No, of course not," I pressed on, "because I wasn't supposed to survive, was I?"

"It was a mercy, my pet."

"A what? Are you serious? Mercy, for me, by throwing me off the fortieth story?"

"What do you think they would have done to you when they caught you, pet?" His cane clicked as he walked to the window. "Do you think they're kind? Three-square-meals a day, respectful and sensitive guards, and time off for good behavior? You wouldn't have survived the night, pet."

"That wasn't your decision." I shot back hotly. "Never was, and never will be. I gave you control, but only under the trust—"

"You didn't want me to have control, pet." He turned towards me again and held his cane in front of him. His tail squirmed behind like an agitated snake. "You wanted me to have you."

"Is that what you thought? Is that what you convinced yourself I wanted?"

"Of course pet. I saw how you desperately you craved to be rid of every bit I took from you. And now here you are, and I see in you more of me than I see of who you used to be." He pointed out at the city, with thin plumes of smoke rising like banners from every district center. "Look at what we've made, my pet. I could not have made this without you."

"Don't include me in your delusions of grandeur. I'm just a—"

"Was. You may not say what you are, pet. That is my privilege alone. You were a scared girl, fresh from the country and barely come to grips with her own power. Now you are a force to be reckoned with. You are the face to Demosthenes' crusade! When you speak, heads will turn and ears will open and minds will churn. You don't know what you are now, because so much of what you are is me!"

"Maybe." I gritted my teeth. "But the rest of me wants what you've stolen back."

His smile fell, and I saw such sadness. "You've such a dream ahead of you, my pet. Don't spoil this moment with a childish tantrum. Come join me at the window and I will show you the new age you've ushered in."

"No."

"Then you are no Demosthenes" He lifted his cane, and almost too late I saw the smooth bore in its base.

Now, A55a55inyou.

My final jacker, waiting in the wings since my break on the twenty-third floor, came with a rush. His instinct pulled me down and to the left. I felt the flare of gunfire scorch my back, and a burning pain lit the end of my tail. A55a55inyou ignored it, and performed a forward roll, then flip. Master's eyes widened in shock as the leap covered the span between us in fractions of a second. Before he could lower his cane, I grabbed its middle and yanked it from his grip.

It was a dizzying ride to watch as my jacker spun and ducked. My leg shot out and swept Master's out from under him. Without his cane to steady him, he dropped heavily on his tail end. A55a55inyou twirled the cane until its business end pointed down at Master's striped face.

Do it, now.

"Now I see how you've done it. How many did it take, pet? Three? Five? Ten? How many have ridden you like a prize horse to get to this finish line?

A55a55inyou fumbled with the cane. While he searched for the trigger mechanism, Master didn't even budge.

"Oh, how rude of me. That's not you, pet, is it? Let me introduce myself. I'm the Master."

Don't let him talk, dammit, I let you in to finish this, so finish it!

My fingers finally stumbled across a nub in the cane that wiggled under my grip. A55a55inyou steadied himself then pointed the cane down between Master's eyes.

"So, are you a professional? Will you look me in the eyes as you burn me and my dreams away?"

Stop dawdling, A55a55in. This is what you wanted to do!

My eyes closed, and my finger played across the trigger. My claw traced over the cane's intricate grain. "I..."

"No, I guess not. A talented hobbyist killer, then? Only take lives on the weekends?" Master scoffed. He hadn't moved an inch.

"I can't." My finger eased off the trigger.

Oh for fucks sake. It's your god damn name. 'Cupcake apocalypse'.

I've read that it hurts to be booted by safeword. I hoped so.

I opened my eyes. I could look into Master's eyes when he ended. I was strong—he'd made me strong.

"Oh, are you back now, pet?"

"If you need something done—" I mumbled between gritted teeth. My finger felt for that trigger I'd felt. It made sense that it was well protected—wouldn't want it going off unless you absolutely meant to fire.

"Do it yourself? I disagree, pet, but at least find a worthy proxy. Pet, please." He reached up and took hold of the cane, but he didn't move it away. He held it centered between his eyes. "Before you put an end to me, may I show you something? You may keep the cane, and at any time you believe you've seen enough you can always pull the trigger then. After all you've proved to me, could I stop you?"

"You can't buy your life back, Master. What you've done to me, that can never be undone."

"And I wouldn't undo it, even had I the chance." My finger finally found the little nub, but I hesitated, just like A55a55inyou had hesitated before me. Just one little squeeze, and this could all end, and I'd go back to... No, after what Master had made me do. I'd be better off turning the gun on myself after this, rather than be caught. Mercy, Master had called it. "I wish instead to show you what you need to see. I want your decision to end me be an informed one."

Keeping my finger on the trigger now that I'd found it again, I stood back. Master let go of the cane and painstakingly pushed himself up to his knees. Hobbling without his cane, he made his way to the center of the room where a titanic holo screen hung suspended in air. He picked up a small remote, and the screen sprung to life.

"—advising residents to stay indoors. Anyone seen on the streets will be considered a rioter and will be dealt with harshly."

On the screen, the view from above one of the ruined streets— just next to one of the district gates—wobbled and tilted alarmingly, then steadied. It was probably being shot from an eye-bot, especially as there was no sound. Below, frightened and angry citizens crowded around the gate. Some of them waved their citizenship cards, others pushed at the security gate, desperate to get through.

"I repeat, the station is being warned that the police have been authorized to deal with any gathering of three or more people. We are advising residents to stay indoors. Anyone seen on the—oh god."

There was a flash from the gate, and the crowd fell back. I couldn't immediately tell what had happened or who had fired the first shot, but from the lack of uniforms on the bodies laying in front of the district gate, it quickly became apparent. The rest of the officers lowered their firearms, and another three flashes lit the camera. Before the feed cut out, I caught just a glimpse—a frame or two—of the bodies laying three-thick, dead where they'd fallen.

Even though I imagined myself cold to the violence of the night's riots at this point, I still felt a chill that seeped down my spine. "Are you actually proud of what you've done? This is sick, this is—"

"Not me. Did I jack in to force the police to pull their triggers? Did I write the laws that allow them to do so? Did I hire the bastards willing to do so in the first place? No, I think not."

"It was your twisted idea of a 'fun night out' that's made this all possible. Don't tell me that you didn't think it would happen."

"I knew it would happen." He turned away from the screen again as the news station tried to cut to another eye-bot, but apparently the scene wasn't available for broadcasting anymore. He pressed a button, and another clip from the night popped up. Without preamble, policemen were plowing through a gang of wolves—incendiary rounds leaving charred flesh behind as the members of the gang ran. One of the wolves surrendered, hands in the air before he went to his knees. One officer walked calmly up behind him and fired another shot into the wolf's back. "I knew this is what they were capable of. How can you watch this, pet, and not feel anger?"

I bristled and growled, holding the cane up and fingering the trigger. "Of course I'm angry, Master, but this is what is. The fact that you stirred the wasp's nest, knowing nothing would change, makes you responsible for this!"

"Pet, if I thought nothing would change, then I would be fighting you for the right to pull that trigger first."

I paused. "But nothing has changed. Look out there. Everyone out in the streets, they're dead walking. Even if the police don't catch them now, all those names and faces, it's just cataloged down somewhere, and tomorrow, or next week, or next month there'll be a knock at the front door for them. For me, Master! I'll be first on that list, because nothing will have changed."

"Nothing has changed yet. Pet, this was only the first step."

"Oh, don't lie to me. I—You killed a bunch of assholes in suits, but it'll pick right back up. It'll be the same group of bastards at the top."

"No, no, no, nothing so benign, pet." He hobbled over to the side table and picked up a different remote. "I was waiting for the right time, you see."

"What, and all those people in the crowd, the time wasn't right for them?"

"No. They were necessary."

I shook my head. "Nothing like that is ever necessary."

"No? Think, pet. You told me that everyone's name and face was being logged and tracked. You're right. It's an ingenious system, a network that spans the whole city, co-located in fourteen different complexes at police stations, redundancy so many layers deep that it'd take fourteen simultaneous wipes of the entire network to take down."

He held up the remote and hobbled towards me. It took a few moments for what he was suggesting to sink in.

"Fourteen... You mean to take the whole network down."

"Not the network, no. The data they contain, yes. Do you know, it's not just criminal records they store. It's the occupations and social status archives, so they can keep the downtrodden from bothering the elite with their problems. It's citizenship so they can properly contain immigrants. It's the surveillance and the grades and the certifications of loyalty to the state. Can you see what would happen if we could banish that wraith from the public consciousness? It's a new start, my pet."

"Bought with blood."

"The only currency worth spending." He confirmed, and he gave me the remote. "Fourteen more presents like the one you saw earlier tonight, placed strategically over the fourteen interdistrict hubs."

I gazed down at the remote in my hands. "This is all I was, then. A distraction."

"You were a match, there to set the fuse on the powder keg. Does it disturb you to think of yourself as a tool?"

I ran my hands over their occupants. In one, the trigger of the cane had warmed under my fingerpad. In the other, the remote was cold and heavy in my palm. They were both so simple.

"No, Master." He had that cocky little grin again. How long had he known what I'd choose? From the moment I'd agreed to listen? Before? Damn him, he had me. I felt a slow shudder pass through my legs as he stood to his full height and reached out.

"I..." I gripped the cane and the remote, and an evil little thought came to me. Why choose? A smile spread to my face. "Master, I could always do both."

He paused. Had he not even considered the option? It was a

victory to see him suddenly so unsure. "You could."

"And why shouldn't I? I will bring about your glorious revolution, erase myself from the archives so I can live my own little life, and at the same time wipe your twisted face from the history books."

He lowered his hand and stood back from me. He visibly deflated. I toyed with the trigger on the cane. It'd be so easy, and he'd already given me the tools I needed to save myself. Just one little squeeze, and the architect of so nearly my demise would face his own justice.

"Move to the window, Master." He jerked, then followed my lead as I pointed the cane at his chest. "And tell me, when you decided that I needed to be 'sacrificed' for your cause, did you hesitate at all? Did it give you pause?"

He opened his mouth, then turned away from me, facing into the dawn as the sun crept just above the jagged skyline.

"And what about the people in the streets? Waiting for the right time? Watching them die from your safe little haven, did you reconsider? Did you mourn for your pawns?"

He didn't answer for long minutes. The sun had crested over the Crown Royal, tall and imposing in the distance, by the time he answered.

"Would you believe that I didn't want anyone hurt? No, I don't mean those nobodies that called themselves our selfless leaders. I meant everyone else. You, the people on the street, the gangs— you are all my people."

"Believe? You seemed perfectly willing to—"

"Willingly is not gladly, pet. Everyone makes sacrifices out of necessity. Those unfortunates down in the streets, they needed to be there. The survivors need to see what they've sold their freedom for, so when the city is rebuilt it doesn't wear the same mask." He put his hands on the glass and stared out into city center over the glowing blue of the district wall.

"Master..."

"And you. I needed to find the head of the snake so I could cut if off. Can't you see what you've been a part of? This is a new dawn, my pet, and willing or not. You were to welcome it in. On my hands are the stains of their blood, but in yours you hold their broken chains. That was always my gift to you, pet.

"Remember when I told you that you'd see the stars one day, pet? I fooled myself into believing it, even though I knew in just half an hour I'd throw you bodily from the top of the crown. Can you believe that? I've become so good at lying that even I believed it." He sighed and ran his fingers over the window.

I followed his gaze out into the city. The highrise district cut the early sunlight into jigsaw pieces. Even though the smog, it was gorgeous.

"Master, close your eyes."

His head hung, and in the reflection of the window, I saw his eyes close. Then I squeezed with my thumb.

There was no noise, at least not yet, but the light was so bright that even through my eyelids I felt it sear my retinas. It was painful, yes, but it was a pain I was willing to bear. The initial flash only lasted a few seconds, then I opened my eyes to new stars rise in the city's sky, one for each district in view.

"Enough people have died today, Master. I can always kill you tomorrow."

He took the cane from my hands when I offered it, then he took my hand and stood with me at the window, watching the many-sun-rise over the City as the thunder rolled in.

Editorial Interjections

I try to avoid these types of comments in any project; however, I have had to break that rule in regards to this story. If you read my opening note, which I hope you have, I mentioned a tragedy was included in this collection. Well here it is just as I promised. It is a powerful and emotionally charged story that works to encourage the reader to follow the mental turmoil of the character, you. That's not a typo—you are the character and this is your adventure.

The Hardest Dance

Tarl "Voice" Hoch

You don't know why you did it.

Jonathan is, no was, your best friend, and now he's nothing. Nothing, because of you.

The blood is cooling on your fur, seeping through each hair, chilling your skin. You look at your paws in shock; your muzzle works in small noises before your eyes fall upon Jonathan and your legs feel weak. Ears lowering you let out a small cry and fall to your knees.

Why, why did you do it?

Helen …

You had been so angry at Jonathan, so confused, so frustrated. The anger had come far too easily, a boiling point finally reached. You hadn't expected him to do what he had, to say what he had. Nausea rolls over you as what he had said echoes in your mind.

You crawl over to the prone body of the wolf, your nose dripping onto the plush white carpet you hated so much. It always showed your russet fur anytime you shed on it, which annoyed you because it made you feel dirty, but Jonathan had loved it. Now it was turning crimson as Jonathan's blood soaked into it. Your ears drooped.

What have you done?

Where was Helen? Your ears raise and swivel, catching her crying in the other room. You hear her voice talking to someone but it had only been you three in the house when it had happened.

The police, she must be calling the police.

Your heart jumps in panic tugging at your ribs, trying to pull them further into your chest.

How had this happened? Your life with Jonathan had been wonderful. You loved him and now he lay before you, still, never to hold you again. You close your eyes as fresh tears tumble down your cheek fur.

***

You had met Jonathan in Intro to Calculus when you had forgotten your calculator. The wolf had smiled at you, flashing beautiful white teeth and handed you a spare before asking if you wanted to sit with him. How could you not accept? He was fit, a runner you later found out; the thrill of his leg against yours while you took notes that first day fuelled many masturbation fantasies while you lay in bed late at night.

They always started out the same; his heavy paws would push up your shirt and run along your white chest fur. Your muzzles would meet, his tongue seeking yours out as if they belonged together. He tasted like blueberries you would later discover when you kissed for the first time at the transit station two weeks later. You always nipped his throat playfully and in your fantasies this would cause him to tear off his shirt and rip your shorts off.

By now your paw would be caressing your own tod-hood, teasing the pink tip as it slowly rose from its sheath, dew collecting on its tip. Small chirps of pleasure would be echoing throughout the room in your dream as well as in reality. You would imagine him freeing himself and you could almost feel the heat of his arousal press under the base of your tail as you rolled onto your chest and raised yourself to him.

He was a wolf; he deserved to be the top.

At least that's what you told yourself when he finally took you in reality, back at his flat. When fantasy had become reality; the moment he entered you, filling you with his need. You had cried out when he had pushed deeper than any lover you had had before. His paws had grabbed your waist and pulled you further onto him until his knot throbbed against your ring.

Oh how you had screamed his name, your body shivering as he started to ride you. He was rough as he yanked your tail and scratched your back all while you had torn the sheets with your claws. You came before he did, you always did no matter how often you tried to outlast him. He was a god in the sack, and you loved every minute of him, every minute submitting to his desires.

When you had finished you had been a quivering mess. The feel of him oozing out of you had brought you back to readiness. But he had left you wanting, even in your fantasies, making you wait until you saw him again. Perhaps that's why you finally broke down when you and Helen started talking. Wanting lovers always swam in troubled waters.

She came into the picture after you and Jonathan had been dating for a few months, though you often questioned if it was dating or not. He was regularly out and tended not to answer your calls as often as you liked. But you were used to that treatment from Brent, an ex you had dated for a couple years and who you had clung to despite him treating your relationship as anything but. Brent used you and then had tossed you to the curb like soiled trash with no thought to your feelings or your time together. It had hurt, but Jonathan wasn't Brent, so you didn't think too much about it. Helen, however, always made it apparent what she wanted—

You …

You met her at a party that Jonathan had taken you to. You both had dressed up, dress-pants and clean shirts. He had already rolled up the sleeves of his dress shirt, unbuttoning the first few buttons so the lighter grey of his chest peeked through the black material he had chosen. You wore white at his suggestion, he said it reminded him of pirates, and he thought pirates were sexy. So you had gone with the colour, surprised that it actually did look good on you. The way Jonathan had pressed against you, part of him warm against your hip had let you know he thought so as well.

You both had looked gorgeous and it was hard to not notice all the looks that Jonathan was getting when you both walked into the back yard where a bonfire roared. It was a typical college affair you had often read about but never thought you would see in person. There had to be about a good sixty people there, mixed species and sexes all drinking and chatting. Some wore suits, others next to nothing as they danced close to the fire, careful not to singe their fur. The music had been superb.

That's when you had first seen Helen, her lithe feline form leaping around the fire like someone possessed. Jonathan had been talking to a kangaroo exchange student so you felt comfortable to watch her dance. The firelight glinted off her calico coat, throwing her colours into a sensory riot. She was a flicker of colour, moving with the lash of the flames as they danced in the air. Her thin dreads whipped around like a scourge, the beads cracking when she snapped her head. Sand and ash coated her body, giving her a primal appearance.

You watched her in awe. How anyone could move in such a fashion you didn't know. It seemed unnatural, flame given life, or some pagan rite long forgotten.

Jonathan had gripped your shoulder and you had jumped in embarrassment. He had leaned in close, his breath caressing the fine hairs along the back of your ear, which caused it to twitch. It had excited you, though you were already hard from watching the feline dance, despite her being a woman.

"Alex says he knows her. I know you have always loved dance. You should talk to her; maybe she knows a good studio."

Jonathan had noticed you watching the woman and you had blushed fiercely under your fur. If he was jealous he showed no signs of it. You hadn't known why but you had wanted to meet her and Jonathan had smiled when you nodded, not trusting your voice. The wolf had exchanged a few more words with the kangaroo and suddenly you were moving to where the feline had moved away from the fire.

"Helen, this is Jonathan and his mate. They wanted to talk to you after that stunning performance. It was moving by the way, as always." Alex had stepped aside and let you and Jonathan move forward. Your tail had swayed nervously behind you while Jonathan reached out and shook her delicate paw.

"You put on quite the performance. I haven't seen some of those moves since I was a cub. Where do you study?"

Helen had smiled, toweling the sand and ash off her fur, cleaning the sweat from her paws and nose. Her voice had been soft, filled with hidden promises whispered in the dark.

"There's a dance studio on tenth and sixteenth street, just look for the kids milling about outside between classes. You thinking of taking it up?" Blue eyes had moved down Jonathan's chest to his crotch and back up as if they were appraising some piece of jewelry. He shook his head as you moved closer and wrapped your arms around him protectively.

"So you then?" She looked at you, her eyes doing the same travel, but when they rise to meet yours they sparkle with something you aren't sure of.

It took a moment to find your voice. "Yes. I have always liked dancers."

Jonathan chuckled beside you. He reached over and put his

arm around your shoulder, the familiar weight helping you to find your voice a little easier.

"I watched a lot of television as a child and always wanted to dance," you had said while your tail started to wag behind you. Dancing had always been a favourite topic of yours. "—but my parents were your typical straight kid parents. They had wanted me to do BMXing, guitar, or something..."

"Manly." Helen finished for you. Her fangs peeked through her lips and your eyes were drawn to them. You nod, suddenly feeling a little uncomfortable under your mate's arm.

"Pretty much. But now that I am away from the den and after seeing you dance so well, I find myself feeling inspired." None of it was a lie; you really wanted to dance. She smiled as if she had found meaning in your words that you had not intended. Jonathan suddenly removed his arm from around you, calling out to someone else in the crowd, and with a quick kiss, he vanished.

You stand there, suddenly nervous about being alone with Helen. She watched you for a moment, her eyes half open, her pupils so large they almost make her eyes look black. Her head tilts and you hear the soft clink of the beads in her hair. They reminded you of wind-chimes.

"Here, let's get some drinks," she said as she took your paw. Her touch had been soft, her pads smooth and silky unlike Jonathan's. His were rough from working out, not that you didn't love it; but right then you were drawn by the change in feeling while she pulled you to a bathtub filled with ice.

Two drinks later you were chatting it up pretty well. You saw Jonathan moving around the crowd, talking to various people. But as the drinks continued and the night moved on you started paying less and less attention to him while he seemed to spend more of his time with others rather than coming over to see how you were doing. Meanwhile Helen continued to talk to you, making you laugh, moving closer to you.

It had been obvious in hindsight. You should have seen it coming. Alcohol has that effect on you and you ignored your limit of five drinks. Did you forget about what happened at Christmas? Hell, there are still pictures of you out on the internet floating around. Hell, you had become a damn meme. Did you really want that to happen again?

But she had moved so close and her body had been so warm. Then again you were feeling pretty warm yourself, the booze heating you up, giving you a warm blush. But that wasn't all of it, and you found yourself shifting from time to time trying to ignore the bulge in your pants. You desperately hoped she wouldn't notice it, but when she leaned over and brushed along it as she reached for a beer, you knew she had.

The rush felt...alive, and suddenly you found yourself wishing she would do it again. Had she done it intentionally? Your mind warred with itself and you tried to follow her conversation about roller coasters until she reached up and made a comment about your hair. Her paw moved and you felt her tracing a claw through it before moving down along the back of your neck. As she had leaned in you had desperately searched the crowd for Jonathan.

He was nowhere in sight.

Where was he?

She purred into your ear.

"Want to go into the hot tub?"

You gasped like something stung you and she laughed, rich and feminine.

"I...I don't have trunks." You managed to stammer out. She smiled.

"Neither do I. Just wear your underwear." She had pulled you to your feet, her paw tight around yours. You had flushed in embarrassment while you tried to hide your arousal from anyone who might have been looking. If Jonathan found out, he would be unhappy, perhaps angry. You did not want to see him angry. You had known this would lead to trouble, and yet you followed her, your paw in hers.

The hot tub had a pair of otter girls in it drinking tall long island ice teas who giggled as you and Helen approached.

"Okay, then strip and get in." Helen commanded you. Your blush had deepened and you had almost left then. But the otter girls had started chanting '*Strip, strip, strip!*' and you peeled your shirt off to their catcalls and hoots. Their cheers got louder when you unbuckled your pants and slid them off. Thankfully your embarrassment had reduced you to just a slightly swollen sheath. But they still giggled and whispered to each other as only women can do while you stepped into the water. You had been thankful you hadn't worn white boxers that night.

"See, that's not so bad now, is it?" Helen smiled down at you before she hooked her thumbs into the waistband of her shorts and started to peel them off. You tried not to stare at the curve of her hips as the shorts had slid off her, partially dragging her white and blue striped panties after them before she paused to pull them up. Finally she kicked the shorts off her foot.

The tank top was off in a flash and she had held out her hand for you to take and help her in. It was hard for you to ignore the way the water lapped against her fur when she stepped in. It rose slowly up her legs with each step, dampening her fur higher and higher until it lapped against her panties. You swallowed as the water turned the fabric slightly transparent and caused them to cling to her. Thankfully she was under the water in a moment and you took a deep breath, relaxing deeper into the water until only your head was above the surface.

The otter girls continued to giggle, though after awhile they turned and started to eye up men while they walked past. From their conversations you can tell they liked the same type you do, and for once you start to relax, the soothing water helping the tension to flow from your body.

And then Helen touched you.

You felt it against your leg and you had to fight not to jump. She had moved closer while you had been listening to the otters talk about men and what their cocks must look like. You glanced at her, your ears splayed in confusion. Helen carried the same half lidded look from before, and you could hear her purring as the sound rippled along the water. The otters must not have been able to hear it over the jets that foamed the water or they would have giggled at you then.

"Told you this was a good idea." She whispered, her voice low and heavy. Her hand brushed along your upper thigh and you resisted the urge to bolt from the hot tub, if only to spare you from the embarrassment of running around in just sopping wet boxers. Not to mention that the alcohol had made you feel more receptive to her advances. Women had never been your core interest, and you were curious about them still, having not experienced life as a straight male before you had come out of the closet, unlike Jonathan.

Her fingertip had twirled a circular pattern on your thigh and your body reacted under the water. The throb had pulsed through your entire abdomen as your cock had pushed against your wet boxers. Your muzzle had opened then, panting, your tongue to the side as you watched her eyes as she smiled, her fingers ever moving closer to your raised excitement.

And then a lone paw-pad brushed your tip. You felt it like an electric spark, which had caused your eyes to close. Your breathing had been heavy and you had sat up, though now you can't remember if it was to escape or to give her an easier chance to touch you.

Where was Jonathan?

Her paw continued to move around your hard-on, caresses that darted and teased. When she finally pressed her palm over your length you almost came from the sheer rush of it, your body quivered like a leaf in a storm. The otter girls had been on their third drink then and were laughing while they splashed water at each other. Helen pretended to watch them while her hand moved along you, feeling the seams of your fly. Then suddenly you had been free, standing hard and proud in the water.

Her digits had wrapped around you, the paw pads soft against the tender skin of your cock while you had panted, eyes unfocused. The feline's paw had moved up and down with all the grace of her dancing as she dragged each stroke out. She turned and met your eyes.

"So, how does it feel?"

You licked your muzzle before panting again. All you had been able to think about was what if Jonathan came by, what if he—

"Well there you two are."

If she hadn't squeezed you then you would have screamed in surprise. Instead your ears had perked up painfully as you turned to see Jonathan with a beer in his paw, his other arm around a burly black bear you had hung out with a couple times. His name was Ted, wasn't it?

"I have been looking all over for you two. Glad to see you are getting along. Hey look, Ted's going to show me his car. He says he has a pretty sweet hook up in it. I'll come back as soon as we are done. You about ready to head home?" He broke away from Ted and lowered down to whisper in your ear. "I can't wait until we get home. There must be something in the punch because damn, I want you!"

He nipped the back of your neck and you yelped which drew laughter from the otter girls who were still watching. You had shivered and mewled under him as his teeth had pressed against the tender furs there. Helen's paw on your cock had tightened and your body had started to tighten, your cock throbbing as you were about to come. Suddenly the pressure released and Jonathan chuckled deep in his chest. Helen's paw clamped on the base of your cock painfully, stopping your orgasm in its tracks. Your wolf ruffled your hair and had kissed the back of your neck where he had bitten. It soothed a bit of the pain from it, but also sent a shiver through your body. Then he and Ted had walked off, laughter echoing with the otter girls as they watched you while you shivered.

You had wanted it so bad right then. Your cock pulsed under the water and your hips quivering with need. The otters must have known because they had been blushing, their eyes continually darting from each other to you.

It was then that Helen's paw started to move, her fingers tight around you. Up and down, up and down she caressed your flesh, her pace increasing with each stroke. Your muzzle opened and your breathing was quick. The otters had started to pant along with you as they finally clued onto what was going on. All you could see from them was the movements of their paws between the other's legs. Was that what you had looked like right then? Then Helen leaned in, her breath had brushed your cheek while her whiskers tickled your fur.

"Cum for me baby; cum for me."

She had rubbed her pawpads over your tip while she spoke just before plunging her fist down on you. You had bitten your lip when your body started to jerk as your cock pulsed, pumping your seed into the water. The otter girls hadn't noticed while they made out, their paws caressing each other in a mad passion as you shivered under Helen's paw while it continued to move almost leisurely over you.

When you finally calmed down she pushed you back through the fly of your boxers and smiled, raising her paw out of the water before she licked her fingers. She had been purring even louder, though the otters were making quite the racket and had started to draw a crowd.

"Next time I will use my tongue. Let's see your boyfriend beat me at that! After all, what are friends for?" She left the words hanging as she rose. Your eyes followed the water trails as they glistened down her body. It was hard not to notice the lips of her sex when she bent over to grab her clothes. They pressed against the damp fabric, soft and inviting. You had wanted to reach out and touch them right then. Under the water you started to get hard again despite your climax and you had swallowed.

Damn, what would Jonathan say if he found out about what had happened?

He wouldn't.

You made the decision in a heartbeat. He would not find out.

Everyone had been drinking, especially the otters. No one would know.

And it definitely wouldn't happen again.

You promised yourself that while you watched the feline saunter away, joining the other males that turned their heads as she passed. Under the water your cock continued to throb.

You had been such a fool.

***

True to his word, Jonathan had taken you that night. It had been rough, hard, and oddly, unsatisfying. You lay there afterwards wondering where the spark had gone. You loved him dearly, the way his masculinity matched your tendancy to bottom. You loved the feel of his rough paw pads, the way he worked his long tongue along your length when he decided to please you, and the way he filled you stretching every part of you.

So why didn't you feel satisfied after that night? What was wrong?

Helen.

It had to be her and what had happened. That was the only explanation. Yet as you lay there you couldn't help but remember the softness of her paw on you, the way her body had moved in the firelight, and the way that her panties had hugged her body. Was this what straight men felt? What was wrong with you?

Jonathan kept pushing you over the next few days to go check out the dance studio. He even offered to go with you, which you finally submitted to just to get him to stop bothering you with it. He kissed you and gave you a long hug as if he was proud you for finally giving into him. He liked seeing you happy, and even though classes were gearing up for midterms he bought you and him a bottle of wine to share that night. You had even shared your suite's tiny tub in an attempt to be romantic. Hell, he even had brought candles and bubble bath. It was oddly feminine of him and you had wagged your tail when he had opened the shopping bag.

But while he had petted your coat, running a wet brush through your fur and gave you small nips and licks in the tub, your mind could only think back to the night in the hot tub. It took him twice as long to get you hard and you think he got frustrated after awhile. You couldn't blame him, you had tried to stay in the moment, but your thoughts kept going back to Helen.

What the hell had she done to you? Jonathan didn't cuddle you that night and you felt like crying into your pillow, which would have just soured the night further. Already you were dreading the dance studio the next day when your first lesson started. But you dared not cancel it, especially after all Jonathan had done for you that night. No, you went with him after the alarm went off. You two barely said two words to each other while you drove around trying to find it. When you did, true to Helen's words, there were students of a varying degree standing outside chatting. Some of the young girls giggled as you walked past. Jonathan ignored them but your tail had tucked between your legs.

Thankfully Helen wasn't there. Instead you got to talk to one of the instructors, and you couldn't help but wag your tail when she named a price that was well in your price range. Jonathan had surprised you by paying and despite the previous night he kissed you and told you that if it would make you happy, then that was all that mattered. You couldn't stop smiling after that and had taken his paw into yours.

***

Even now that memory is enough to make you choke on a sob. You must have blacked out because you are leaning against the sofa in Jonathan's apartment. You can feel his body nearby, but you can't look knowing that if you did you might not stop screaming. He had done so many things just to see you smile, to see you wag your tail or let out a yip of excitement. Even through the worst times he was always there trying to make you happy. That's all he wanted, and your ears press against your head.

This is how you repaid him?

You don't know where you find the tears, you've cried so hard you are surprised you have anything left. Your body feels like it's trying to empty itself of all the guilt, sadness, and shame as the pile of vomit that smears the carpet attests. Your fur dampens and you cradle your muzzle in your paws, wishing to the heavens you could just wake up.

But no, Helen's crying in the next room and the smell of blood that clogs your nose reminds you that you aren't asleep. Your shoulder aches where the knife had slashed your skin and you know you should clean it, or do something, but you can't seem to care anymore.

Jonathan is dead.

The only man who made you feel special was gone and you were the reason. Your vision swims before you as you rest your forehead on your knees.

***

Learning to dance had been fun. You went a few days a week and always found yourself wagging your tail on the way home no matter how sore you were. Jonathan had even come to your classes once and awhile to watch, something that made you feel important and special. Sure he got teased by the mothers who were there but he took it in stride. He was doing it for you. It was hard not to smile whenever you thought about him sitting in those plastic chairs, his eyes watching while you moved across the dance floor.

You couldn't help but feel sexy in front of him, tights hugging your body. A body that was starting to trim up with the constant exercise. You felt sexy, more limber, more flexible and more importantly, more confident. Your sex life even improved, though you were still always the bottom. You didn't mind most of the time, it gave you a way to show off how flexible you were. But once and awhile you still thought about Helen's paw on you when he pawed you off in the shower or when he would bend over to show you an ass you had never penetrated.

You were unprepared the next time you saw Helen, your guard down after weeks of not seeing her. The school was generally empty in the evenings around suppertime except for one or two classes and you had gone there to practice while Jonathan had gone to his parents. His parents were amazing, but Jonathan had insisted you practice since there was a recital coming up and you had been nervous about more than a few of the moves you would have to do. Jonathan had promised his parents would understand. So you had packed your gym bag and headed to the dance hall. It had been storming by the time you got there on foot and you had gratefully peeled off your damp clothes in the locker room.

"I've been waiting for you."

Your gasp echoed against the tiles as her voice purred through the room. You turned; bringing your towel up to cover yourself, suddenly wishing you hadn't come, that you had insisted on going to his parents house. You could cry out, there were instructors in the building teaching a hip hop class a couple of rooms away from the change room. You could even hear the bass beat thumping through the walls, but what would they say—what would they do?

"It's been awhile. I was hoping you would follow my advice and come dancing here." Helen advanced on you as you backed up until the lockers thud into your back. You yelped and she had laughed at it, the sound like silk on stone as she pressed up against you. She was wearing nothing more than a t-shirt and panties. Even now you couldn't figure out how she had made it into the men's locker room dressed in so little.

She had leaned in and you could smell her, all of her. Your head had felt foggy as you recognized the scent of arousal. Your whiskers quivered as despite yourself, you drew in longer breaths through your nose, her scent heavy and cloying. If she had asked you to follow her you would have right then as your body's reactions screamed in some primal part of your brain.

"See, I knew you would remember me." She nuzzled your neck, her small tongue brushing along your fur while she pressed her hips against you. Your body pushed back yet you managed to keep the towel between you.

"I have a boyfriend!" You managed to choke out as you tried to slide away only to corner yourself between two lockers. She followed, her tail snaking behind her, paws reached out and pressed to your chest.

"I know, and so do I. But that doesn't mean we can't just have a little fun." She kissed you then. Her lips pressing against your muzzle, which you held closed, until she caressed your neck, claws scraping along your skin. You gasped and her tongue rolled its way into your muzzle. She kissed like she was trying to pour herself into you, her paws pulling your head to hers, fingers tangled in your hair. You moaned into her mouth as you felt yourself grow hard, pressing against the towel. She paused to tear it aside and smiled when she looked downwards.

"Remember what I told you?" She bit her bottom lip when she looked at you from under the few dreads that had fallen in front of her eyes. Slowly she had lowered herself to her knees, her paws running down your chest and inner thighs. You groaned, the fur and skin under her touch trembling. Had you felt regret then? Or just lust? In the end you had forgotten it all when her tongue touched your length, running from sheath to tip. There had only been one thing on your mind then.

You'd never had a blowjob from a feline, and her muzzle, though shorter, held a tongue of such dexterity that she had to tug at your balls to stop you from spilling your seed too quickly. The small nubs on her tongue tugged at you while they caressed your nerves when they slid along your skin. She sucked you in as much as she could, sometimes so far that she would gag before coming up for air. While you watched her head bob over your erection you placed your paws on her head, feeling the thin tangles of hair flowing around your fingers with each movement of her muzzle.

Her paws massaged your balls before moving further, finally finding your tight hole and you gasped in surprise when she wigged a slicked digit into you.

When she finally let you come you let out a loud growl, your fingers tightening in her hair while you forced her muzzle as far onto your cock as you could. Stream after stream jetted into her muzzle while she purred, slurping at you while thin lines of cum and saliva dripped off of her chin. When she finally pulled away from you she met your eyes while she licked the last of your semen off of your tip, then her lips. It was all you could do just to lean against the lockers while you tried to collect your thoughts. Helen smiled as she rose to her feet and gave you a chaste kiss on the cheek.

"Let's see your wolfie top that." She turned and had walked back towards the door. You watched her go, the rolling of her hips, the curve of her tail, the way they seemed to invite you to ravage her. You'd never been allowed to do that with Jonathan or any boyfriend for that matter. You had never felt this dominant, never wanted to be the one doing the topping, yet her body screamed for you to take her. You wanted to part her lips and shove yourself into her, to rut with her like your primal ancestors, to force your knot into her until she cried out and came over you in a sticky mess.

You didn't end up practicing that night. Instead you tried to shower away the memory of Helen's mouth on you. Even relieving yourself twice didn't help and only left you feeling raw and with aching balls. Finally you left the dance hall, your thoughts trailing after Helen and her body. It wasn't until you got home to find Jonathan wearing nothing but boxer shorts and a grin that your heart sank and the guilt hit.

Jonathan's frustration at being unable to get you off bordered on anger that night. You couldn't help but feel bad when he took you rougher than you were used to. You had tried to take it without complaint, knowing that it was because he had been unable to get you off with his mouth. It had been a treat, something rarely done. He had worked you with tongue and paw until they both had given out and he had thrown you onto your stomach and taken you with a snarl filled with frustration and anger. Even when he came you hadn't reached climax, though you had faked it the best you could, hiding the fact that there was no mess beneath you when he finally flopped beside you.

That night you didn't cuddle and you spent long hours staring at his back. What was he thinking? You must have asked yourself that a dozen times as your gaze followed the line of his broad shoulders down along his spine to a bushy tail and muscled ass. Yet even while you thought about reaching out and caressing it, the fantasy turned to Helen's tail, Helen's ass. With a groan you rolled over and squeezed your eyes shut.

The next morning Jonathan didn't even kiss you goodbye when he left for his morning classes. You watched him leave from the open door, your ears lowered, tears vibrating behind your eyes. You wanted to rush to him, to grab him, kiss him, tell him that you loved him despite the sex. Jonathan believed that sex was a large part of a relationship, that if the sex failed then the relationship was failing as well. And as much as you didn't want to admit it to yourself, you were starting to believe the same.

The recital passed and you had done alright. Jonathan had shown up late. Despite the fights that were starting to happen between you he still stood and applauded when you finished your routine. Later after changing you had run to him and lavished his face with licks and kisses. That night you had almost been able to forget the fights and remember why you loved him so much. You had gone for a delicious supper at O'Malley's, somewhere you hadn't been to since you two had started the awkward pre-dating phase. It had been the first place he had taken you to dinner. Then later you had even slow danced in a park where a small group of musicians had been playing. Not even the few whispers or stares at you and Jonathan had ruined that moment for you, gazing up into his eyes while he gazed into yours.

***

You're crying now, the sobs coming from so deep in you it feels as if you're going to throw up again. Jonathan's paw is in yours, the digits dead in your grasp as you cradle them like he is going to grip you back and tell you that it will be all alright.

Why won't he tell you that it's just a nightmare?

You look at his face and that's a mistake. Golden eyes stare out at nothing. You watch them, willing them to blink, to turn to you, but they stay motionless. You dry heave in your sobs as you crawl to his head and place it in your lap. You caress his hair with your blood soaked paws. He would be angry with his hair this messy so you try to fix it. He doesn't move.

You want to kiss him but are too scared.

"What are you doing?" Helen sobs from the entrance to the living room. She's still naked, though there's a stunned look to her and she seems to be swaying. She keeps glancing from you to Jonathan's head cradled in your paws. You look at her and suddenly you're hugging Jonathan's head to your chest as you start screaming.

***

The fighting had gotten worse as finals loomed. Not only were both you and Jonathan worried about the multitude of finals coming up, but also having less time for each other was starting to take its toll. Whenever one of you would be able to find time for the other, either you got shot down or you both ended up working on homework or studying. You had only made love once that month, but it had been a brief and emotionless affair.

Helen, you only saw a handful of times at the dance studio, and twice on campus. Each time she would smile at you before sauntering off, hips swaying as if she could feel your gaze as it caressed her hips and ass. Once at the dance studio you had walked in on her almost nude in the locker room. She had kissed you then, long and drawn out that had left your tail fluffed and your whiskers quivering. If it hadn't been for one of the instructors walking in you hadn't known what you two would have done.

But it was the fights that were getting to you the most. They were over the stupidest things and yet you and Jonathan both seemed to relish a chance to butt heads against each other. Things like the dishes at either of your places, leaving clothes lying around after a visit, or even not cleaning the sheets after that one love making session. You had only managed to climax that night by fantasizing about Helen anyway. The thing that hurt you the most was that you hadn't even felt guilty about doing it.

You found yourself with the phone in your paw more than once, a digit raised to dial his number and break things off. Yet each time you had hung up the phone with a sigh and forced yourself to go for a walk just so you wouldn't cry. Yet you still found your heart leaping when he called, even as bad as things had gotten. You told yourself again and again that once exams were over things would change. It would be summer vacation and you would have a lot more time for each other. Perhaps you would be able to have a vacation and get away from everything, including Helen.

That was if you lasted that long.

Jonathan surprised you with the offer of dinner at his place the day of his last final exam. You had finished up two days earlier and had been near to driving yourself insane pacing around your apartment with nothing to do besides the internet and a few games. You didn't dare go to the dance studio, not with the chance that Helen would be there. She had started to infect your thoughts no matter what you were doing. It felt like you were in heat constantly, a burning need to take her and push yourself into her. Jerking off had become a chore that only seemed to aggravate you more. So when you finally heard from Jonathan you had sighed in relief.

Finally you would be able to start your summer together! With all the stress gone he might let you top him in bed, which you were pretty sure would get the fantasy of Helen out of your head once and for all. Or maybe you would suggest that one of your gay friends like Donnie join you. He was enough of a gay boi that given a skirt and tight top you could imagine him being Helen. Hadn't Jonathan had a thing with Donnie a couple years ago, you can't remember anymore.

All these thoughts rushed through your head while the day seemed to crawl by. You resisted the urge to pleasure yourself, knowing that you might make love that night and you wanted to be able to find release with Jonathan. When the alarm on your cell finally rang you had dashed out of your apartment taking the stairs two at a time. No more fights, no more nights unable to make love, no more Helen! It was hard for you not to skip as you walked down the street, your tail wagging back and forth at a furious pace. You were practically vibrating when you finally found yourself at his door.

When he opened the door your muzzle had fallen open. He was dressed to the nines. Suit, dress pants, even a tie. Your eyes travelled up and down him and you felt the blood in your veins start to pump faster for the first time in what felt like months. You wanted to leap into his arms and have him carry you to the bedroom. But when he met your eyes your heart sank. He only ever looked at you like that when he was about to give you bad news.

"I have to run to a quick meeting. I'll be back soon hun, and then I hope I can explain why I have been so moody as of late. Then we can have a wonderful evening together, okay? I'll be right back, I promise."

You stood in the kitchen and listened to his car pull away. Why had he scheduled a meeting when he knew you were coming over? Was it a surprise thing? You paced back and forth, your tail no longer wagging. What did he have to tell you after all? Did he know about what had happened in the hot tub? You knew those otter girls looked like they would start shit!

Snarling didn't make you feel any better. Nor did moving from room to room; the wolf's scent permeated everything. You found yourself pacing again in his living room, thoughts snowballing through your head as you tried to work out what he might have to tell you. He knew you hated it when people did that to you, and yet he still had done it.

You were clenching your jaw and fists when you heard the knock on the front door. It caught you off guard and you stubbed your knee on the coffee table as you moved to the door. Jonathan often ordered ancient records for his collection of vinyl and you might as well get it. You opened the door expecting to see a UPS canine standing there in their ugly uniform.

It was Helen.

You took a step back and she followed you, glancing around as if she was searching for something. She was wearing a hemp sundress that flowed around her like water, her hair loose, the beads clicking while she turned her head. When you had recovered enough from your shock to push her back out the door she had already placed a paw on your chest.

"Jonathan's not here is he?"

You shook your head. "No, he went out to a meeting. He'll be back soon." You stressed the last part as hard as you could hoping she would clue in.

Instead she moved further into the house, turning around to face you. You wanted to yell at her to get out in case Jonathan came back. Instead she smiled and held up a record.

"Jonathan wanted me to deliver this to him today. I think he was hoping I'd get it here before you showed up. Bit late I guess." She smiled and sat the shrink wrapped square of cardboard in the coffee table. You recognized the band, it was one you and Jonathan both loved. In fact you had made love the first time listening to a digital copy.

You raised an eyebrow. "You know Jonathan?"

She winked as she moved up to you and pressed her paws against your chest again. "Hun, we've been hanging out ever since the party. We share a passion for old vinyl, though he tends to like a bit different stuff than I do. He didn't tell you?"

Jonathan had never mentioned Helen whenever you had talked. Why had he kept it a secret? Were they sleeping together behind your back? No, Jonathan was too gay for that, or so you hoped. Something in the back of your head nagged you while your mind tried to piece together everything. Helen moved to a shelf of books and traced her fingertip along the spines.

"You haven't..." the words are out of your mouth before you realized you had said them. She just laughed before grinning at you.

"Oh no sweetie, no. Your man has a thing for dominating men, not women. No, we only talk about music and things like that. But I'm sorry; I've got to use the bathroom if you don't mind. Nature calls."

She headed to the bathroom with the confidence of someone who had been in the house more than once. You caught yourself watching the sway of her tail and hips before forcing your gaze to the bookshelf. Helen reached the bathroom and you heard a gasp. You gave into your curiosity and moved to where she stood just inside the door of the bathroom.

Helen had stopped you with a paw.

"Hun, what do you know about what Jonathan does when you aren't around?"

"What do you mean?" Your chest had clenched and it had become hard to breath.

"Have you had sex with him anytime recently?"

You had shaken your head and she gave you a hug.

"I'm sorry hun." She moved to the side and you looked where she pointed. Draped on top of the bin by the toilet are three used condoms, shriveled and dried. Wrappers lay nearby. The world had lurched to the side as you dropped to your knees.

"He … he's cheating on me?"

Helen's paws had come to rest on your shoulder. "I had my suspicions. He talks a lot when we get together. There's been a lot of talk about Ted and cars."

You had nodded.

"Here, come into the living room."

She helped you rise to shaky legs and guided you back into the living room where you fell to the couch like dead weight. Helen sat beside you and wrapped her arms around you. You had felt like crying but after the last few months it all made sense to you. It hadn't been Helen's fault that Jonathan had been cheating on you. If anything she had, in her own way, been trying to spare you. That's why you had started to fight, that's why he had grown distant. That's why your sex had faltered, he had been getting it somewhere else. Suddenly you hadn't felt so guilty about the things you and Helen had done.

You sat there in silence while your thoughts tore through the last few months. Your anger rose and you found yourself fantasizing about what you were going to do when Jonathan came through the front door. Yelling to start. Yes, there would be a lot of yelling.

Helen had nuzzled against your neck and your thoughts suddenly crashed to a halt.

If Jonathan was cheating on you, then you could cheat on him!

You turned to Helen and she looked at you as her eyes searched yours. You had reached out and caressed her cheek, moving your paw to the back of her head and drawing her muzzle to yours. She gasped when your muzzles met, her hands moving to your shoulders. Her fingers clenched your shirt as your tongues fed off of each other, your breaths quick. You moved your mouth to her neck, nipped and licked her fur while she gasped, her paws scattering buttons as she tore your shirt off. She had licked your chest, the tip of her tongue passing over each nipple, the tiny nubs sending zips of pleasure to your balls with each pass.

Helen had stood and you were suddenly thankful that she was wearing a dress. It slid off the feline's shoulders to her hips where she pushed it to the floor. Your gaze had travelled over her fur while you had risen to meet her, your mouth finding hers while her paws moved to your pants. Your belt and buttons had flown off in a flash as your pants joined her dress on the floor, weeks and weeks of tension finally finding release.

She pressed her chest to yours, your nipples brushing each other as your paws slid down her back to grab her ass. Feminine noises escaped her muzzle when you pulled her hips to you, your fingers sliding over the flimsy material of her panties. Her paws worked along your back, each claw sent shivers through you while she gently played them along your spine.

Then Helen had shoved you back, lowering herself in front of you. Soft fingers hooked their tips into your waistband and yanked your boxers down. Her mouth found you and your muzzle opened in a gasp, your paws moving to her head as you tangled your fingers in the strands of her hair. She had purred and the vibrations moved along your length while you thrust in and out of her muzzle. But this wasn't what you had wanted, not even close.

You had pulled her up by the hair as she let out a gasp that was more pleasure than pain. Your muzzles met and she had writhed in your grasp like a serpent until you broke the kiss and turned her around. She had glanced over her shoulder, her eyes wide and her ears perked. It was the first signs of uncertainty you had ever seen on her.

It had only made you harder.

You pushed her over the arm of the sofa and she instinctively raised her tail and widened her stance. There was a glimmer of something wet trailing down between her thighs and for reasons you weren't sure of, it made your cock pulse.

Guiding yourself with your paw you slid your tip along her. You had never been this close to a woman's sex before and the scent was intoxicating. Not the sharp musky scent of a male, but more akin to the scent of a rose. Sharp yet pleasant. Your cock throbbed when you found her entrance and started to push into her.

Helen had made a noise and gripped the cushions while she watched you from eyes that slid in and out of focus until you filled her to your knot. It was different from a male, softer, wetter, warmer. Helen had moaned as you had reached down to take her hips while instinct drove you to slid out of her before you hammered back inside her entrance. She quaked and let out a cry as you thrust in her again and again while your balls slapped against her with each thrust.

Someone was growling and it took you a moment to realize it was you.

The feline slashed the upholstery as her tail thrashed along her back. You slammed harder and harder into her when you realized the harder you went, the more she cried out in pleasure. No wonder Jonathan had took so much pleasure from being the dominant one in bed. Your nails dug into her calico pelt as you felt her wetness slide down your cock and over your balls. Each thrust brought your knot against her lips and her entrance slid further and further along it each time your hips met hers.

Then suddenly you had pressed hard enough that it slid into her, filling her, tying her.

Helen had screamed as her body shook itself apart, her inner walls pressing against you as they gripped you. She had climaxed and that thought was enough to drive you over the edge with a roar. Your cock had let out a massive pulse as you started to spill your seed into her depths. Helen continued to shake and scream, her tail wrapped around your arm while she shook under you.

When she finally settled down you had massaged her back, kneading her muscles while you waited for your knot to shrink enough to pull out. She still quivered with each of its pulses, eyes closed and a content smile on her muzzle.

That's when you both heard the keys in the lock. Her eyes flashed open and you tried to pull yourself from her only to get a squeak of pain.

The look Jonathan gave you when he opened the door was like a knife to your soul. Cheater or not, at that exact moment you knew you had broken his heart. The wolf's muzzle opened and his keys fell from his paw to the floor with a loud crash.

"What are—"

You finally managed to pull away from Helen, your cock dripping with your combined fluids as you turned to face your former mate. All the arguments you had been planning came to the forefront of your brain and fanned your anger back to a blaze despite the endorphins that were still in your system.

"How dare you! How dare you cheat on me!" You had known it

would start with yelling, and even the fact that you were standing there with another person's fluids coating you, you still dared to call him a cheater.

"Wha—"

"You and Ted. I saw the condoms in the bathroom. How long Jonathan? How long!"

Helen had moved away from the couch and slinked away from you as the wolf slammed the door behind him. The bang of the door had cut through the room.

"What condoms?" He yelled back.

Something nagged at you. "In the bathroom! How dare you do this to me! I loved you!"

Jonathan had stalked over to the bathroom and flicked on the light. After a moment he had come back out again. "Those aren't mine."

"Bullshit!"

"Those aren't mine!" His paws had turned into fists and his ears had lain back against his skull. Canines flashed as his lips had pulled back. Jonathan snarled at you. "Did you look at the packaging? No, you didn't did you! You know I only use one brand because it's latex free. I told you I am allergic to latex and those are latex condoms. Latex condoms!"

The pit of your stomach dropped and you had stumbled back. Breathing was difficult and you had reached out to steady yourself on the couch.

"Where?" You raised your paw to your forehead, trying to think. Helen gave you the answer a moment later.

"It was me. I wanted to be yours. Jonathan doesn't understand you like I do."

You had glanced at her and back at Jonathan. The pit in your stomach deepened.

"I—" tears had started to darken your cheek fur. "I'm sorry...oh my god I'm sorry Jonathan. I—"

Helen took a step forward from where she had been slinking behind Jonathan and the wolf growled at her, driving her back. Instead it was him that moved to your side and wrapped his strong arms around you. You remembered what it had felt like when he had first hugged you, how safe you had felt. It was all wrecked now because of you. How could he still want to touch you?

"Shh..." he whispered to you while you sobbed into his chest. "it's okay. It may take some time but we can work through this. I'm sorry. If I hadn't been so busy trying to get a house finally I would have had more time to spend with you. It's not all your fault."

You had looked into his eyes then. House? Jonathan had been talking about getting a house since you two had started dating. It had always been one of his goals. That was why he had been so distant? You tried to smile but the betrayal still felt too deep.

"No, I screwed this up Jonathan; I screwed us up."

"Let me ask you this?" The wolf had run his paw through your hair. "Who would you rather have, Helen, or me?"

You had glanced to where Helen glared from over Jonathan's shoulder at the wolf and then back into his eyes. It was amazing that those eyes were still filled with love, even after all of what he had just seen. Love you didn't deserve. And yet it had been there.

"You." You had whispered.

"NO!"

Helen's shout had bought your eyes up in time to see the flash of metal before you had fallen back as pain had ripped through your shoulder. You had thought Jonathan was choking until he had fallen to the floor and you saw the blood running down his chest. The world had spun and your paw had come away from your shoulder red. Helen stood over the wolf, a butcher's blade in her hand, each rise and fall of the knife splashed red over Jonathan's white carpet.

***

Helen's crying again, sitting by the door. She's rocking back and forth as she sobs.

Your tears have stopped and now you just hold Jonathan as you listen to the sirens get closer.

You're telling him that you are sorry for everything.

That he was your best friend and you should have trusted him.

That you should have been faithful to him and that you didn't deserve the love he had shown you.

You whisper that you wished you could have moved into his house and kissed him every morning before classes.

That you wished you could have him hold you in the dead of night and find safety in his arms.

You kiss his muzzle one last time and tell him the one thing you will never get to tell him again.

That you love him.

And goodbye.

ABOUT THE AUTHORS

Whyte Yoté has been writing erotic furry fiction since 1995 when he was probably far too young to be doing such a thing, and he has been seriously pursuing his craft since 2000. His works have appeared multiple times in the anthologies FANG and ROAR as well as Heat magazine and many other anthologies. When he's not writing, he...oh wait, nevermind. He juggles personal work with anthology submissions as well as commissions and collaborations.

Kansan by birth, South Dakotan by grace and Californian by convenience, Whyte Yoté currently lives in Sacramento with writer/graphic designer Tym, his forever boyfriend since 2004.

www.furaffinity.net/user/whyteyote/
inkbunny.net/WhyteYote
whyte-yote.sofurry.com/stories
https://www.weasyl.com/profile/whyteyote
www.twitter.com/WhyteYote

Ianus J. Wolf lives in the DC area and writes furry fiction that usually falls into the categories of horror or erotica, with a healthy dash of other speculative fiction on the side. His short stories have been in Will of the Alpha, and will be featured in the upcoming Abandoned Places and Taboo from FurPlanet. He

is also the editor of Trick or Treat and the upcoming Pulp! Two-Pawed Tales of Adventure from Rabbit Valley. When not writing, he shares his life with his mate Ashe and their lovable labradusky Bandit and enjoys tabletop gaming, reading, horror movies, and a smattering of other hobbies. He welcomes contact at ianusjwolf@gmail.com and can be found online here:
Twitter: @IanusJWolf
FurAffinity: http://www.furaffinity.net/user/ianusjwolf/
SoFurry: https://ianusjwolf.sofurry.com/

Sorin is an author of anthropomorphic fiction, science fiction and romance. He lives and works in the Denver Metro area with his partner in a house full of critters including cats, ferrets, turtles, and critters of the human persuasion. Sorin's short stories have been published in anthologies and on many anthropomorphic websites.

NightEyes DaySpring is a known troublemaker who is rumored to have a penchant for coffee and an interest in dead ancient civilizations. His stories have appeared in ROAR 3, ROAR 4, Fang Claw & Steel 13, Trick or Treat, and Taboo. So far, NightEyes has stuck to writing short stories, but he has an incomplete first novel that he needs to someday complete.
He resides in Florida with his boyfriend.
More information about NightEyes can be found at http://www.furaffinity.net/user/nighteyes/
For day-to-day nonsense, follow @wolfwithcoffee

on twitter.

Zantal is young in his career as an author; this is the first of his works to be professionally published. This has a special significance for him as he would consider his own efforts to be inspired by the quality of storytelling and imagination he saw in previous editions of FANG. He only hopes this in some small way lives up to the impressive works that have come before him, and continue to push his own efforts forward toward ever more enthralling and enjoyable works.

In "Competitive Nature," Zantal explores the world of two individuals whose rivalry, like many organic things, grows in a strange and unexpected way. Like nature, it produces something beautiful nonetheless. Predator and prey develop alike, and both learn effective techniques to use on each other ...

Tarl "Voice" Hoch is a horror/erotica writer based out of the frozen, cowboy infested north that is Alberta, Canada. His works have been featured in a number of places, chief among them 'Will of the Alpha" by FurPlanet, 'Trick or Treat' by Rabbit Valley, as well as 'Fifty Shades of Decay' by Angelic Knight Press. He is also head editor for FurPlanet's upcoming horror anthology 'Abandoned Places'.

When not boner killing with his stories, Tarl can be found reading anything he can get his hands on, wishing everyday was Halloween, or secretly feeding treats to his feline overlords when his fiancee isn't looking. Find his work on Twitter @voicespider or on Facebook at https://www.facebook.com/TarlWriter